SEE YOU

IN MY

DREAMS

EVERY NIGHT THEY MEET IN A SHARED DREAM
WHERE THEY ARE YOUNG LOVERS ON A DESERT ISLAND

SEE YOU IN MY DREAMS

MICHAEL EDWIN Q.

See You In My Dreams by Michael Edwin Q.

ISBN: 978-1-59755-662-0

Published by: ADVANTAGE BOOKS™
Longwood, Florida, USA
www.advbookstore.com

Library of Congress Catalog Number: 2021944659

1. Fiction: Romance – Fantasy
2. Fiction: Romance – General

Cover Design: Alexander von Ness
Editor: nancysabatinicopyedit@gmail.com

First Printing: October 2021
21 22 23 24 25 26 10 9 8 7 6 5 4 3 2 1

One

Follow that dream

Follow that dream, I gotta follow that dream
Keep a-movin, move along, keep moving
I got to follow that dream wherever that dream may lead
I got to follow that dream to find the love I need

Word and music by Fred Wise – Ben Weisman

THE JOURNEY

The old man stood on the side of the road in front of a cornfield. Not one car passed by in the last hour. Finally, a dilapidated pickup, filled with field hands in the back, stopped. Sitting alone, the young farmhand driving the truck hollered out the truck window.

"Hey, old man, what'cha doing out in the middle of nowhere? Practicing to be a scarecrow?"

The old man walked over to the passenger's side.

"Unless times have changed, a man on the side of the road with his thumb in the air meant he was hitchhiking. Now if you'd prefer me to stick up another finger other than my thumb, you just keep running your mouth."

"Relax, what'd you do, leave your funny bone in your other pair of pants? Where you getting to?"

"I need to get downtown."

"We pass that way. I can drop you just outside town. Hop in."

The young farmhand reached over and opened the door. The old man struggled and grunted to get in and sit; he placed a small black gym bag at his feet.

As they barreled down the dirt roads, the old man held on tight not to bounce out of his seat. When they got on the highway, he relaxed, placing his hands in his lap.

The young farmhand was tall and sinewy. His clothes faded from a million washes. He needed a shave, although clearly too young to grow a decent beard if he wanted to. His face was long, horse-like, with sharp features – a pointed nose and chin. Definitely, not a pretty-boy, nevertheless he was attractive enough that there'd be at least one woman in the world who'd have him. He kept his eyes on the road, save for sneaking side glances at his passenger, now and then.

"So, does your mother know you're out on your own?" laughed the young man.

"My mother's been dead more years than you've been alive."

"Hey, don't take what I say wrong. It's just my style; I like shucking and jiving."

"Sorry," said the old man, "I got a lot on my mind."

The young man let some time elapse before speaking again.

"So, what's downtown?"

"The bus station, the train station, I got to get out of this town."

"Where you going?"

"San Diego, California."

"Oh, that's a long ways from Texas! What's out there?"

The old man didn't answer. The young man apologized.

"Sorry, old-timer, I didn't mean to be so nosy."

Another moment of silence oozed by. "My girlfriend's in California. I'm going to see my girlfriend."

The young man burst into laughter. When he looked over, the old man's face was stern. He stopped laughing.

"I'm sorry for laughing. It's just I wouldn't think an old guy like you would have a girlfriend."

"I'm old, I ain't dead."

"Yeah, right." The man felt free to laugh again. "Tell me, how did you and your girlfriend hook-up, living so far from each other – on the internet?"

"No, I see her every night in my dreams."

"Yeah, right, sure." He stopped laughing. "So, what are you, like, seventy-five?"

"Thanks for the compliment. You better add ten years to that; I'm eighty-five."

"And how old is your girlfriend."

"Eighty-four, a year younger."

"Wow, eighty-four and eighty-five. We'd better hurry up; times a-waste-in." He gunned down on the accelerator.

One mile out from downtown, an electric traffic sign hovers over the highway. It cautions of traffic jams, accidents, bad weather warnings, and advises drivers not to drink and drive. Some days it tells stories of woe – missing children, stolen cars and such. Today the sign read:

ALERT – MISSING SENIOR, MALE, ON FOOT,
LAST SEEN WEARING BROWN CORDUROY PANTS,
TAN SHIRT AND GRAY FEDORA

The young man looked over to refresh his memory. As he remembered, the old man wore brown corduroy pants, a tan shirt and a gray fedora. The tires screeched as he took the road going into downtown. The old man looked at him, questioning.

"I just remembered I need to do something downtown….good for you, ay?"

He parked the truck in front of the police station.

"I'll be right back; then I'll drive you to your bus."

Two minutes later the young man came running out of the police station followed by two policemen. The front seat was empty.

"He was here! I swear it!" He ran to the passengers sitting in the back of the truck. "The old guy, where'd he go?" The men shrugged their shoulders and shook their heads. He turned to the policemen. "He said he was either going to catch a train or a bus. He's on his way to California."

****

The phone rang, Beth ran to get it.

"Mrs. Bouchard, this is Sergeant Hall; someone spotted your father downtown."

"Do you have him? Is he all right? Let me speak with him."

"He's not here, Mrs. Bouchard. He was hitchhiking; someone drove him downtown, and gave us a heads-up."

"What person picks up an eight-five year old man and just drops him off downtown?" She sounded angry and worried.

"Try not to worry, Mrs. Bouchard. We do know he plans to either catch a bus or a train out of town. We've all the stations covered."

"Leaving town, where could he be going?"

"That brings up my next question, Mrs. Bouchard. Does your father have any friends or family in California, especially San Diego?"

"I don't think so; I don't think he's even been that far west in his life."

"The person who picked him up said your father told him he was off to San Diego to see his girlfriend."

"Girlfriend! He must be going senile. My father doesn't have a girlfriend. He's outlived all his friends. My mother's been dead for ten years. When she died, my father never even considered dating another woman. There's no way! Sergeant, my father's never been to

Californian, he hasn't been out of Texas in twenty years, and he hasn't been out of this house in five!"

"Try not to worry, Mrs. Bouchard. We've got men stationed everywhere. He won't get far. Keep your phone line open; I'll call you."

"As soon as you know something, call me, no matter what the hour."

"I will, Mrs. Bouchard."

She hung up and turned to her husband.

"He's been seen downtown. He hitchhiked downtown! Do you believe it? He told someone he was heading to California to see his girlfriend in San Diego. He's not only lost his marbles, they've rolled out the door, never to be seen again. What are we going to do?"

Walter took her gently and sat her on the couch. "There, there, Beth, he won't get far. He's easy to spot. They'll have him home before dark."

Their youngest son, Walter Jr. stood up and started for the door.

"Junior, where are you going?" asked his father.

"I can't just sit here. I'm taking my car; I'm going downtown to look for Grandpa."

"Don't stay out late," said his mother through her sobbing.

"I won't."

"Call if you're going to be late."

"I will."

****

Walter Jr., or Junior as called by everyone from day one, was the poster child for the "Boomerang Generation". He'd gone straight from high school to college and after four years emerged onto the job market. After a year of mailing out hundreds of résumés, countless job interviews, and living on ramen noodle soup, moving back in with his folks was his only alternative. It was that or the street. At twenty-six he felt a complete failure, unlike his older brother, Dave, who was doing well in insurance, and his sister, Jenny who married into money.

He had his father's brains and his mother's good looks. Still, he couldn't get his life rolling. Living at home was hell. Though never actually spending any time in hell, he could presume living at home was worse. The only saving grace was Grandpa. Sure, the old man could throw harsh words at him, only he did listen and was always open to discussion, unlike his parents.

He parked his rundown jalopy – a gift from his Grandpa. He appreciated the gesture, except he felt he should be mature enough to get his own transportation, another reason to feel insignificant. He entered the bus station, walked over and sat on one of the wooden benches. He wasn't sure why he was there. Surely the police watched the bus and train stations for his grandfather. He kept telling himself he was there because he feared for the safety of his grandfather, not because he believed one word the old man said when he confided in him about his dream-girlfriend. It was a far-fetched story. He was not there because he believed the old man's story. It was because the old man believed it – and that's what counts.

Junior's mind went into detective mode. Knowing the old man truly believed what he believed – he was without a doubt on his way to San Diego. The family treated the old man like he was a child, just as they treated him. After hours of talking with his grandfather, he knew the old man was still sharp as a tack, perhaps a little nutty – all that dream-girl stuff – nevertheless, he was nobody's fool.

Keeping that in mind, he knew his grandfather was smart enough to outmaneuver the police. If they knew he was on his way to San Diego, he wouldn't take the direct route. Junior walked over to the information booth.

"Excuse me, have there been any buses to southern California today."

"You looking for that old guy, too? The police are way ahead of you. They asked me all about it, earlier. I'll tell you what I told them. I never seen any such guy. And there ain't any buses to California till tomorrow morning."

"Has there been any buses going out of state in the past four hours?"

"Just two, one to Miami, the other to Denver. Only, like I said, I ain't seen your old guy."

Junior went back into detective mode. Denver would be the perfect roundabout way of going to California. Except his grandfather never bought a ticket, never came in the station. Then it dawned on him.

"That bus to Denver, what's its first stop?"

The man looked at the schedule. "First stop, Denton, north, halfway between Dallas and the Texas border, going into Oklahoma."

"Thank you." Junior walked out of the bus station. On the corner was a taxi station. The cabbies were socializing under a streetlamp.

"Excuse me, gentlemen. Have any of you had a fare, an old man, going up to Denton."

One short stout cabbie stepped forward. "I did. Crazy old coot, I told him he could catch the bus going north to Denton for a fraction of the price. He said he didn't care; he wanted to go by taxi."

"So, what did you do?"

"What do you think? I took him to Denton. It cost him an arm and leg. he didn't care. Gave me a good tip, too."

"Where in Denton did you take him?"

"That's the crazy part. He had me drop him off at the Denton bus station."

****

An hour and half later, Junior was at the Denton bus station. He walked up to the ticket booth. A plump, gum popping, country girl smiled at him. Junior backed off a little, just enough to not get the full force of her perfume.

"Can I hep ya?"

"Yes, did a bus just leave for Denver?"

She looked at the schedule.

"Sure did, not long ago."

"I'm looking for my grandfather. Did you happen to notice if he bought a ticket and if he might be on that bus?"

"Sorry, sweetie, I couldn't tell ya; I just got on shift and that bus left half an hour ago."

"Where's its next stop?"

She referred to the schedule. "Let's see. Oh, here it is. Next stop, Oklahoma City; they pull in at six in the morning."

"Thank you, you've been most kind."

"Hope ya find your grandpa."

****

The phone rang once; his mother answered.

"Mom, I don't think I can make it back home any time soon."

He could hear her screaming across the room to his father. "It's your son; he says he's not coming home tonight." Then she bellowed into the receiver. "What do you mean you're not coming home tonight?"

"I'm too tired to drive. I'm going to sleep in the car for a few hours, then I'm going to keep looking for Grandpa."

"Sleep in the car! I don't know what's come over you, Junior! You're nothing like your brother. You're turning into a damn…a damn…a damn hippy!"

"Mom there's no more hippies; Dad was a hippy. I gotta go. I'll call you tomorrow." He hung up.

He stretched out in the backseat of the car. As he slowly drifted off to sleep, he rehashed the stories his grandfather told him – how when the dreams first started, about his Dream-girl, why he needed to go to her.

Two

Dream, when you're feeling blue

Dream, when you're feeling blue
Dream, that's the thing to do
Just watch the smoke rings rise in the air
You'll find your share of memories there

Words and Music by Johnny Mercer

BEFORE THE JOURNEY

The old man sat at the breakfast table, sulking. It was their anniversary, their fiftieth wedding anniversary. His wife, Phyllis, died ten years earlier. However, that didn't change anything. It was their fiftieth wedding anniversary and no one remembered, no one cared enough to remember, except him.

His daughter, Beth, stood over the stove in three-inch heels, her dark hair held high in a bouffant by multiple layers of hairspray. She wore a full apron over her gray flannel dress; she held a spatula in one hand and a lit cigarette in the other.

"How do you want your eggs, Daddy?" she asked.

"I'm not hungry," he said softly.

"Daddy, you got to eat something."

His son-in-law, Walter Sr., came out from behind the morning paper just long enough to make a proclamation.

"Says here the unemployment rate is going down again… If you ask me, I think they're fudging the numbers." Walter Sr. shoveled the last of his breakfast into his mouth and slurped down his coffee. He spoke with his mouth full as he stood up. "Well, it's off to the rat race."

The old man didn't hate Walter Sr., he just didn't like him, he bored him. Sad to say, he felt the same about his daughter, Beth. He wasn't fond of her, even when she was a child. Now she was a grown married woman with three kids, and the years had only added to the strength of his dislike for her. Oh, he loved her, loved her with all his heart. He'd cut off his right arm up to there for her. He just was never fond of her company.

Actually, he had nothing to beef about. Most folks don't get to be eighty-five; none of his and Phyllis' friends made it. He had a good clean room and bed; he was well-fed, and well-cared for. He wanted for nothing. He had no complaints there.

He'd been a restless youth. Raised in Beaumont, Texas, after high school he was out of there. He joined the navy to see New Jersey. And after a four-year stint, he, Christopher Goodman, left the navy with a few thousand dollars in his pocket and commanding skills in the art of metal welding.

He moved back to Texas, Fort Worth, where he worked the next few years as a master welder welding oil rigs. After years of saving, plus what money he had from his navy hitch, he moved southeast to Venus, Texas and started "Goodman's Trailer Sales and Truck Rentals".

He was not an overnight success. Still everyone knew Chris Goodman was a fair man and a good ole boy, and in time he was the richest man in Venus. Having money and good looks made Chris the most eligible bachelor in the Ellis and Johnson counties. Only, Chris had eyes for no one except Phyllis Duffy, the Mayor's daughter. After one year of courting they married. He bought her one the nicest track homes south of Dallas. After one year of marriage, they had Beth. And as they say, they lived happily ever after. Except no one tells you there's a time limit to ever after.

After college, Beth married Walter and moved to Waco. They made Phyllis and Chris proud grandparents three times over – Dave, Jenny, and Walter Jr., in that order.

Time did what time does. It goes and it goes too fast. When they were both seventy-five, Phyllis died – the cancer. After one year, it was clear to all that Chris could not take proper care of himself.

Beth, Walter, and their brood of three moved in with him. He signed everything, the house and his bank account over to them. Walter Sr. gave up his profitable insurance business to run Goodman's. Chris signed the company over to Beth and Walter Sr. with one stipulation, that it always bear the name Goodman's.

Now most people might call this a recipe for disaster. However, Beth loved and respected her father and Walter Sr. loved and adored his wife. They never took advantage of him, never spoke in disrespect to him. They vowed to make his golden years – shine.

To give him more room and privacy, they hired a contractor to build an addition to the house, a good sized bedroom with its own bathroom. The three grandchildren loved and cherished their grandfather. In time, all three left the nest. Chris was now in his eighties and seemingly forced to live out his days with Beth and Walter Sr., the most boring people he could think of.

When Walter Sr. started out of the kitchen, the front door bell rang. Beth opened the door to find her youngest son, Walter Jr., his luggage on the floor around him, an alarm clock radio under one arm, and a toaster oven under the other. A taxi cab drove off.

"Junior," cried his mother. Walter Sr. stood behind her. "My God, son, what are you doing here?"

He looked at the ground, unable to look either of them in the eye. "I had no place else to go. I'm broke."

"Why didn't you call us?" asked Beth. Junior didn't respond; he didn't look up. They ushered him into the house. "Have you eaten?" asked Beth. They shepherded him into the kitchen. "Here, sit down; I'll fix you something."

"Hey, Grandpa," said Junior, bending and kissing the old man's cheek. He sat down.

"We'll talk tonight; I gotta go," Walter Sr. said.

"It's okay, Dad," said Junior.

Beth and Chris listened to Junior's stories of woe.

The old man pressed his hand down on his grandson's. "Rough out there?"

"You ain't just whistling Dixie."

"Don't worry, we'll find an answer, together," said the old man.

After breakfast, as Junior brought his things into his old room, he caught his grandfather in the hall.

"You okay, Grandpa. You look down-and-out."

His grandson's honest concern touched him.

"Today would have been your grandmother and my fiftieth wedding anniversary."

"Wow, that's great, I guess. It's difficult for me; I hardly remember her."

There were tears in Chris' eyes. "I hardly remember her, too."

****

It was days later at the breakfast table. Walter Sr. left for work. Beth ran off to a woman's Bible study at the church. It was just Junior and his grandfather.

"What'cha thinking about, Grandpa?"

Chris answered with a question. "You know what old folks mostly think about?"

"What's that?"

"There are only two things old people think about; that's the future, because it scares the hell out of 'em, and the past because there is where they feel the safest."

"And what are you thinking about, Grandpa?"

"Surprisingly, it's not the past or the future."

"The present?"

"Not really, something more than past, present or future. Something in between all of them – dreams."

The young man looked at the old man, confused.

"It's hard to explain," said Chris. "If you promise me you won't tell your folks, I'll tell you."

"You've always kept my secrets from my parents; I can only do the same for you."

"Well then, I'll do my best," said Chris.

****

Christopher Goodman woke up in a dream. He found himself lyng on a satin tan beach, the sand virgin and smooth. He assumed he'd been sleeping. On waking in this dream, he stood up and looked out at the ocean. It was so blue you could almost taste it, and the sky, a paler shade of the same color seemed to blend into the sea. What few white clouds there were gave the impression of cherubs floating in peaceful grace. The horizon hung on to eternity. Chris knew he was dreaming; except this was like no other dream.

First, he was well aware it was a dream, which is uncommon in most dreams. And there was a realism about it that was equal to reality. He knew he was dreaming; if he didn't know he was dreaming he would have not acted normal. Yet he did act normal, because there was an uncommon reality to the dream – awfully strange.

He looked back at the impression his body left in the sand. It was not his body, at least not the one he remembered. It was short with muscle tone. He examined himself. His body was firm, tan, healthy, and a million years younger than his true age. His arms, chest, and legs were muscular. He wore only a dark brown leather loincloth, similar to what Johnny Weissmuller wore in all his Tarzan movies.

He was on an island. Where was the island? How big was it? Was he alone? Only from the top peak could he assume an answer. He ran up the hill to the highest point on the island. It amazed him how effortlessly he was able to do this, although, of course, anything is possible in dreams. Standing atop of the highest peak, he looked in all directions – nothing other than blue water as far as the eye could see. There was a small pool of water. He looked at his reflection. It was him, only it was he a million years ago. He was young, handsome, and buff, like he was when he first came out of the navy. He laughed and the dream disappeared.

No one would think it strange, an old man dreaming he is once again healthy and strong. Only the next night the dream continued, starting where the last dream left off, again, not so far-fetched. Each night the dream continued – linear – as if no time elapsed since the last dream. He harvested coconuts and bananas, fished in the ocean, collected firewood, built a small hut, living his life on the island.

It was paradise. However would Eden be paradise for Adam without Eve? "It's not good for man to be alone", echoed in his head. He searched the island, finding no one or a trace of anyone. Till one night, he found evidence he wasn't alone. A charred group of sticks denoting a fire, bent branches, empty coconuts, fish bones, banana peels, and fruit pits, all signs of someone else on the island.

The most definite proof came in the form of a footprint in the wet sand at the shore's edge. Chris placed his foot next to it, in comparison. It was small, a woman's footprint. His first thought was that it was his wife's footprint. It made all the sense in the world, an old man dreaming he was young on an island with a woman. To be united with Phyllis, in his dreams, seemed only logical.

During one dream, Chris sat at the island's highest point near a fire he'd made, cooking the catch of the day. The sun was setting; sunset colors filled the sky. He looked down at the beach. A woman was walking along the water's edge. Chris stood on top of a rock, waving his arms, he called out to her. She stopped and looked up. That was all; he woke up.

The next few dreams were all the same. He shouted to the woman below, and then woke. In his real life, he wondered who she might be. Only inwardly, he was sure it was Phyllis. Why would he dream of anyone else?

Finally, one dream lasted long enough for Chris to find out more. He ran down the hill to the beach. The woman stopped in her tracks. She was young and beautiful; dressed in a scantily body covering similar to his. She was Jane to his Tarzan. She didn't look familiar.

"Phyllis, is that you?" he cried.

"I'm sorry, I'm not Phyllis. Who are you?"

"You're not Phyllis?"

"Again, I'm sorry, but I'm not Phyllis."

"Then why are you here?"

"I don't know, you tell me?"

"Phyllis was my wife. I thought…I hoped…you were she."

"My name is Irene Cooper. I'm not sure what's going on, either. I've been living on the other side of the island. Just recently I've felt an urge to come to this part of the island."

"Have you been alone on the island long?"

"I'm not sure. It seems like a long time. Only, I'm not sure. What about you?"

"I can't explain it. I've been in this dream only the past few nights."

"There must be some reason we're here."

Chris didn't know what to say. "Are you hungry? I've some fish."

"I'd love some," said Irene. "I can't remember the last time I ate."

She followed him up to his camp. Sitting near the fire, they shared a meal.

"That was wonderful," said Irene. "It must be weeks since I last had something to eat."

"That's impossible," said Chris. "You'd be dead by now."

"This is a dream," she said. "Anything can happen in a dream."

"I suppose you're right."

Suddenly, his face grew pale.

"Are you all right?" she asked.

"I don't know; I feel strange."

"Maybe it was the fish?"

"I don't think so," he said, placing his hands over his face. "I've felt this way before. I have to leave this dream. I'm waking up."

"I understand," said Irene. "Don't worry; I'll be here when you return."

Three

Life could be a dream

Hey nonny, ding dong, alang, alang, alang
Boom ba-doh, ba-doo ba-doodle-ay

Oh, life could be a dream (Sh-boom)
If I could take you up in paradise up above (Sh-boom)
If you would tell me I'm the only one that you love
Life could be a dream, sweetheart
(Hello, hello again, Sh-boom and hopin' we'll meet again)

Words and Music by The Chords

THE JOURNEY

It was still dark when Walter Jr. woke up in the backseat of his car. He stepped out and stretched. Being cramped for so long left him with a stiff back and a knot in his neck. He didn't bother to check what time it was, the car radio and clock didn't work – he'd got it that way. He knew he needed to hustle if he was to make it to the Oklahoma City bus terminal by six in the morning.

He drove north slightly under the speed limit. He couldn't afford another speeding ticket. Besides, his inspection sticker expired month's ago – another misfortune for being jobless.

Downtown Oklahoma City, he parked the car and walked to the bus station. The overhead clock read quarter to seven. He was too late. Just to be sure, he walked over to the ticket booth.

"Excuse me, sir; has the bus to Denver left yet?"

Looking at the schedule, "Sorry, you just missed her. They arrived on time at six, laid over for half an hour, and left on time at six-thirty. There's another bus to Denver leaving at six this evening."

"That's all right; thank you," said Junior as he slowly turned.

On the other end of the terminal was a café – The Starlight – twenty-four-seven – have a home-cooked meal away from home. Coffee sounded good.

The Starlight was empty. There were three seating choices – a booth, a table, or at the counter. He thought if Grandpa ate breakfast here a half hour ago, where would he sit? Where else other than where the coffee and conversation flows – he'd sit at the counter.

A pretty, middle-aged black woman stood behind the counter in front of him.

"Coffee, please."

"Would you care for anything else?" she asked as she placed down the coffee and cream.

He didn't speak right away. He'd fixed his attention on her hair; the ends were bright pink, reminding him of some rare and beautiful African flower. He read her nametag – Lily.

"Could you tell me if an old gentleman was here about half an hour ago? He always orders coffee and a bowl of grits with plenty of butter and maple syrup."

An ear to ear smile grew on her face.

"Sure-nuff was here. Sweet old guy and talk-a-tive..." She laughed with her whole body, and then went stern. "Old man like that shouldn't be out on his lonesome."

"He's my grandpa. We're supposed to be traveling together, except I got detained. I'm trying to catch up with him. Did he say anything...like where he was going?"

"I asked him just that. I said, 'Sugar, where you going all by your lonesome?' and he says he's going to a wedding. So I say, 'who's gettin' married?' and he says he is. Cracked me up...!" She began laughing again. "Left a good tip, too."

Now he had a full-fledged dilemma on his hands. What should he do? He now knew for certain his grandfather was on a bus on its way to Denver. All he needed to do was phone the police or his parents and let them take care of it. Only, that left him with a feeling of betraying his grandfather. He could let things play out the way they were going, without interfering, except that felt wrong, too – for two reasons.

One – his grandfather, a frail old man was on his lonesome (as Lily put it). He was defenseless.

Second – not doing anything meant he was buying into his grandfather's delusion.

So what's wrong with that? Why does it have to be a delusion? Why can't it be true? There are more things in heaven and earth, Horatio, then are dreamed of in your philosophy. Then why not the dream of an old man? Is there no more love, hope, or miracles in the world?

He knew if he accepted what his grandfather told him to be true he would have to accept it one hundred percent. That meant finding his grandfather and getting him safely to his destination.

It would be foolish to follow the bus in route; he'd never catch up with it. The best thing to do was skip going to Denver and try to overtake him in California. Knowing his grandfather's love of trains, he felt sure that was the way he'd go. And a train heading west from Denver to California meant only one place – the end of the line – the Los Angeles train station. He'd drive west, camp out at the L.A. train station till his grandfather's train came in. There was only one problem – money.

He could only think of one solution. He hated the idea. He found a payphone and dialed. He knew what he had to do. The operator got the ball rolling.

"I have a collect call from a Mr. Walter Bouchard Junior. Will you accept the charges?"

"Yeah, I guess so. Hey, little brother, a collect call, ay. I guess that means you still ain't found a job, yet. If you're thinking of putting the bite on me, you can save your breath and me some money by hanging up right now."

Junior bit down gently on his tongue, inhaled deeply and slowly let it out.

"Dave, you know I hate calling you as much as you hate me calling. But this is an emergency."

"What's wrong? Is Mom and Pop all right?"

"They're fine. It's Grandpa; he's run off."

"Have you called the police?"

"Of course, we have. Listen, Dave, I'm just going to come right out and say it. I think I know where he's going. I want to try to head him off."

"Why don't you just call the police?"

"Because, if I do, they'll stop him and then he won't get to his destination."

"Where's he going to?"

"I'd rather not tell you, Dave. You have to trust me."

"This is silly. Don't you think Grandpa's a little old to go running away from home?"

"He's not running from; he's running to, Dave! Haven't you ever wanted something so bad you were willing to put it all on the line? Or have you always been a stick-in-the-mud?"

There was a long silence.

"I know you won't do it for me; only do it for him. He's always been there for us. When did he ever ask anything of any of us? He wants this so bad, Dave. Let's not let him down."

There was another even longer silence.

"How much do you need?"

"A thousand. I'm in Oklahoma City."

"I'll telegraph five hundred."

"Thanks, Dave. Say, do me another favor. Don't tell Mom or Pop about this."

"You're a piece of work, Junior. You know that?"

He picked up the money at Western Union. He bought a small cooler and filled it with bottled water, white bread and baloney. After filling the gas tank, he got on the freeway and headed west.

Four

Beautiful Dreamer

Beautiful Dreamer, out on the sea
Mermaids are chanting the wild Lorelei;
Over the streamlet vapors are borne,
Waiting to fade at the bright coming morn.

Words and Music by Stephen Foster

BEFORE THE JOURNEY

A week after Walter Junior's return home, things again became routine. Chris felt glad he told Walter Jr. about his dream world and his dream lady. However, it wasn't enough; he wanted to tell others. There was a newfound joy running through his old veins; a joy he'd long since forgotten; and he wanted to share. It was just a dream and dreams can be strange. Surely no one would think him foolish. If so, then all people are fools for all people dream.

That night at dinner, in the middle of cutting his chicken-fried steak, he announced, "I've been having the strangest dreams, lately. Actually, I should say dream, just one dream. It continues every night where I left off the night before. I dream I'm young and I live on a desert island. I saw a woman walking on the beach. I thought it was Phyllis, except when I ran to her I found out it wasn't. She said her name was Irene Cooper. I don't think I've ever met anyone named Irene Cooper. I'll ask her about that tonight. I have to admit I'm excited about seeing her again. The strange thing about these dreams, or dream, is it all feels as real as when I'm awake."

Walter Jr. gently kicked his grandfather's leg under the table as a warning for saying too much. The old man looked at him, as if not understanding.

Walter Sr. spoke without looking at the old man. His mouth was full. "I would image most old folks dream about being young again. It seems only natural to me."

Beth saw it in a different light. "Daddy, have you been taking your vitamins? That can have an affect on your sleep."

"I tell you, Beth, I'm thinking this island and this lady are real."

"The nurse will be here Friday for your weekly checkup. You tell her all about it. And I bet cha I know what she'll say – vitamins."

Walter Jr. let out a sigh of relief because no one believed his grandfather.

Chris let out a sigh of despair because no one believed him.

****

Chris liked Nurse Molly. She was forever smiling. She was his squatty, little marshmallow lady in her starched white uniform.

He sat on the edge of his bed, as she slipped her stethoscope up the back of his shirt and pressed it against his skin.

"Now, breathe in, good, now, let it out slowly." She removed the stethoscope and held his wrist to take his pulse. "Your daughter tells me you're not taking your vitamins."

"What's the difference? It's too late to die young."

"It's never too late to live well. Follow my finger."

"Molly?"

"Mmm?"

"Can you write prescriptions?"

"Why, what do you need?"

"Sleeping pills."

"Aren't you sleeping well?"

"I get up at least twice a night to go to the bathroom."

"That's not uncommon for a man your age."

"Yeah, it can be embarrassing. Say for instance, you're talking to someone in your dream, when suddenly you have to excuse yourself because you have to wake up and go to the bathroom. Then you tell them to wait there, you'll be right back. It's embarrassing."

"Chris, I've no idea what you're talking about."

"I keep having the same dream every night. I'm young; I live on an island with this girl…"

"Knowing you, I'm not surprised there's a woman involved."

"Molly, this is serious."

"Okay. I'll tell your daughter to pick you up some over-the-counter sleeping pills, nothing strong. Let's see if those help."

"Molly, tell me straight. Am I crazy?"

"No, I'd say you just got a bad case of the human condition."

****

That night when Chris woke in the dream, he was lying on the beach again. Only this time his head rested in Irene's lap. She smiled down on him, running her hands through his hair.

"Are you all right?" she asked.

"Never better," he said as he quickly jumped to his feet. He felt uneasy in the delight of her touch. Looking at her beauty aroused long forgotten feelings.

"We need to talk," he said. "We need to find some answers."

"Answers?"

"Yes, answers. I know this is a dream. Only why are you here? I don't know anyone named Irene Cooper."

"Cooper was just my married name. My maiden name was Kelly."

"I used to date a girl in high school named Irene Kelly."

"I only dated one boy in high school and his name was Chris Goodman."

"That's me!" shouted Chris. "I'm Chris Goodman! Now I think I understand.

"Understand what?"

"It's simple. I'm an eighty-five year old man. It's only natural that I dream every night that I'm young again. And to make the dream complete, my mind is trying to recapture my youth by conjuring up my first love, Irene Kelly."

"There's only one problem with your theory," she said, folding her arms.

"What's that?"

"This isn't your dream; it's mine!"

"Oh, this is rich! This is a hoot!" He laughed and danced in the sand in front of her. "The figment of my imagination is telling me I'm a figment of its imagination!"

With her arms still folded, "I was just about to say the same about you!"

He stopped dancing. "This is serious. One of us must be wrong."

She unfolded her arms, her face grew soft again. "Not necessarily, what if we're both right? What if we're both sharing the same dream?"

"Is that possible?"

"I can't see why not. Anything is possible in a dream."

"But for what reason?"

"I'm not sure. I guess we'll find out."

They both instinctively sat down in the sand, staring out at the ocean.

"So, Chris, tell me, where do you live?"

"With my daughter and son-in-law in Venus, Texas…it's not bad."

"Still in Texas, ay?"

"What about you?"

"I live in a nursing home in San Diego, the Blue Jay Nursing Home; it's not bad."

"I guess we've got a lot of catching up to do? You know, I remember you. You were the first girl I ever kissed; I mean, really kissed."

She smiled. "I never forgot you. You were my first love. A girl never forgets her first love. Who knows, maybe that's why we're here together on this island."

"Why's that?"

"I don't know, recapture what we lost, find something we missed, get it right...for once."

"Say, didn't you used to wear your hair scrunched in the back."

"It's called a ponytail."

"Yeah, I remember. We sure had some good times. I can't remember why we broke up."

She laughed even harder and gently bumped into him, causing him to rock in the sand.

"Well, I sure do! There were lots of reasons we broke up and all of them were you."

"Me?"

"Yeah, you! You were too immature at the time. When things started to look serious, you got cold feet and ran off to join the navy. I'll tell you the main reason we broke up."

"What's that?"

"I wouldn't go all the way with you, that's what. I bet if I did, you would have stayed. We probably would have married." She closed her eyes and smiled. "You sure did look good in that sailor uniform."

"When did you ever see me in my uniform?"

"At the Christmas dance. You were home on leave. You came over to say hello. I thought I would cry. I was with Mark Cooper, remember?"

He spun around in the sand and pointed at her. "Mark Cooper...Cooper...Irene Cooper...you married Mark Cooper!"

"Sure did."

"How is old Mark?"

"He died about ten years ago."

"That's about the same time I lost Phyllis," he said sadly.

"Guess we both have a story to tell."

"Yeah, and from the looks of it we'll have plenty of time to tell it."

He suddenly jumped up. "Oh, oh, I'm sorry but there's something I've got to do. I'll be right back."

"I'll be waiting."

He faded out of the dream.

****

Old Chris slid slowly off the side of the bed till his feet were in his slippers. He carefully made his way through the dark and into the bathroom. It was a clearly noticeable difference in the way he felt now from the way he felt only a minute ago on the island.

Washing his hands, he could see himself in the mirror. He thought, "I don't want her to ever see me like this. Irene must never see the real me."

Slipping back into bed, he looked at the clock. The sleeping pills helped. He'd never slept so long without the need to go to the bathroom. Yet, it still wasn't enough.

In bed, he pulled the covers up and closed his eyes.

****

Chris appeared at the water's edge. He looked both ways up and down the beach. He was alone. He backed up into the water, turned to face the island, cupped his hands around his mouth and shouted. "Irene! Irene!" He saw movement at the top of the hill.

"Chris! Up here!" she called down, waving her arms.

He laughed, as he ran. One minute earlier he struggled in pain to get to the bathroom. Now, he moved with no effort like the wind.

She'd lit a fire and was cooking fish. They picnicked overlooking the ocean below.

"When I was gone just now, how long did it feel to you?"

She thought for a moment. "Four or five hours."

"Really, for me it was only five minutes. I guess time moves slower in dreams."

He leaned back and rested on his elbows, picking his teeth with a fishbone. "I don't see why you should go back to your side of the island. It makes more sense for both of us to live on the same side."

"I agree," she said. "We should build two huts to sleep in – one for you and one for me."

"Mine can be there on the beach; you can stay up here, in case any ships pass."

"What makes you think there are any ships?"

"Like you said, anything's possible in a dream."

"Whoever heard of being rescued from a dream?"

****

All afternoon they gathered palm leaves to make the huts. The warm sun slowly baked their skins to golden bronze. Finally, when the heat of the day became too much to bear, they ran waist-deep into the ocean's waves, laughing and splashing each other.

Without warning, Chris went somber. In response, she did the same.

"Irene, I'm so glad we're here together. I really like you."

"I've always liked you, Chris."

"Irene, there's something I want to say. Please don't be upset with me, I've got to say it or I'll burst." He hesitated and then continued, "I can't stop looking at you, your legs, your arms, your eyes and hair; I want so badly to just reach out and touch you." He hesitated again. "You're not mad at me, are you?"

"No, I'm not mad." She smiled. "I have to confess I feel the same way about you."

"You do?"

"Sure; why do you think I suggested separate huts?"

Suddenly the air was shattered by a loud shrill sound that dug into their eardrums like a power drill. They covered their ears with their hands.

"What is that?" she screamed.

"It's my alarm clock! It's gone off! It's time for me to get up. I'm sorry. I've got to go."

"I'll be here waiting."

He faded out of the dream.

The instant Chris woke, before opening his eyes; he reached across the bed and shut off his alarm.

Five

What a day for a daydream

What a day for a daydream
What a day for a daydreamin' boy
And I'm lost in a daydream
Dreamin' 'bout my bundle of joy

Words and Music by John Sebastian

THE JOURNEY

They say God watches over drunks and small children. It would seem He also has a soft heart for little old men. Chris is living proof of that. Denver is a big town and easy to get lost in, although, with the help of some friendly locals, Chris found his way from the bus terminal to the train station.

He wasted no time buying his ticket. He'd always loved trains, and this was sure to be the trip of a lifetime. His heart quickened as he held his ticket. He sat on a bench in the station's main hall. It would be a long wait. The train leaving Denver to L.A. wouldn't leave till six the next morning. His grumbling stomach reminded him he hadn't eaten anything since his bowl of grits in Oklahoma City. It was then he realized he'd left his hat on the bus.

****

If they ever have a waitress' hall of fame, a large portrait of Hilda Broz would be the first thing you see when you enter the building. Hilda worked at the Colonial Diner, across from the train station for over thirty years. She'd raised her three children single-handed. She worked hard to put all three through college – proof she did have a heart.

She could recall up to twenty orders and which customers got what. Your food was always hot and your plate removed just after the last bite. She could carry four plates on each arm and pull a twelve hour shift six days a week.

Years of working with the public left her an extremely private person with a dreadfully cold heart. Every night, at home, as she soaked her feet, she'd erase every face she came across that day from her memory. She wanted nothing to do with the human race.

The Colonial Diner was packed. Chris waited for a seat at the counter.

"What'll it be?" Hilda asked in arctic tones.

"I'd like an order of buttered toast and a cup of hot water, please."

"White, pumpernickel, or whole wheat?"

"White, please."

"You know we do have tea bags, if that's what the hot water's for."

"No, thank you. I'd just like a cup of hot water, please."

After placing his order in front of him, Hilda backed off and watched. The old man reached for the ketchup and stirred two tablespoons of it into the hot water. He salt and peppered it, and began dunking his toast in the mixture.

He looked up to see Hilda's questioning face.

"I've gotta watch my pennies, while I'm traveling. It don't taste as good as tomato soup from a can, but it cuts the hunger."

Hilda walked away, shaking her head in disgust and disapproval, only to return with a hamburger and an order of fries. She plopped it down on the counter.

"I'm sorry, but I didn't order this," said Chris.

"Fellow at the other end of the counter ordered this and decided he didn't want it."

"Really?"

"Have I ever lied to you?" asked Hilda.

"Not lately," said Chris.

"Listen, you want it or not? If not it goes into the trash."

"Oh yes, please, thank you so much."

Chris dug in with both hands.

Hilda went into the kitchen where she was sure no one would see her and did something she hadn't done in a very long time. She smiled.

****

Walter Jr. sat in the front seat of his car, parked in the parking lot of the Blue Oyster Diner, preparing a baloney sandwich. He hid the sandwich in his coat pocket and entered the diner. Budget or not, he needed a cup of coffee. The sign out front "Free Refills of the World's Best Coffee". That remained to be tasted. Especially since the sign also proclaimed oysters on the half shell were the house specialty – a bold boast for a diner in New Mexico.

He sat at the far end of the counter, so he could eat his sandwich undetected. The waitress placed his coffee in front of him.

"Anything else…?"

"Just coffee, thanks."

She laid his receipt down next to his cup.

It wasn't the world's best coffee, still, it was hot and there were free refills.

Though the counter was nearly empty, a young well-dressed gentleman took the stool next to him, on his right. The young gentleman had no need of a menu. He recited what he wanted from memory.

"I'll have a full dozen oysters on the half shell, shrimp cocktail, a bowl of chowder, a green salad with thousand island dressing, the six ounce rib eye – medium rare – baked potato, and string beans. To drink, I'd like a vanilla shake, and for dessert I'll have the New York cheesecake and a cup of coffee."

It's hard not to admire someone with such a grand appetite who remains slender. As the young gentleman slurped down his full dozen, Walter Jr. sipped his coffee. With one hand in his pocket, he tore off small bites of his baloney sandwich and popped them in his mouth – hopefully unnoticed. However, the stranger at his side noticed.

"What's the matter? Down on your luck?" asked the young gentleman.

"No, just on a tight budget."

"Not me," snapped the stranger. "I know what I want and I take it." He tapped the side of his head with his forefinger. "Positive thinking! Know what you want and take it."

Before Walter Jr. finished his second cup of coffee, the stranger wolfed down his entire meal. Before leaving, the young gentleman stood up and spoke to Walter Jr., again tapping the side of his head, "Remember! Positive thinking! Know what you want and take it."

When the young gentleman left the diner, Walter Jr. felt relieved to be rid of him. After his fourth cup of coffee, Walter Jr. had had enough. He grabbed his receipt and walked to the front of the diner. A short, bald, burly man behind the cash register rang him up.

"That will be thirty-nine, ninety-five, plus tax."

"No, that's not right! All I had was coffee."

"That's not what it says here, pal. This says you had a pretty big meal."

"No, you see, that was the other fellow. I only had coffee."

"Marge," hollered the burly man. "Call the police."

"The police! What for?"

"I know your game, pal. You and that other guy are running a scam. You sit next to each other, pretending you don't know each other. He orders a big meal and you order coffee. You switch checks. He pays the coffee tab, and then you complain about having the wrong check. You pay for your coffee, and then the two of you do it again at the next diner down the road. Only this time, you eat the big meal and he orders the coffee. I've seen this scam a hundred times. Marge, call the police!"

"No, wait, there's been a mistake. Don't call the police. I'll pay the check."

Walter Jr. handed him a fifty dollar bill. The burly man rang it up. Walter Jr. stood silently.

"What are you waiting for?" asked the burly man.

"My change?"

"Tip," he said as he slammed closed the drawer of the cash register.

Back in his car, Walter Jr. was still hungry. He made another sandwich and drove off holding it in one hand. His stomach became upset. The ordeal, two baloney sandwiches, four cups of coffee, and the lingering smell of oysters were the cause.

****

Chris positioned himself in the corner of one of the high-back wooden benches in the main hall of the Denver train station. With enough back support, he could sleep sitting up while waiting for the morning train. There were a few other travelers scattered about the hall trying to do the same. Yet, no one could sleep. A young couple seated alone in the middle of the hall was in the midst of warfare – a spat, an argument, a quarrel. Their voices were loud, and echoed off the high ceiling, the marble floor, and the plaster walls. No one could sleep.

With closed eyes, Chris listened to every venomous word they threw at each other. They hurled blame, accusations, and called each other rude names. Clearly, each of their goals was to hurt the other.

Chris rose and kicked his gym bag under the bench to hide it. He walked and stood before the couple. They stopped arguing and looked at him. The old man's eyes were wide and unblinking. They sat silently with their eyes fixed on him. His body shook violently, as if he were going into convolutions.

"Stop it! Just stop it!" he shouted. "Can't you see what you're doing? Why are you trying to hurt each other? If you hate each other that much, shake hands and go your separate ways. But don't attack each other, clawing and biting like two wild animals!"

"But..." whimpered the young woman.

"But you love each other," bellowed Chris. "Well then, act like it! If it's love, then treat it so. Treat it as what it is – something rare and beautiful. Do you know how many people go an entire lifetime never knowing love? Or they receive it too late or lose it too soon? Love isn't free. You pay for it everyday with every breath! Either part from each other or cling to each other! But, stop it! Just stop it!"

They remained silent, as they watched him walk away. Chris sat back in his seat and closed his eyes. He heard them whispering.

Had his words made a difference? It didn't matter to him. He'd offered them the gospel according to Christopher Goodman. He'd planted a seed. Now it was up to them to decide what to do with it.

****

Few people know the many colors of the desert, especially at sunrise. Walter Jr. felt he drove on holy ground – driving through a church. Now and then, he'd drive through small towns, so small that if you blinked you'd miss them. He decided to stop for coffee at one of these towns. In the heart of this small nameless town was a two-block stretch of stores. In the middle of the second block was a café – Patty's Cake House – world's best pancakes – breakfast all-day.

An old International Harvester truck was parked out front. Household items filled the back of the truck – a couch, a bed, a crib, and such. The hood of the truck was up. A tall, slender, young cowboy worked on the engine. His sleeves rolled up and his cowboy hat tilted back. Standing near him, leaning against the side of the truck was a willowy, young black woman. Her beauty equal to any model or actress, she wore a tan tee-shirt, and military green pants tucked into high and heavy army boots. She held a baby in her arms.

As he passed by, Walter Jr. heard the cowboy cursing the engine.

"Can I help?" Walter Jr. asked.

The cowboy came out from under the hood and adjusted his hat.

"I'd appreciate it. I ain't gettin' nowheres with her."

Walter Jr. got under the hood and began to tinker.

"You a mechanic?" asked the cowboy.

"No, only I've owned enough piles of junk to know my way around them." Walter Jr. stepped back. "Go head, try her."

The cowboy jumped behind the wheel and turned the key. It kicked over. He pressed down on the gas, the engine roared. He shut it off and started it again with no problem. He turned it off, again, got out and slammed down the hood.

"We really appreciate this, mister. Say, we were just goin' to go in and have breakfast. Why don't you join us? It's on us. It's the least we can do. What do you think, honey?" He directed this last remark to the woman who nodded in agreement.

The thought of another baloney sandwich made his stomach twitch; pancakes sounded like heaven.

Entering the café, nothing short of storming in with guns blazing would have gotten more attention than a multiracial family. All the local patrons never saw a mixed couple and child before – in the flesh, you might say. Other than the surprised look on their faces, it was difficult to say what they were thinking.

However, it was immediately obvious what their waitress thought. She tossed the menus onto the center of the table and plopped their glasses of water down so hard that water spilled everywhere. She walked off without a word.

His newfound cowboy friend smiled. "You get used to it."

"Really…?" Walter Jr. thought.

"So, what's your name?" asked the cowboy. "This here's my lovely wife, Felicia and our son, Tyrone. My name's Travis Wilkins."

The two men shook hands; Felicia and Walter Jr. nodded and smiled at each other.

"My name's Walter. It's a pleasure to meet you."

"The pleasure's all ours. I don't know where we'd be if it wasn't for you."

Between his cowboy clothes, mannerisms, and twang in his voice, it was easy to peg Travis as a country boy. Felicia spoke without a hint of accent. Their baby boy, Tyrone, looked an unmistakable combination of both his parents. He was beautiful.

The waitress returned, holding her pad and pencil.

"What'll it be?" she asked coldly.

While waiting on their breakfast, the conversation became cozy.

"So, Walter, where you heading?"

"California. I'm going to spend some time with my grandfather. How about you folks? Where you heading?"

"Don't know," said Travis. "I guess you could say we're on the run."

"Don't look so worried," laughed Felicia. "We're not killers or anything like that."

"Ever hear of King's Corner, Nebraska?" asked Travis.

Walter Jr. shook his head.

"I'm not surprised," laughed Travis. "It's not even a pimple on the map. That's where we're from. I lived there all my life. My parents are prominent citizens there. Get this, my father is not only the mayor, he's the preacher at the only church."

"Talk about your separation of church and state," added Felicia.

"Well, when Felicia and I hooked up, my parents disowned me. The whole town wanted nothing to do with us."

"What did we care," said Felicia, taking hold of her husband's hand, "as long as I had my sweet *Electric Horseman*."

He looked deep into her eyes. "And I had my beautiful *African Queen*." He turned to Walter Jr., "I guess you can tell we're movie buffs. Well, anyways, everything changed when little Tyrone, here, arrived. My parents said they wanted to be part of his life. Which sounded like it might be a good idea, at first."

"Until they called child services on us," added Felicia. "They claimed we weren't fit parents, and they wanted custody."

"I thought that was the funniest thing I ever heard," said Travis, "my parents wanting a baby who's half black and only half redneck."

"You don't have a redneck, do you, sweetie?" whispered Felicia to Baby Tryon, kissing the nape of his neck.

Just then the waitress returned with their food. She placed the plates down as hard as she had the water glasses. When she left, Walter Jr. just had to ask.

"Doesn't that bother you?"

"It used to," said Felicia. "Now we just ignore it."

"Ignorance, just plain ignorance," Travis huffed.

As they ate, they talked.

"How can your folks say that you're not good parents?" Walter Jr. asked.

"They say we don't make much money. That's true. We live in a trailer, which is some kind of no-no. They say it ain't right Felicia is away so often, seeing how she's in the Army."

"You're in the military?" Walter Jr. asked.

"Sure am," said Felicia. "Officially AWOL, as of yesterday…"

"What do child services say about your parents?" continued Walter Jr., "They don't have any real grounds to take Little Tyrone away from you, do they?"

"Certainly not," snapped Travis. "But they've got enough power, connections, and money to make our lives miserable. So we packed all our stuff in the old International and skedaddled."

When they'd finished eating, every eye followed them, as they left the café.

Outside, they said their good-byes. The men shook hands. Felicia kissed Walter Jr. on the cheek. She and Baby Tyrone got in on the passenger side.

"Well, you take care, Walter," Travis said as he got behind the wheel. He made one last statement to Walter Jr. before driving off.

"One other thing I think you might get a kick out of. My parents told child services that a trailer was no place for a grandchild of theirs to live in. If they had custody, he could live in their million dollar mansion. So, you know what we did? Before we left town, I put a match to it. Down to the ground, baby! I wrote a postcard to my folks from Albuquerque saying if they needed a place to stay, they were welcome to the trailer. Hee-haw!"

Walter Jr. heard Travis' laughter as they drove off.

Six

In Dreams

A candy-colored clown they call the sandman
Tiptoes to my room every night
Just to sprinkle stardust and to whisper
"Go to sleep; everything is alright."

I close my eyes, then I drift away
Into the magic night, I softly sway
Oh, smile and pray like dreamers do
Then I fall asleep, to dream my dreams of you.

In dreams. . .I walk with you
In dreams. . .I talk with you
In dreams. . .you're mine

Words and Music by Roy Orbison

BEFORE THE JOURNEY

Walter Jr. was no slacker. The day after he moved back home, he got right into looking for a job. He spent his time looking at job postings on the internet, he sent out résumés, made phone calls. Since they lived far from town, far from the main roads, if he got an interview, his father dropped him off at the bus stop on his way to work – five miles away. To get downtown, he needed to buy an exchange ticket and take three different buses. It was a three-hour trek.

The waiting rooms of these companies were full of other hopefuls, like himself, also there for an interview. Some of them had years of experience, which out weighed just having a college degree.

After the interview, Walter Jr. ate lunch at one of the hot dog stands – to save money. Then with his exchange ticket, he'd ride the three buses for the three hour journey back. At the last bus stop, he still had a mile hike home. The entire day was shot. He'd get home just in time for dinner.

Most mornings, Walter Jr. waited in his room till Walter Sr. left for work. He avoided his father whenever possible. He knew his father loved him, as he loved his father, except lately, all they did was argue. His father often barraged him with harsh clichés: a man needs to stand on his own two feet, you need to start acting like an adult and be more responsible, you need to set goals and follow through. You need…you need…you need! He offered plenty of criticism, none of it constructive.

One morning, less than a month after his return, Walter Jr. waited in his room for his father to leave for work. He couldn't make out the words, although, he heard his parents talking at the breakfast table. He was sure his grandfather was with them.

The door bell rang. Beth placed her coffee down and her cigarette safely out in the ashtray, and went to answer it. A young man dressed in blue overalls, sporting a close-cropped crew cut, stood at the bottom of the stairs, holding a clipboard.

He didn't look up, staring at the clipboard. "I have a delivery for a Mr. Goodman."

Beth looked out, in the driveway was a tow truck, and attached to the back was an old jalopy.

"What's this all about?" asked Beth.

"I'm supposed to deliver this car to a Mr. Goodman."

Beth hollered through the house. "Daddy, it's for you?" She turned again to the young man. "There must be some kind of mistake."

"I don't know, lady, I just deliver them."

Her father and Walter Sr. came up behind her.

"I'm Christopher Goodman," announced the old man.

The young man handed over his pad and pen. "Just sign here, Mr. Goodman."

Unable to ignore the commotion, Walter Jr. showed up.

"Daddy, what's this all about?" asked Beth.

"What does it look like; I bought a car."

"A car? You can't drive; you're too old!"

"It's not for me; it's for Junior."

"Junior? What for?"

"So he can go on interviews."

Walter Sr. pushed forward. "Now, Dad, Beth and I appreciate what you're trying to do. But the boy needs to stand on his own two feet. He needs to learn about life."

"I agree," said Chris. "But he's not going to learn it sitting on a bus for six hours everyday."

They watched the man detach the jalopy from the tow truck. Walter Jr. stood on the lawn, smiling, and then he turned to his grandfather.

"Daddy's right, Grandpa. I appreciate it, but I can't accept this."

"Then don't. Think of it as a loan," said Chris. "It cost me eight hundred. When you get a job, you can pay me back in installments."

Junior looked to his father who nodded in approval.

"It's a deal," said Walter Jr., shaking his grandfather's hand.

"Here are your keys, Mr. Goodman." The young man held them out to Chris.

"No, they go to this young gentleman, here," said Chris pointing to his grandson.

"Well, now that that's done, let's all go back inside and finish breakfast," announced Beth.

"Junior and I will have breakfast later. I want him to take me for a ride in his new car," said Chris.

Beth shook her head, "I don't know if that's such a good idea, Daddy."

"We won't be long. I'll just drive around a mile or two," said Walter Jr. as he opened the passenger side door for his grandfather. "Don't worry. I'll take good care of Grandpa. We'll be right back."

****

"Engine sounds pretty good," said Chris. Walter Jr. reached over to turn on the radio – nothing. "Sorry about that; we can get that fixed."

"No, this is great, Grandpa! I love it. I really do."

"My first car was a Hudson. We didn't have power steering in those days. It was all muscle power. You'd break out in a sweat trying to get into a parking space."

Walter Jr. wasn't sure why he asked what he asked. He wasn't sure if it would please his grandfather or not. Perhaps, he was just being nosy, nevertheless, he felt compelled to ask.

"So, Grandpa, how's everything on the island?"

The question surprised Chris.

"Just fine. Irene and I just built two huts, one for her at the top of the hill and one for me on the beach."

"Why not just one hut?" Walter Jr. snickered.

"Take your mind out of the gutter. We're from a different generation. We never pushed the envelope like your so-called progressive generation does. Sure, we thought about it, only we tried not to act on it. Still, I don't blame you. It was easy to do, then. We had the whole world behind us. Our parents didn't want us to act on our impulses, nor did our music, or the movies, or society. Now the whole world tells you if it feels good – do it!" He looked over at Walter Jr., "Am I sounding like an old man?"

"Just a little, Grandpa."

"I hate when I do that! But what else do you expect an old man to sound like?"

"Grandpa, I just meant do you like this Irene?"

"Yes, I do very much."

"Do you think you'll ever like her as much or more than Grandma?"

"Funny you should ask that. I was thinking the same thing, myself. Then I realized the question's all wrong. It isn't how much more or less, it's how. Your grandmother and Irene are two completely different people. And the way I feel about each of them is completely different. That makes any sense?"

"I guess it does, somehow."

When they returned home, Walter Jr. pointed to a car parked out-front. "Hey, Nurse Molly's here."

****

"Have you been taking your vitamins?" asked Nurse Molly, shining a light in his eyes.

"Yes, mother," Chris said sarcastically.

"Don't get smart with me, Christopher Goodman."

"No worry of that ever happening. In all my eighty-five years no one ever accused me of being smart."

"Now who's being smart?" she laughed. "Did those over-the-counter sleeping pills help?"

"In a way. I didn't need to get up till later, although I did get up the same amount of times."

"Have you ever considered wearing padded underwear to bed and trying to sleep through it?"

"You mean a diaper."

Just the sound of the word made both of them cringe. "I guess a mild sedative wouldn't hurt. I'll call it in, and your daughter can pick them up for you. Just remember, they're mild but they're not candy. Only one at night, you understand?"

"Yes, mother."

****

The hope of sleeping through the night without getting up even once was all Chris could think about. In anticipation, he took one of the tablets during dinner. It hit him earlier than he expected. After dinner, the family watched television. Chris excused himself.

"You feeling all right, Daddy?" asked Beth, in a worrisome tone.

"Just fine, darling, I guess I should have waited to take one of those new pills. I'm already sleepy."

"You need any help, Daddy?"

"No, thank you, sweetheart. I'll be just fine. See you in the morning."

****

Chris woke in his dream; he stood at the water's edge, his feet planted deep in the wet sand. It was night. He looked a few yards up the beach. Irene sat next to a blazing fire. He walked over.

"You like lobster?" she asked.

"Love 'em."

"Good, I caught a few earlier. I just put them in the fire."

"Irene, tell me, why is it you're always here before me?"

"I guess I go to bed earlier than you."

"I don't know, tonight I fell asleep after dinner. That's early for me."

"Really?" she said. "Sometimes I don't even make it to dinner. Most times when they call us to the dining hall at the home, I'm already in bed and fast asleep."

"I took a mild sleeping pill tonight. I'm hoping I can get through an entire dream without having to go to the bathroom." He looked up at the night sky. The stars twinkled and a full moon shown next to its reflection in the water. "This is great," remarked Chris. "I've never been here at night. It's beautiful."

"Like a dream," added Irene in a slight giggle.

"Yeah, like a dream," chuckled Chris.

"Come and get it," cried Irene.

They placed the hot lobsters on flat stones and cracked the shells with sharp rocks. The meat was juicy and sweet.

"What was your wife like?"

"Phyllis, she was wonderful."

"You don't mind me asking, do you?"

"No, I don't mind; I could talk about Phyllis for days."

"You loved her very much?"

"Yes, I did, with all my heart from the instant I laid my eyes on her to the moment of her last breath."

"Tell me about her."

"What's to tell? She was beautiful, loving, fun, smart and so much more. My only regrets are that we met late in life, and it ended way too soon. After I started my own business, we married. We had one child, our daughter, Beth. I told you I live with her and her husband. Beth means well, she's…I don't…she's just Beth."

"I know exactly what you mean. We had three kids and not one turned out the way I hoped."

"Three! That must have been a handful?"

"You said it; and Mark was never there to help. Oh, he was a good provider, and I know he loved us, but his career came first."

"What did he do?"

"He was a zoologist. That's how I wound up in San Diego. He worked for the San Diego Zoo. Don't get me wrong, his putting in so many hours is my only complaint. No question, I loved him like he was the only man in the world."

"What about your kids?"

She hesitated. "That's strange; I know we had three children, two boys and one girl, only I can't remember their names. Lately, it's all becoming a blur."

"Tell me about it," said Chris. "It's like watching television with the sound turned down and picture out of focus. It seems like everything moves farther away everyday, out of grasp, out of sight; and everyday moves by faster."

"I know what you mean."

He reached over and placed his hand on hers. She responded like a grateful child hungry for attention and took his hand tightly in hers. She lifted it up and held it to her cheek. They sat warm and hypnotized by the flames.

"Chris?" she asked finally. "When you first saw me on the beach, you thought I was Phyllis. Are you sorry I'm not her?"

"When I think about Phyllis, I'm disappointed anyone is near, except her. I loved her. Except when I think of you, I know I wouldn't want to be with anyone else."

"I know it's strange, I feel the same way," whispered Irene to herself, the fire, and Chris.

"It's funny you asked me about Phyllis. My grandson did the same thing today."

"Did what?"

"Asked me if I cared for you more than his grandmother."

"Why would he do that? Does he know about us?"

"Yeah, I told him all about us. Well, almost all."

"I envy you. I'd so want to share with someone. My granddaughter, Olivia, visits me often, except we don't really talk. I could never share anything like this with her. What's your grandson's name; what is he like?"

"His name is Walter Jr.; only he's nothing like his father. We mostly call him Junior. He's a good kid, fresh out of college; but he's never been able to find a job. I just bought him a car; he wouldn't accept it unless I let him pay me back for it, once he's settled. You got to admire his spunk."

Irene moved closer to him. She wrapped both her arms around his arm and placed her head on his shoulder. They sat that way for a long time, staring into the fire and listening to the crackle of the burning driftwood. Chris felt a strong urge to wake up and go to bathroom. He fought it, till the feeling passed. He could only hope he hadn't wet the bed.

Finally, when he felt she would fall asleep on his arm, he broke the silence.

"Irene?"

"Yes," she whispered into the flames.

"May I kiss you?"

"You can, if you walk me home to my hut on the hill."

He stood up and raised her up with him. Without taking their arms from around each other, they slowly walked to the highest point of the island. Standing in front of her hut, they stood holding hands. The full moon was large and bright; it had now risen to where it seemed only inches above their heads.

He pressed his face against hers. "I'd give you the moon, if I could," he sighed into her hair.

"I don't need or want the moon, only you."

He reached out, as if trying to catch the moon. Remarkably, as his hand smoothed across the silver orb, it wiggled like a pond when you throw a pebble into it. Silvery moon dust covered his hand, like fluorescent fairy dust. She reached out with both hands and did the same. Both hands were shining. Again, he dipped his hands into the sphere above them. They laughingly painted each other with the glow of the moon. He held her and pulled her in close to him.

"Goodnight, my love."

"Chris, you've walked me home. You can claim your kiss, now."

And he did, it was a young man's, young woman's kiss, something long forgotten. He backed away slightly to look at her. The silver moon dust made her look like an angel.

"Goodnight, my love," he said again.

"Are you saying you love me?" she asked.

"Without question, I do."

"Then fear not," she said in a low voice. "You are not alone in this. I love you, too. I don't know what the future may bring, what it may hold; I only know I want to do it with you."

He kissed her again and again, till the moon and stars fell, till the island disappeared, till he woke up in his wet bed.

Chapter Seven

All I have to do is dream

Drea-ea-ea-ea-eam, dream, dream, dream
Drea-ea-ea-ea-eam, dream, dream, dream
When I want you in my arms
When I want you and all your charms
Whenever I want you, all I have to do is
Drea-ea-ea-ea-eam, dream, dream, dream

When I feel blue in the night
And I need you to hold me tight
Whenever I want you, all I have to do is
Drea-ea-ea-ea-eam

Words and Music by Felice & Boudleaux Bryant

BEFORE THE JOURNEY

"It's all your fault," said Chris. "You jinxed me. Now I've got to wear diapers every night. And Beth put down plastic slipcovers. What's next a crib?"

"I should have known those sleeping pills were a bad idea," said Nurse Molly. "At least before you woke up to go to the bathroom, with the pills you sleep right through it."

"Like heck I do. I still wake up four to five times a night. Only difference is now when I wake there ain't no use in going to the bathroom, I'm soaking wet! What I need are stronger sleeping pills so I can sleep through the entire night."

"I don't know about that, Chris."

"What's the difference, either way I've got to wear a diaper and wake up in the morning soaked. At least with stronger pills I'd get a full undisturbed night's sleep."

"Chris, what is with you lately about not wanting to wake up in the middle of the night? It's become an obsession with you. You almost sound like you fear it."

He leaned over and whispered as if telling her the deepest of secrets. "Do you know the time ratio between real life and a dream is sixty to one? If I wake up in the middle of the night, and if I'm up for only one minute, the person I left in the dream has to wait an entire hour for me to return. And if I can't get back to sleep right away, and I'm up for say twenty minutes, that person in the dream has to wait twenty hours, nearly a full day, before they see me, again."

"Chris, who's waiting for you in what dream?"

"Irene," he said even softer.

"Oh, I get it. This Irene is that girl on the island you keep dreaming about."

"Every night, I just go to sleep and there I am and there she is. We're both young and in love. And I want to spend every sleeping minute with her, I don't want to miss a thing, and I don't want her waiting days for me to get back from the bathroom!"

"Chris, that's just…crazy."

"I asked you weeks ago if I'm crazy and you said I wasn't!" he fussed at her.

"I'm not saying you're crazy; I'm saying *that's* crazy."

He calmed down and again spoke softly. "Listen, I'm just an old man. I've got foolish ideas. I talk nonsense sometimes. I don't know any better; it comes with age. I probably won't live much longer. Why not just humor me? Please, Molly, give me the pills."

She thought long and hard. "Okay, but on one condition. You never have those pills in your possession. Your daughter picks them up, she keeps hold of them, and gives you one every night – and one only. You never have access to them."

He didn't have to think twice. "It's a deal. Here, let's shake on it."

"I'm not going to shake on it," she laughed.

He grabbed her hand and shook it. "There, now it's official."

****

That afternoon was one of those rare times when Chris found himself in the house alone. He picked up the phone in the kitchen. Getting the number from information, he dialed. A bright friendly voice answered.

"Blue Jay Adult Living, where your golden years shine. May I help you?"

"Yes, I'd like to speak with Mrs. Irene Cooper."

"One moment, please."

The line went silent. He waited. Then with a sharp click the bright friendly voice returned.

"I'm sorry, there's no answer at her room. Would you like to leave a message?"

"Then, you do have an Irene Cooper there?"

"Excuse me, sir?"

"I mean, I've got the right number? Irene Cooper does live there?"

"Yes, sir. She's probably not in her room. We have bingo in the main hall, today. Most of our guests are there. Would you like to leave a message?"

"Just tell her that Chris called."

****

After dinner, Chris, Beth and Walter Sr. sat in the living room watching television. Walter Jr. went straight to his room. Chris got up, went to the kitchen and came back holding a glass of water. He didn't want to look anxious, however he was. He stood at the living room door.

"Beth?"

"Yes, Daddy?" she asked, not taking her eyes from the screen.

"Did you pick up my pills? I'd like to go to bed, now."

Without flinching, she tapped the shoulder of her husband seated next to her. "Walter, hand me my purse." He obeyed. She rummaged through her purse without looking. She took one pill out and handed it to her father. "Here, you are, Daddy. Remember, Nurse Molly says you only get one per night, no more."

"I understand. Thank you. Goodnight."

"Goodnight, Dad," Walter Sr. mumbled.

"Goodnight, Daddy," said Beth.

After taking the pill, Chris returned the glass to the kitchen. On his way to his room, he passed young Walter's room. He heard typing. He knocked on the door.

"Who is it?"

"J. Edgar Hoover; we got word you've been passing counterfeit thousand dollar bills."

"Come in, Grandpa."

Not wanting to intrude on his privacy, Chris stood in the doorway.

"How's the job hunting going?"

"Slow. I just sent off three applications."

"That's good. Keep it up. It'll pay off soon."

"I hope so."

"It will." Chris waited a minute, before changing the subject. "You know the old saying, *'All work and no play make Jack a dull boy'*?"

"Yeah, what about it…?"

"Well, Junior, I'm suspecting you're turning into a dull boy. When was the last time you spent some time with a woman?"

Walter Jr. laughed.

"That long," said Chris. He pulled a twenty dollar bill out and held it out to Walter Jr., "Here, take this. It ain't much, but you need to get out. Find a friendly bar, have a drink, meet some girl."

"No offense, Grandpa, twenty dollars won't make much of an impression on women today."

"Never did. That's why you got to fill in the gaps with personality. You got personality, don't cha boy?" You got some of my blood running through your veins; you must have some, because I got personality coming out of the wha-zoo."

"Thanks, Grandpa, except I owe you enough money already."

"This ain't a loan; this is a gift. Think of it as a birthday present for the birthdays you'll have after I'm gone."

"You ain't ever going to go, Grandpa."

"How's that saying go, '*Get behind me, Satan*'? Heck, of course I'm going to go. In many ways, I'm looking forward to it. Now, I want you to take this twenty, find a friendly bar. First, you order a drink, get yourself loose. Then I want you to walk over to the most beautiful woman at the bar and offer to buy her a drink. Then I want you to tell her the truth – everything about you. Any intelligent woman will respond. Some women want handsome, security, money, but a true woman's more attracted to a caring, loving, truthful man."

"You sure?"

"Trust me."

****

Johnny Friendly's bar was anything but that. It was dark, the music was loud, it smelled of stale beer, and no one – that is no one – was friendly. They argued over who played what on the jukebox. They argued who was next at the pool table. The waitresses were cursed for being too slow, and the bartenders for shortchanging the customers both in money and the small amount of alcohol in the drinks.

Walter Jr. sipped his beer and examined his surroundings. Sitting at the other end of the bar was a woman. Only, not just any woman, perhaps the most beautiful woman Walter Jr. could remember laying eyes on in a long time. He hesitated at first, yet the words of his grandfather pressed him on. He walked over and sat next to her. There was a strange look about her. It was difficult to read what was going on inside her mind. Her face showed no evidence of happiness, sadness, anger, love, or any other emotion. She was a blank slate, waiting for someone to write something on.

"Buy you a drink?" Walter Jr. asked.

"If you like?" she said unfeelingly.

He motioned to the bartender. For awhile, they sipped in silence.

"What's your name?" he asked.

"Sandy."

"My name's Walter."

When they finished their drinks, Walter Jr. ordered another round. His grandfather's voice echoed in his head. He decided to go for it.

"My grandfather told me a true woman wants caring and truthfulness in a man, more than wealth or looks."

"Your grandfather's no dope."

"To be honest, that's the last drink I can buy. I've got no more money. I don't have a job and I live with my parents. I think you're the most beautiful woman I've seen in a long time, and I thank you for giving me the pleasure of your company. You have a good night."

He excused himself, rose from his stool, and headed out of the bar. Just a foot from the door, unexpectedly, he felt someone tugging at his sleeve. He turned to see Sandy. She slipped a piece of paper into his hand.

"It's my number. Call me when you get back on your feet." She reached up and kissed his cheek.

He took the slip of paper. "Thank you; I will." Driving home, he held a vision of getting a job and calling Sandy for a date. He vowed to spend his entire first paycheck on her.

****

Once Chris hit the bed, the pill took its toll. An instant after closing his eyes, he awoke in his dream. Irene was there waiting.

"You grow more beautiful every day," he said.

"You mean every night, don't you?"

They both laughed and hugged.

"I took a stronger sleeping pill; I hope, we can spend the entire night together, undisturbed."

"What about if you have to you-know-what?" she asked.

"It doesn't matter," he said, gesturing his hands across his front. He whispered, "I'm wearing one of those what-cha-call-its to bed."

She laughed. "Don't sound so ashamed. I wear one of those what-cha-call-its both day and night. It just comes with the territory. Getting old ain't for sissies."

He guided her to the shade, away from the blistering tropical sun. They sat in the sand, holding hands.

"I tried calling you, today."

"You did? What did I say?"

"We never spoke. They said you were playing bingo. Don't you remember?"

"Not really. For some reason, you have a better memory of the waking world, better than I do. When I'm here, everything else is a blur, like that was the dream." She reached out and lovingly brushed his bangs from his eyes. "Chris, why did you call? You had doubts about me being real, didn't you?"

"I'm sorry. I just had to be sure."

"I understand, but have a little faith in us. And please, Chris, don't call me again. This is our world. That old woman and that old man have nothing to do with us. We live here; they don't."

She saw in his eyes how sorry he felt and how desperately he wanted to change the mood. She kissed him and jumped to her feet.

"Race you to the water. Last one in is an old maid."

****

As if by magic, a small caldron washed up on the shore. They decided a seafood stew would be the perfect evening supper. They spent the afternoon filling the caldron with everything they could get their hands on. They dug along the beach for clams and oysters. Slow moving crabs and lobsters in the shallow water were easy pickings by hand.

As the sun sank low into position for a perfect sunset, they cleaned their harvest in the freshwater atop the hill. They covered everything in the pot with a mixture of half freshwater and half coconut milk. Irene added a few strips of seaweed for seasoning. Making a small fire, they placed the caldron in the center.

They sat hand in hand, his arm over her shoulders, watching the sunset as dinner simmered.

Using large shells as bowls, they sipped the rich broth, and ripped the sweetmeat apart with their fingers and popped small pieces into each other's mouth.

"That was good," remarked Chris, lying back, flat on the sand. Irene cuddled closer, placing her head on his chest. He listened to the crackling of the fire; she listened to his heart. She closed her eyes. He stroked her hair and counted the stars.

Perhaps a minute passed in the real world, or an hour in their dream. Chris only knew some time passed, only not how long. Irene remained motionless.

"Sweetheart, are you awake?"

"Just barely," she sighed.

He somehow maneuvered himself to his feet. He bent down and took her up in his arms. He gently placed her in her hut, and kissed her forehead. "Goodnight, sweetheart."

He stood in the doorway, unable to take his eyes off her. She spoke softly, like a child ready to drift off to sleep.

"Chris, I never knew you could fall asleep in a dream. Do you think I'll dream? I mean, can you dream while you're dreaming? And if I do, maybe I'll dream I'm an old lady living in a nursing home in southern California. Perhaps, that's really the dream and this is what's real."

The notion made his head swim.

"Sleep well, darling."

She didn't respond. She was fast asleep.

He carefully made his way down to the beach. Lying in his hut, he felt sleep take him gently by the hand.

"If I do dream, please, let me dream I'm on an island with Irene. Amen."

****

He woke to the sound of crashing thunder. He jumped to his feet. Great winds tore his hut apart and tossed the pieces into his face and then down the beach. Lightning struck trees, splitting them in half. The rain came down hard, like tiny pebbles. He ran up the trail to the top of the hill. The strong winds blew him off the path more than once. Before he was near the top of the hill, he met Irene running down the path. Lightning struck with a loud earsplitting thunder crack, as she ran into his arms, sobbing.

"We've got to find shelter," he shouted.

"The cave," she cried.

"Cave, what cave?"

"On the other side of the island where I came from, there's a cave."

"Do you think you can find it, again?"

"I think so."

"We've got to try for it."

They ran along the beach. He kept her close and tried to shelter her with his arms. The hard rain now mixed with marble-sized hail. The wind ripped bushes out by their roots. Lightning struck the trees, setting them on fire. The thunder roared at their heels like a wild beast in pursuit. They ran long and hard, mostly with their eyes closed.

"This way," shouted Irene, pulling him onto a tiny path leading upward. He could feel sharp rocks shredding the soles of his naked feet. Finally, they tumbled into the mouth of a large cave. They fell to the ground, holding each other tightly. Out of breath, they panted like hunted animals. Only the quick flashes of lightning allowed them a momentary look at their surroundings.

"Is this where you used to stay?" asked Chris.

"Only when it stormed and only here in the opening; it always frightened me."

"You never went inside?"

"Never."

"Maybe we should check it out?" The little boy woke in him. He stood and started slowly into the darkness of the cave.

"Chris, don't! Please come back!"

His voice echoed over and over. "Why, there's nothing to be afraid of. Say, what's this?"

"Chris. . .Chris!"

He came back carrying a candle and a box of wooden matches.

"Do you believe this? Well, like you said, *'Anything can happen in a dream'*."

"It is a dream, isn't it, Chris?"

He purposely ignored answering the question.

"Come on, let's explore."

She held fixed to his arm. When they were well out of the reach of the storm's winds, he lit the candle. The cave became clear. It was a long tight walkway with high walls, just wide enough for the two of them to walk side by side.

"We need to turn back," she warned.

"No, let's see where this leads."

After a hundred yards or so, they came to a large open space. Like an underground Cathedral, perhaps sixteen hundred square feet, the ceiling was twenty feet high with three to four foot-long stalactites hanging from it. In the center of this natural grand hall was a large pool with six stalagmites standing every few feet around it – reminiscent of ancient sentinels guarding the sacred waters.

"It's beautiful," said Irene, aloud. Her words slammed against every nook and cranny and echoed six or seven times back to them. It frightened her. She whispered to avoid the effect. "It's beautiful."

Chris picked up a stone; he was just about to toss it into the water when Irene grabbed his wrist to stop him.

"No, please, don't. We should leave everything undisturbed. This place frightens me."

"We'll leave," he said, taking her by the arm.

As they turned to go back the way they came, the candlelight shown on the far wall. Its surface was rough like the rest of the cave; only in the center, clearly, someone purposely made the surface smooth. Coming closer, they saw charcoal hand-markings.

"Who could have made these?" she asked.

"Your guess is as good as mine."

"They look almost like hieroglyphics, only more primitive."

"It's some sort of picture book story. Look at the way the people are sketched. Stick people, as if a child drew it."

They followed the wall. There were two lines of illustrations, one under the other. At the end of these lines, someone drew a strange symbol. After the symbol, the characters of both lines were not only erased; but chiseled out of the wall.

"Here, hold these," said Chris, handing her the box of matches and the candle. He reached down and came up with a chisel and mallet someone left on the ground.

"Someone wanted the last parts of these two lines removed, for sure." He looked back at the other characters. "Even if we do learn what it says, we'll never know their ending."

Suddenly, the chisel and mallet fell from his hand. He looked at her with fear in his eyes.

"Chris, what's wrong?"

"I'm waking up!"

"No, Chris, not now! You can't leave me here alone! Not now! Not here!"

She reached out to grab him, except he vanished in her arms. The candle fell to the ground and snuffed out. She was by herself in complete darkness.

Eight

Dream a little dream of me

Sweet dreams till sunbeams find you
Sweet dreams that leave all worries behind you
But in dreams whatever they be
Dream a little dream of me

Music by Fabian Andre & Wilbur Schwandt
Words by Gus Kahn

THE JOURNEY

"America the Beautiful," announced Chris.

"Excuse me, did you say something?" asked the woman seated across from him. A little girl in a bright yellow sundress with matching blouse and leggings sat leaning against her, trying not to fall asleep.

Chris gestured at the panoramic Colorado landscape appearing and disappearing across their train window. "I was just commenting on how beautiful it is."

"It is, isn't it? We just love living in Colorado. Are you from Colorado, Mr....?"

"Goodman, but call me Chris. No, I'm from Texas. It's not as pretty as Colorado, but we like her." He looked at the small child, trying desperately to stay awake. "They sure hate to miss anything, don't they?"

"Especially this one; she's always worried she's going to miss out on something. She'll sleep with one eye open for hours. We have a sleeping compartment; however, she wanted to be out and about."

"How old is she?"

"Just turned four; her name is Sara."

He leaned forward. "Please to meet you, Sara. Go to sleep. Don't worry. If anything happens I promise we'll wake you." He looked closer at her. "Didn't seem to make a difference."

"Oh, not with Sara. My name is Trisha Millwood. It's a pleasure to meet you."

It was too awkward to shake hands so they just nodded graciously to each other.

"I've got a daughter, too," he bragged. "Of course, she's older than you are." They both smiled. He checked out the little girl, again. "Looks like she finally conked out."

"Yeah, she may fight him tooth and nail, but she's no match for the sandman."

Again, Chris turned his attention to the window. Now and then everything would go dark as they passed through mountain tunnels, only to emerge into bright sunlight that glared off the snow peaks, causing you to squint. Looking down, there were lakes shimmering in the valleys below. The mountains rose and fell, as the train sped by like waves out at sea. He looked to the sky.

"Oh, beautiful for spacious skies…! I'm just beginning to understand what that song is all about."

"So, Chris, how far are you going?"

"All the way to the end of the line, Los Angles, and then some, down to San Diego."

"What's in San Diego, if I may ask?"

"Promise you won't laugh."

"I promise."

"I'm going there to see my girlfriend."

"Now, why would I laugh at that? No woman in her right mind would ever laugh at love."

"Well, some folks do. What with me being an old geezer and all, some people find it funny."

"I don't. You're never too old for love." She looked at her daughter. "That's like saying someone is too young for love. No one ever laughs at that."

"Trisha, is that right, Trisha? How far are you going, if I may ask?"

"End of the line, L.A, same as you. We're heading south, just not as far as you. We're going to Disneyland. It's always been Sara's wish to go to Disneyland."

"My wife and I wanted to take our daughter a few times, except we were always either short on time or money…or both."

"Bill, that's my husband, would have loved for to come. Unfortunately, they only pay enough for the child and one escort. You see *Dream Makers* is paying for everything."

"Dream Makers, isn't that the…" His voice trailed off and he looked at the sleeping child.

"Yes, they're the organization that makes dreams come true for children with incurable illnesses."

"But she looks so healthy?"

Trisha looked down, admiring her daughter, also. "Yes, she does, doesn't she? I only hope she stays that way. It's bad enough with her looking healthy."

Chris no longer saw the scenery passing by. There was no sky, no lakes, valleys or mountains, only the small sleeping child before him.

"Should we wake her?" he asked.

"Now you're thinking like I did at first. She has so little time; she shouldn't miss a minute." She stroked Sara's hair. "No, children need their sleep."

All at once, Chris felt confused, ill at ease, embarrassed, and full of a sorrow he'd not known since Phyllis passed away. He wanted so much to help; except he was helpless. He wanted to run away, than face another minute.

He stood up. "I'm going to the dining car for coffee. Would you like me to bring you something back?"

She looked up into his eyes; they were welling up with tears.

"Chris, I'm sorry if I'd made you feel uncomfortable."

He fell into full-blown crying. "I'm sorry. I just can't look at her right now. I've got to get away just for a few minutes. I'll be all right. I'll be back, I promise. See, I left my travel bag," he said, as if that sealed the deal, showed his sincerity.

They looked at each other for a few seconds. Chris blinked over and over till the tears stopped. He sniffled and then spoke.

"How do you do it? How do you handle it?"

"The best I can, one day at a time. It's my job. I never cry. Somewhere there's a large bottle full of my tears, and one day, I hope not too soon, I'll empty it…but not today."

"Do you want me to bring you back anything?" he asked.

"Sara likes cookies."

He nodded and began to walk off. Trisha reached out, grabbed his hand, and took it to her cheek.

"Thank you," she whispered.

****

It was late morning; the dining car was nearly empty. There was a tall dark man in a dark suit seated in the corner. A young couple in love, capturing all eyes, as they carried on like young lovers do, and an old woman seated by a window, wearing the strangest and largest of hats, sipping tea and admiring the countryside. Two waiters, elderly men, stood, waiting for breakfast to be over, when they could eat and drink as well.

When Chris sat down, one of the waiters approached him.

"May I help you, sir?"

"Oh, just coffee, please."

Alone, he examined the menu. He could think of hundreds of things besides just coffee. Only he needed to watch his pennies, especially if he wanted to bring back cookies for Sara. The tall dark man in the corner rose and left the dining car, the woman with the large hat hadn't moved, the young couple were kissing. The waiter returned with his coffee and a tray of food.

"I'm sorry, I didn't order this."

"It's all right. The tall gentleman who just left paid for everything."

Besides the coffee, there was a plate of two eggs – over medium, the way he liked them – two sausages, two strips of crisp bacon, toast, and a small bowl of grits with plenty of butter and maple syrup.

"Did he tell you his name?" asked Chris.

"No, sir. I am supposed to give you something else. He specified not to give it to you till you finished eating."

"What is it?"

"I'm afraid, sir, I can't say."

He paid little attention to the tall dark strange; now he wished he had.

Not wanting to look a gift-horse in the mouth, Chris enjoyed his breakfast. He held deep thoughts. Who knew of his preference for grits with butter and maple syrup? No one knew except close friends (all of whom were now dead) and family who would surely want him to return home immediately. This was a mystery.

When he finished, the waiter returned with a small paper bag. Inside were two cookies and a small container of milk.

"The gentleman said you'd want this."

"True," thought Chris, "only how would anyone know that?"

The waiter also handed him a small folded slip of paper.

"The gentleman said to give this to you last. He said it might disturb you, and he didn't want to ruin you appetite, so I was to give it to you last."

"Thank you," said Chris, looking through his wallet for a tip.

"That won't be necessary, sir. The gentleman gave me a generous tip." He walked away.

Chris took the note and opened it. It was in ink, and in the most superb handwriting. It read:

One or both of you must leave the island, as soon a possible.
Talk it over. I'll be in contact.

Chris' hands shook, as fear seized him. His mind reeled in search of possibilities; he could think of none. He read it again. There was no signature. He placed the slip of paper down on the table and sipped the last of his coffee. He picked it up again, to look at it once more. A chill ran over him. There wasn't anything written on it; it was blank.

When Chris returned, Sara was awake and ready for adventure. Standing in front of the window, her mouth open in awe, she pointed out everything that caught her eye to her mother. She turned to look at Chris, as he sat down. She wore an inquisitive look, as if sizing him up. A smile burst on her face.

"Pawpaw!" she cried as she jumped at him, throwing her arms around his neck.

"No, sweetheart, I'm not…"

"That's right," Trisha broke in. "This is Pawpaw number three. You're so lucky. You're the only little girl in the world with three Pawpaws."

Chris closed his eyes and held her in his arms, soaking up the sweet milk of a child's kindness. He wished it could last forever. However, the attention span of a four-year-old is shorter than that of an eighty-five-year-old. She kissed his cheek and hopped back to the window.

"Oh, look!" she said joyfully, again pointing at the whole beautiful world racing passed her window.

Chris handed the paper bag to Trisha. She looked inside.

"Sara, look what Pawpaw number three got you – cookies and milk."

Nothing could sway the child's attention from the window.

Trisha looked at Chris. "How much do I…"

He stopped her with a wave of his hand, shook his head with a pantomime *No* on his lips.

"Thank you," she said.

She took out one of the cookies and handed it to Sara. The child nibbled at it. Trisha gave Sara sips of milk between bites. The girl never took her eyes away from the window.

"I enjoy your company, Chris; however, if there's something you'd rather be doing, don't feel like you have to stay with us all the time."

"There is something I'd like to look into," said Chris. "I think I saw a friend of mine on the train; I'd like to try to find him. Can you keep an eye on my bag for me?"

"Sure. And if we have to leave, I'll take it with me. You can always find us at our compartment, number 191."

****

Chris walked the full-length of the train. From caboose, through baggage cars, passenger cars, dining cars, observation cars, more passenger cars, sleeper cars, and finally to the engine. He turned around and walked back to the caboose. He saw no sign of the mysterious man. Of course, he might have spent his time in hiding in a private compartment. Chris watched the lunch rush into the dining cars; then he watched throughout dinner. He saw no dark stranger. Was he real?

When he returned to his seat, Trisha and Sara were gone, as was his little black gym bag. He felt sure his possessions were in good hands. He sat back in his seat. The darkness took over. There was nothing to look at through the window – just black; the glass was like a mirror. He closed his eyes. He needed to sleep. He needed to be on the island. He needed to talk things out with Irene.

****

Many miles away, Walter Jr. continued driving through the desert. There was nothing to look at save for a vast scope of sandy flatlands dotted with rocks and cactus, with dry brown mountains always looming off in the distance. The road was so straight; he played a game with himself to see how long he could keep his hands off the steering wheel. Without a working clock, he had to count in his head. The longest was a count to one hundred and twenty-seven, before needing to put his hands back on the wheel.

Under such conditions, it was easy to spot the hitchhiker a mile up the road. As bored and lonely as he was, Walter Jr. decided he'd pick him up, that is considering the man didn't look like a fiend.

As he approached the figure standing on the side of the road, he realized it was just a young boy. His clothes were dusted by the sands of the desert. He carried a backpack and wore a wide-brim hat with his long hair tuck into it. Walter Jr. stopped a few yards after the boy. The boy ran, opened the car door and hopped in.

"Gee, thanks. I've been on the side of the road since yesterday."

"Where you going to?"

"Up to the next junction, then I need to go north."

"Me too," said Walter Jr., "How far north?"

"Montana."

"Well, I'm not going that far north, although, I could get you into Nevada."

"That would be great! Thanks!"

"You hungry?"

"Does the Pope wear a funny hat? I'm starved!"

Walter Jr. handed him a baloney sandwich.

"Gee, thanks," he said, taking off his hat.

This is the part in the story where anyone who is anyone who reads books or watches movies knows what happened next. It wasn't a young boy, it was a girl. Walter Jr. masked his surprise, although inwardly he was floored.

"So, you a gambler?" she asked, munching at large bits she'd stuffed in her mouth.

"What makes you think I'm a gambler?"

"You're going to Nevada. I just figured you're going to Vegas or Reno."

"No, once I get to Nevada, I turn west to California."

"What's happening there, if you don't mind me being nosy?"

"I'm going to see my grandfather."

"Cool," she said, wadding the last of the sandwich into her mouth.

"You still hungry?"

"A little."

He handed her another sandwich, which she woofed down faster than the first.

"Before we go any further," asked Walter Jr., "how old are you?"

"Don't worry, don't worry, I'm over eighteen," she said, rolling her eyes.

"How much over eighteen?"

"Eighteen and four months, I'm legal. So don't go freaking-out."

"Do your folks know where you are?"

"I just told you I'm over eighteen. It's none of their business." She spoke under her breath, "Not that it would matter to them, if they did know."

"What's your name?"

"Megan; what's yours?"

"Walter."

"Pleased to make your acquaintance, Walter."

"I told you where I'm going. Tell me, what's in Montana."

"Can you keep an open mind, Walter?"

"I'd like to think I can. Why?"

"There's a ranch in Montana. Well, it's not a real cowboy hee-haw kind of ranch. It's more like a community. It's called the *Church of Inner Peace*. Their spiritual leader is Sri Baba Ram."

"Who…?"

"Sri Baba Ram! You probably never heard of him, but you will. Someday the whole world will hear of him. He's an enlightened being, and he's taken this mortal body to come to earth and teach us how to achieve enlightenment, too."

"Hold your horses; you lost me," said Walter Jr., taking a right at the junction going north. The next few hours, an excited Megan explained the benefits and wisdom of following her teacher. Walter Jr. tried to remember why he stopped to pick her up. Oh, that's right; he felt bored and lonely.

Hours later, Megan was still talking.

"Now, let me get this straight," questioned Walter Jr., "Sri Baba Ram is god, and we're god, too. Only he's an enlightened being and knows he's god, and he's trying to get us to remember that we're god, because we forgot we're god."

"Exactly!"

"And how long have we been gods?"

"Since all eternity."

"And how powerful and smart is god?"

"All-powerful and all-knowing."

"That's where you lose me," said Walter Jr., "If I'm all-powerful and all-knowing, how could I have been so stupid to forget who I am?"

This stumped her, only for a moment.

"See, that's why you need to go learn from Sri Baba Ram. He knows all the answers to the heavy questions." She looked out at the desert. "Gee, it's getting dark." They passed a sign that read: The Desert Flower Motel – clean rooms at reasonable rates. "It's getting late," she said. "Why don't we get a room for the night, get something to eat, and head out early in the morning?"

"Because," Walter Jr. said. "I've only got so much cash. You think I'm living on baloney sandwiches because I like them?"

She waved a credit card in front of his face. "Plastic. . .more valuable than gold."

"Where did you get that?"

"It's mine. And mommy and daddy pay the balance every month like clockwork without question."

"If you've got a credit card, why don't you rent a car?"

"I'm from New York City; I don't know how to drive. Besides, all the great spiritual seekers wandered in the desert – Moses, John the Baptist, Jesus."

"Really, did they have credit cards, too?"

****

The Desert Flower Motel was a flower, a brown withered flower. It was clean, depending on your definition of cleanliness. The rates reasonable compared to the Plaza off Central Park in New York. You could smell the cigarette smoke from the previous occupants in the pillows and sheets. The shower ran lukewarm. The towels smelled of cigarettes, also. The television got only the three local stations – the weather, old reruns, and the gospel hour – all of which were blurry and went off the air at eleven. Still, compared to sleeping in the back of his car, it was a little slice of heaven.

There wasn't a restaurant, just a row of coin-operated snack machines. Megan took a handful of coins from her backpack, left and came back with an armful of sodas, cakes, chips, and tossed them onto the bed. This brings in another problem, as far as Walter Jr. was concerned, there was only one bed.

He took his shower first while Megan watched television. He wore a makeshift toga made from one of the sheets. He washed his clothes in the sink, using a bar of soap. He took his clothes outside and placed them on the hood of his car to dry by the night winds.

"You look like Julius Caesar," said Megan, when he came back in. She tossed him a can of soda and a bag of chips. "I'm going to take a shower. Save me the tortilla chips and the doughnuts."

Walter Jr. got under the covers and stared at the television. An hour and half later Megan stepped out from the bathroom looking clean and new. She pranced around stark naked, which put Walter Jr. on edge. In bed, next to him, she drank a can of soda and ate the chips and doughnuts. At eleven, The Star Spangle Banner played and the television went into white noise.

"We need to get some sleep," said Walter Jr., turning off the light.

A moment later, Megan whispered, "Do you want to get it on?"

"What's that?"

"Do you want to make it? You know…?"

His head was swimming for an answer. "That sounds good. But I need to get some sleep. I'll take a rain check."

"Just trying to be friendly," she said. "After all, you've been so kind. It's the neighborly thing to do."

"Not right now. Thank you, I'm tired."

"I can dig it."

There was nothing more that needed saying. Exhausted, they both fell asleep in the next minute.

****

The morning sunlight squeezed through the small opening between the curtains. The beam worked its way slowly from the foot of the bed to the head of the bed where it pierced his eyes. He woke in a flash.

He left the bed and headed for the bathroom. Looking back, he saw Megan wasn't in the bed. She wasn't in the bathroom, either. His clothes, now dry, lay spread out on the dresser. There was a message scrolled across the mirror, written with a soap bar. It read just one word: SORRY. He ran to the door and opened it. His car was gone.

He dressed quickly and ran to the motel's office.

"The young girl that I was with, did you see her?"

The small dark-haired man with a Mexican accent, answered. "She left hours ago."

"Did she leave any message?"

"No, I thought you left together."

Walter Jr. was unsure what to do. He picked up the phone sitting on the counter. "May I have an outside line, please?" He waited a moment. "Hello, I'd like to place a collect call to Mr. David Bouchard. My name is Walter Bouchard Junior."

After all the incidentals, Dave spoke.

"Walter! Young brother! Don't tell, let me guess. You need more money. How biblical. The prodigal son returns after squandering all his money. Only there's no father to welcome you, nothing left in the cookie jar to share. So, what do you want?"

"I need more money, Dave."

"So?"

"I'll make a deal with you, Dave. Grandpa is old. He won't last much longer. You know as well as I do, he plans to leave us all something. It's got to be at least ten thousand each, and you know it."

"So?"

"So, I'll swap you anything he leaves me for some cash, right now."

"Again, you're being so biblical. Didn't one brother sell his birthright for something to eat, or something like that?"

"It's all yours, Dave. I swear."

"I need it in writing."

"What?"

"You heard me. I want it in writing."

Walter Jr. cupped his hands over the phone's mouthpiece. "Do you have a fax machine?" he asked the man behind the counter.

"Si."

"Dave, give me your fax number. I'll send what you want within the hour."

"For how much?" Dave asked.

"Ten thousand?"

"Once I get the document, I'll wire you two thousand."

The document was brief.

I, Walter Bouchard Jr., being of sound mind, do bestow all and every inheritance I may acquire from my grandfather, Christopher Goodman, at the time of his death, to my brother, David Bouchard. I do this in exchange for two thousand dollars given to me on this date.

True to his word, Dave sent the sum immediately. The desk clerk was helpful. He put Walter Jr. in touch with a used car salesman who sold Walter Jr. another jalopy for five hundred dollars. He was on the road again within four hours. The used car company gave him the car with a full tank of gas. After that, he was on his own. He had little more than fifteen hundred to complete his mission. Strange, he held no ill feeling towards Megan. He only felt sorry for her.

Nine

Darn that dream

Darn that dream
I dream each night
You say you love me and hold me tight
But when I awake and you're out of sight
Oh, darn that dream

Music by Jimmy Van Heusen
Lyrics by Eddie Delange

BEFORE THE JOURNEY

Chris never forgot the night a furious storm hit the island. Without opening his eyes, Chris knew he was awake and back home in his bed. He tried desperately to fall back to sleep. However, the reason he wanted to return to the dream was causing him to remain awake and alert. He'd left Irene alone in that dark cave, with a hurricane raging outside. He needed to get back to her. He looked at the alarm clock next to his bed – it was six in the morning. He closed his eyes and tried again; nothing. He looked at the clock again; it was six-o-two. If she hadn't found her way out of the cave, that meant she spent the last two hours – in dreamtime – in that horrible place. He tried hard, except that only made it more impossible. The clock read six-o-three. Another hour of dreamtime had passed. Hopefully, she woke in her room in the nursing home, leaving the cave. Then it dawned on him.

"That's it," he said out loud, getting out of bed. "I need to wake her up."

He quietly found his way through the house in the dark. He put the kitchen phone to his ear. He knew the number by heart. A recorded voice greeted him

"Blue Jay Adult Living, where your golden years shine. We're sorry; our office is closed at this time. We are open seven a.m. to nine p.m. everyday. If you'd like to leave a message, press one. If this is an emergency, press two."

He pressed two.

"Answering service. May I help you?"

"Yes, I need to speak with someone at the Blue Jay Home."

"I'm sorry their office is closed right now."

"I don't want to talk to someone in the office; I want to talk with one of the residents, Irene Cooper."

"I'm sorry I don't have the ability to ring any particular room. May I ask the nature of your call?"

"It's an emergency. She needs to wake up."

"You do understand, sir, it's only four in the morning. If you are not more specific, I can't help you."

The time difference, he forgot there was a two-hour difference between Central and Pacific Time Zones, him in Texas, her in California. Even if they woke her at six in the morning, in dreamtime she could have spent hours alone in that cave.

"Are you still there, sir?"

He hung up. He made his way to Beth and Walter Senior's bedroom. As quietly as he could, he opened the door, walked passed the bed holding the sleeping Mr. and Mrs. Bouchard. In the bathroom, he rummaged through the medicine cabinet. It woke Beth.

"Daddy, what are you doing?"

"I'm looking for my sleeping pills. I woke at six, and I want to get back to sleep. I need to get back to sleep."

Walter Sr. began to stir. "What's going on?" he mumbled.

"Nothing, honey, go back to sleep," said Beth. To her father, "Daddy, it's six in the morning. If you can't sleep, I'll make you some warm milk. You know as well as I that you're supposed to have only one sleeping pill every twenty-four hours."

"Never mind," said Chris, walking towards the door.

"Give me twenty minutes and I'll start making breakfast," said Beth.

Chris felt helpless. His only hope was that Irene found her way out of the cave or woke early.

****

The entire day Chris thought of nothing other than sleep. He lived for the moment Beth would give him a sleeping pill and he would find out the fate of his beloved Irene. To pass the time, he scrawled from memory the symbols they saw on the cave wall. He looked at them, confused. Then he knew his thoughts only made things more complicated. This was something more…divine, more spiritual than worldly. With a clear mind, he understood the secret of the symbols. Another thing he couldn't wait to share with Irene.

Finally, after dinner, Beth granted him another sleeping pill. He lay in bed, ready to enter the dream, ready to wake on the island, hopefully to a well, safe and happy Irene.

He appeared on the beach. He was alone. He looked up to see smoke on the hill. He smelled fish cooking. He ran as fast as he could. Irene welcomed him with open arms.

"Irene, darling, you're all right!"

"Why wouldn't I be?"

"I left you in that horrible place – that cave. I've been so worried." He began to sob in her arms.

"It's okay. Don't cry. I found my way out. It's all right."

It took some time for Chris to compose himself.

"I tried so hard to get here sooner," he cried.

"I'm fine," she said, caressing his cheek.

It took a moment, and then he found his composure.

"I've been thinking, about the symbols we found on the wall of the cave. I think I know what they mean. Come, I'll show you."

"No," she insisted. "I won't go back to that cave."

It was low tide and there was much wet sand. He took a stick and began to draw.

"If I remember correctly, these are the symbols we saw. There are two lines, one above the other. Think carefully; don't you see. These are the courses of our lives. You're the top line and I'm the bottom. See, this is where we were together, here's where we separated. The boat represents when I was in the Navy. The male stick figure next to the female figure is when you married Mark. These are your three children. These two figures are Phyllis and me. See, we had a little girl, our daughter, Beth. If you follow both lines you can see our life stories. Only, someone took the chisels and mallet and erased our future. They put in this large symbol before they chiseled away our future. Don't you recognize it?"

She shook her head without a clue.

"It's a picture of the island. Our futures have been erased, and now only this island, this dream is our future. Nothing exists for us other than this island."

"But why? How? And by whom?"

"I don't know. I only know I'm here with you, and I haven't been this happy since I don't know when."

They fell into each other's arms.

There were more hugs and kisses during the afternoon they spent on the island. After sunset, they lay on the sand watching the stars. They kissed more and deeply, Chris placed his hand on her leg at the knee and slowly worked it up her thigh. She burst into tears, pushed away from him, and ran up the hill. Confused he ran after her.

"I'm sorry; I just want you so badly."

"I'm not crying because of that. I'm crying because I want you in the same way you want me. Here on the island we're young. I haven't had to deal with those feelings in years. I don't want you to stop! But we're not married. Call me old fashioned; but I am eighty-four. How more old fashion can you get?"

"But it's just a dream," argued Chris.

'So, you're morals don't count in a dream?"

"I don't know, I didn't say that. Nevertheless, it's just a dream," he insisted.

"Chris, this is no ordinary dream, and you know it. If you think it is, you're dreaming."

This sent them both into laughter.

"Then why don't we marry?" he said.

"And who's here to marry us?"

He thought for a moment. "We can marry in the waking world. I'll come to you and we can be married."

"Ridiculous, once we see each other, each of us will back out. Look at me, look at you; we're young, handsome, only just here on this island, in this dream. I don't want to take the chance of losing you. I'm old and undesirable."

"Only I can decide that," he insisted. "Somehow, I'll find a way to your side in the waking world, and I'll marry you."

"I wish you wouldn't. You'll be disappointed."

"I swear, I'm coming to you, and we'll be married."

He'd never forcibly tried to wake himself up; only he felt determined to make his point. As he faded away, he swore his love and his intent. "I'm coming for you, my sweet Irene, and we will be married."

BEFORE THE JOURNEY

The next morning at breakfast, Walter Jr. made one of his rare appearances. He had an early job interview. Walter Sr. alternated sipping coffee and shoveling eggs into his mouth with his right hand. His left hand held the newspaper, which his head hid behind. Beth stood at the stove, holding a spatula in one hand, now and then flipping this and that in one of the frying pans. Chris sat motionless, gazing at his bowl of grits. He lifted his head, and made an announcement that caught everyone off guard; they all stopped and looked intently at him.

"I'm thinking of taking a trip to San Diego, California."

Walter Sr. let his newspaper fall to the side. "Dad, why would you want to go to San Diego?"

"I hear they got a crackerjack zoo out there; and I'd like to see it before I die."

Beth put her cigarette out. "Daddy, you're too old to take on something like that."

"Then, we could all go together. Call it a vacation. I'd pay for everything."

Beth lit another cigarette. "It's not a question of money, Daddy. You know Walter Sr. can only take so much time off from work. If we did, we always go to our time-share on Padre Island in the Texas Gulf."

"Then, if you're afraid of me going alone, have Junior take me."

Beth blew the first puff of smoke to the ceiling, as not to disturb anyone else. "I'm afraid not. I wouldn't trust Junior. He's just not mature enough."

This statement made Junior's stomach tighten. He wanted to strike back; instead he bit his tongue. He was in no position to go toe-to-toe with his mother.

Chris pounded his fist down on the table. "I don't understand. I'm a grown man. I worked hard all my life. I'm nearly at the end of my life. I have money. Yet, I can't do a simple thing like go to a zoo!"

"And that zoo is two thousand miles away!" shouted Beth. "If you want to go to the zoo, we can drive up to Dallas. They got a jim-dandy zoo." She turned to find much of what was in the pans now burned. She shut everything off. "I can't believe you'd bring something up like this now, at breakfast. Walter Sr. has to get to work, Junior has a morning interview, and I've got a headache to beat the band. Can't we discuss this at another time?"

"I want to go to San Diego," insisted the old man.

"We'll discuss it at another time," Beth said through tight clenched teeth.

Chris knew what she was actually saying. She hoped in time he would forget such foolishness. Either way, if he wanted to go to San Diego, he needed to find other means.

Chris knew if he was to go it alone, he needed a plan. First, he needed money. All smart elderly people have a cash stash hidden somewhere. Chris was no exception, although the amount he had was not enough.

It was on an afternoon when only he and Walter Jr. were in the house. He knocked on Junior's door.

"Who is it?"

"It's me."

"Come in, Grandpa."

He stood in the doorway. "I need a favor. I need you to drive me someplace."

"Sure I will, Grandpa; where to?"

"Amanda's"

****

Amanda's Pawnshop was not any better than any other pawnshop. Yet it was cleaner than most, which seemingly made a difference to Chris. A husky old gent sat behind the counter.

"I suspect you're not Amanda?" said Chris.

"Amanda, shoo, she's been gone these past thirty years. Would have pawned the gold in your teeth; she was something else. How can I hep ya?"

"I'd like to hock this watch."

He placed an old solid gold pocket watch on the counter. The man picked it up. He took out a kit and ran some tests.

"You know this is solid gold?"

"Yes, I do," said Chris.

"You know this is a hock shop. I'm not going to give you what this is truly worth. I can only give the going rate for gold."

"I understand," said Chris.

"I'll tell you what; sixteen hundred is the best I can do."

"I'll take it."

"You understand, it's worth twice that; it's just I'm in no position to give you more."

"It's all right. I understand. I'm grateful for your honesty; but I need the money right now."

The man pushed a paper and pen towards Chris. "Well, if you're fine with it then so am I. Just fill out this form."

When Chris finished filling out the form, he pushed it back across the counter.

"Now, if I can just see some identification?" said the man.

Chris fumbled through his wallet and handed over his driver's license.

"I'm sorry, sir, but this license expired fifteen years ago. Do you have any other forms of identification?"

"No, I'm afraid I don't."

"Well, then, I'm sorry; I can't process this loan."

Chris thought for a moment, and then he pointed to Walter Jr., "This is my grandson. What if I gave him the watch and he pawned it?"

"Fine by me, as long as he has a valid driver's license."

Chris handed Walter Jr. the watch. "Here, it's yours now. If you please, I'd like to pawn it."

The man slipped Walter Jr. a new form.

Ten minutes later, the man handed Walter Jr. sixteen-hundred in cash.

"You understand that you can reclaim the pawned item as yours up to thirty days from today. There's a ten percent charge added each week. After thirty days, it becomes the property of Amanda's Pawnshop. You understand?"

Walter Jr. looked to his grandfather who signaled him it was all right. He nodded to the man.

Outside, Walter Jr. tried to hand the money to his grandfather.

"Here you are, Grandpa."

"No, you were the one to hock it; the money is yours."

"But it's your watch, Grandpa."

"It was my grandfather's watch and it would have gone to you. I'll tell you what, let's split it fifty-fifty."

Chris took half the money and put it in his pocket. Walter Jr. held onto eight hundred dollars.

"This isn't right," Walter Jr. said.

"No, no, fifty-fifty is only fair. Now give me the other eight hundred dollars. Good! Now you've paid what you owe me on the car. We're even."

****

Chris poked around in his closet. He needed to travel light if he wanted to go to San Diego on his own. His luggage was old and cumbersome. He found an old black gym bag once belonging to his grandson, Dave, who used it all through high school and college. How it wound up in Chris' closest was a mystery.

He placed the bag on his bed, put in another change of clothes, a comb, toothbrush and toothpaste, and a few razors. He looked through his clothes hanging in the closet. He owned nothing worthy of wearing to a wedding – his wedding.

****

That night at dinner, Chris made another ear catching comment.

"If anyone is free tomorrow, I'd like a ride to Freemans."

"The men's clothing shop," said Beth. "What for?"

"I looked through my closet and realized I don't own a suit."

"What do you need a suit for, Daddy?"

"If I died right now, what would you bury me in, my pajamas?"

He'd made a good point.

"Daddy, you have those nice brown slacks and the dress shirt I bought you for Easter."

"I want to be buried in a suit. Is that too much to ask?"

The man was right. There was no arguing with him. He had the money, and a man with money should own at least one suit, especially one to be buried in.

"I'll take you in the morning," Beth said, not knowing what else to do or say.

****

Freemans is not your everyday, suit off-the-rack establishment. There are patterns to look at and discuss, and material to select.

"May I help you," smiled the salesman.

"Yeah, "said Beth. "We need a suit for a funeral."

"I'm sorry to hear that," said the salesman. "May I ask whose funeral?"

"His," she said, pointing at her father.

They looked at fabrics, patterns, and styles. Finally, Beth chose the perfect elegant black suit.

"I don't know," said Chris. "It's nice, but it's so glum looking. What if I live longer than I expect and I have to go to a wedding?"

"Daddy," said Beth. "Whose wedding are you going to go to?"

He knew if he said his all hell would break loose. He decided to answer the best he could.

"I don't know whose wedding. But if I live long enough to go to a wedding, I'd like to have a suit that doesn't make me look like a walking cadaver."

In the end, all agreed on a dark brown material, and a double-breasted suit, suitable for both funerals and weddings. Delivery would be in a week.

THE JOURNEY

Chris packed his new suit carefully in his black gym bag.

After breakfast, the next morning, he waited till Walker Sr. was gone. After eleven, while Beth took her morning forty winks, Chris walked down to the nearest point he might hitch a ride to downtown – in front of Steward's cornfield.

There wasn't a single car passing, let alone a possible hitch to downtown. For five days, each morning, he stood waiting and remained vigilant.

Finally, a truckload of farmhands took him as their own, and drove him downtown. It was a gift, a mystery, to be judged by those who come after.

He was at last on his way. He hadn't felt this alive in years. He became aware of his manhood returning to his body. Not testosterone, something more powerful and far more important.

Ten

I don't have to dream alone

Dream lover where are you
With a love oh so true
And a hand that I can hold
To feel you near when I grow old
Because I want a girl to call my own
I want a dream lover
So, I don't have to dream alone

Words and Music by Bobby Darin

THE JOURNEY

When Chris woke in his dream, he was lying on the beach with his head in Irene's lap. She curled his hair around her finger, and then ran four fingers through it. He smiled up at her.

"Where are you?" she asked.

"I'm on a train, working my way to you. I'm sleeping in my seat."

"In your seat, why didn't you get space in a sleeping car? A man of your age…"

"Alas, my love, I'm not a rich man. I think you should know that up front."

"And I think you should know that I'm nothing but a blue-haired old biddy. And once you lay your eyes on me…"

"I'll fall in love with you all over again."

"So, there's no way I can get you to go back to Texas?"

"None, whatsoever."

"Very well."

He reached up and kissed her. He sat up and looked at her with all his attention.

"We need to talk," he said.

"What is it, darling?"

"On the train, a man slipped me a note. He warned that one or both of us must leave the island."

She laughed, "That's impossible. How would anyone know about our dreams?"

"I don't know."

"Besides, even if we did want to leave the island, how would we do it?"

He thought for a moment. "I suppose build a raft."

"Would that end the dream?"

"I'm not sure. I don't think so."

"What did he look like? Did he say anything?"

"It was the waiter in the dining car who gave me his note. I paid no attention to him when he left the car. I've been all over the train; I can't find him. The note just said for one or both of us to leave the island and that he'd be in touch."

"Why one or the both of us; what difference would it make?"

"You got me."

"Then we're stuck with a riddle," she said. "We can only wait for him."

"He'll contact us, but how? Another note?"

"The ball is in his court; we can only wait."

Without warning, an angelic voice filled the air. "Pawpaw…!"

"What is that?" asked Irene.

"It's Sara, a child of four, on the train, who's adopted me. You don't mind if I leave?"

"No, of course not; in fact, I envy you."

****

Walter Jr. drove through the dark desert. He could just as well been driving across Mars. There was no light except for his headlights that shown only thirty feet of road ahead. All else was darkness. His eyes became heavy and began to burn. It was a long day. Thankfully, the new car had a working radio. Though there was little more than weather reports, small town preachers, and country music, hour after hour of country music, a blessing to some, a curse to others.

Finally, he could drive no further. He turned off the road and drove nearly a quarter mile into the desert, where he knew he wouldn't be annoyed by other drivers of the night or the police. Cramped in the backseat, he failed to sleep. It was too constrictive and too hot. He got out of the car and hopped up on the roof of the car. He sprawled out, his hands locked behind his head. The cool night air was fresh and a relief. He never saw so many stars in his life, like millions of diamonds twinkling in the sky. Thinking back to his Boy Scout days, he found the North Star with ease. From there he found the Big Dipper, the Little

Dipper, and all the major constellations. He saw Orion, his belt and all, the lion, the ram, the scale, the twins, all of them clear and alive. He understood why they called it the Milky Way. It was as if someone splattered a gallon of heavy cream across a black velvet sheet. As he began falling asleep, he thought of his grandfather. He longed for what Chris had. The old man was out there somewhere, sleeping, happy on his island, holding the love of his life in his arms. A dream refused to Walter Jr., he was destined to dream an unexpected dream, a dream of no consequences, inhabited by people of no account, nothing of importance. Perhaps that's why he never remembered his dreams.

****

Chris woke on the train and smiled to see little Sara leaning on his knees and laughing.

"Pawpaw," she giggled.

Trisha came running up.

"I'm sorry, Chris. As soon as she saw you, she ran from me."

"It's all right; I need to get up anyways."

She leaned down and handed him his gym bag.

"I did like you said; I took your bag with me."

"I knew it was in good hands."

Sara turned her attention to the window. "Look a bird," she shouted, pointing at the sky.

Trisha turned again to Chris. "Did you find your friend, yesterday?"

"No, somehow we missed each other. I guess I'll try again, today. Which reminds me, I'm off to the dining car for some coffee. Would you two ladies care to join me?"

"No, thank you. It's early and it'll probably be crowded. Sara and I will go later, when the rush is over."

"That's why I'm going now. Perhaps I can find my friend. You want me to bring anything back?"

She shook her head, "No, thank you."

****

The dining car was crowded. Chris waited to be seated. While waiting, he eyed every one who came and left – no tall dark stranger. Once seated, he ordered coffee. He felt slightly disappointed when coffee was all that the waiter served – no large breakfast, no grits, and no note.

"That man, the one who sat in that corner, the one dressed in black, the one who bought my breakfast yesterday and left me a note, is he here today?" Chris asked the waiter.

"I'm sorry; sir, I don't recall any of that."

Chris reexamined the man's face. He was sure it was the same waiter.

"Don't you remember? I had grits with maple syrup. You must recollect an order that strange? You handed me a note!"

"I'm sorry; sir, you must have me confused with one of the other waiters."

Chris realized it was useless. "Perhaps you're right," he said, sounding defeated, knowing all too well he was right.

If someone could know what you dream, could write notes that disappear, and themselves vanish into thin air, surely they could make the messenger forget he delivered the message. He decided to be content with sipping his coffee and looking out the window.

An hour passed before he returned. Sara was now wide awake and full of energy.

"The dining car's nearly empty, now," he told Trisha.

"Come, honey, let's go have waffles."

"Waffles!" cried Sara, excitedly turning from the window.

Trisha twirled to look at Chris, as they left. "When we get back, I'm going to take Sara to the observation car. Care to join us?"

"Sounds great, I'll be here."

Again, he focused his attention to the moving world out the window. The mountains were long gone; they were in the desert. The land was flat and brown. At this rate, they'd be in L.A. station by late afternoon.

****

Walter Jr. felt like stopping the car, getting out and dancing. He'd crossed over the Californian state line. He stopped in Bakersfield for a cup of coffee. The temptation was too great. The money his brother, Dave, sent him burned a hole in his pocket. In a moment of weakness, he ordered a hamburger, fries, and a shake – sheer extravagance, and it felt great.

When the waitress gave him his bill, she announced, "The gent who just left paid for everything. He wanted me to give you this note."

Understandably, Walter Jr. was confused. He opened and read the note.

Your grandfather has been warned.
Leave the island or else.
The stakes are high.

"Who told you to give this to me?"

"The same guy who paid your bill."

"And who's that?"

"I don't know, sir."

He stood up and placed a couple of dollars down as a tip and as he was leaving he thought of something else. He rushed back to the waitress. "The man who gave you this note, what did he look like?"

"What are you talking about?"

"The man who paid for my breakfast, what did he look like?"

"No one paid for your breakfast. You didn't have breakfast. You came in, sat down, and without ordering got up and started walking out."

"Then, what about this note?" He held the slip of paper to her.

"What note?"

He looked at the paper in his hand. It was blank.

He left the restaurant, got in his car, and sat there confused. He opened the note once more. Still, there was nothing to read or consider. It was a blank slip of paper.

****

Chris sat next to Trisha in the observation car. She held Sara in her lap. They sat high; the dome covering them was clear glass. They could see the beauty in all direction. Both Sara and Trisha could not contain their excitement; they looked frantically this way and that, trying to take it all in. Chris was more interested in their reactions to the scenery than the scenery. He couldn't take his eyes off them.

There were few others in the observation car. Chris was aware of someone taking a seat behind them. He heard the squashing sound of the leather seat. The voice was cold, dark, and spoke with authority.

"Don't turn around. Keep looking ahead," said the dark voice from behind.

"What?" Chris questioned.

"Did you say something?" asked Trisha.

The voice continued. "She can't hear me. Only you can. Tell her it's nothing."

"No, I didn't say anything."

"Good," said the voice. "Now, listen to me. You read my note. Have you spoken with Irene about this? Just nod."

Chris nodded slightly.

"Good. I imagine you two haven't arrived at a conclusion, yet. I understand, a single note of fair warning can only persuade so much. That's why I'm talking to you now. You need to take this to heart. All hell is about to break loose if you or her or both of you don't leave the island immediately. The storm was only a small sample of what could happen. You have only so much time before you wished you'd acted."

"How?" asked Chris.

Trisha looked at him, questioningly.

"Shut your mouth," said the voice. "I'll give you only so much warning and then...."

"And then what?" shouted Chris, standing up and turning to look behind them. There was no one there.

"Are you all right?" questioned Trisha.

"It's nothing. Forgive me. I'm just an old man, and old men..." he couldn't finish the sentence. "Forgive me," was all he could say.

"Another bird," cried Sara, pointing to the sky.

****

Walter Jr. couldn't stop thinking about what happened in the diner. Nothing like that ever happened to him before. He wasn't crazy. Except, don't most crazy people believe they're sane? It was his word against the waitress'. Maybe she's crazy. No matter what she said, there were still certain facts that couldn't be denied. She said he didn't have anything to eat; only, his stomach felt full and his breath smelled of onions. He recounted his funds and came up two dollars short – the tip. And note or no note, he still had the slip of paper.

Still, what did the message mean? Only he, his grandfather, and, if he believed his grandfather's story, Irene knew about the island. Then he thought, the message was not only a warning, it was also a prediction. The writer of the note knows he will see his grandfather, soon; why bother giving him the message? It was all too mystifying, cosmic, and frightening. He decided to file it all somewhere in the back of his mind for consideration later, and put all his attention into his driving. He was making good time. According to the road signs and his speedometer, he calculated he'd be in L.A. by late afternoon.

****

Trisha insisted Chris use their sleeping compartment for an afternoon nap. Chris didn't argue. He felt tired and a late-in-the-day nap sounded just fine.

He placed his little black gym bag at the foot of the bed, and pulled down the shades. It didn't take long, the hum and rumble of the train induced sleep. Not since his childhood, when being rocked and sung to sleep was the afternoon ritual, had he fallen asleep so quickly and so deeply.

When Chris woke on the island, he began collecting large pieces of wood and vines. He laid them out on the beach.

"What are you doing?" he heard Irene ask. He spun around, surprised to see her.

"What are you doing here?" he said.

"You're not the only old person to take an afternoon nap, you know. Now, tell me, what are you doing?"

"I'm trying to make a raft."

"What for?"

"That fellow I told you about, the one with the note, he's becoming very forceful. I think we need to do something about it."

"And your conclusion is to make a raft and leave. Have you ever made a raft before?"

"Never; but what could there be to it?"

"I used to braid my friend's hair, when I was young. It can't be much different," said Irene, taking up portions of vines.

Hours later, they had what looked like a durable raft. To test it, they pulled it into the water. They watched it fall apart in the waves like a sugar cube melting in warm tea.

"What now?" Irene asked.

"Where there's a will, there's a way. I'll figure this out, one way or another."

She pulled in close to him. "I know you will, my love. I've faith in you."

"We should be coming into L.A. station soon. Forgive me, I need to wake up. I'll be back with a plan for a sturdy raft. Don't worry."

"I'm not worried. I have faith in you."

She waved as he dissolved out of the dream.

****

Many times Walter Jr. drove up to Dallas and Fort Worth, and College Station in south Texas – all fine cities. However, he wasn't ready for L.A.; he doubted anyone is ever ready for L.A., California. It's something you have to ease into like a hot bath. So much happening all at once, he forced himself to ignore most of it and keep his eyes on the road. The honks of cars were constant and coming from all directions. He swiveled his head towards each hoot; he was sure an accident was unavoidable. So many different people, everyone doing common day things like walking and shopping or uncommon things like dancing and singing on street corners, juggling Indian clubs, and gambling with cards atop cardboard boxes.

Walter Jr. stopped at a red light, rolled down his window and shouted.

"Can anyone tell me how to get to the train station?"

A man holding a sign that read *The end is near!* came rushing over.

"What do you want with a train, or a plane, or any other mode of transportation?" shouted the man. "It's all coming to an end; and you can't run away from it!"

"I don't want to catch a train," Walter Jr. shouted back. "I just want to pick up my grandfather at the station."

"Then why didn't you say so?" said the man, sounding much more calm. He lowered his sign and pointed down the road. "You just follow this road and make a right at the third stoplight. It's half a mile down from there; you can't miss it."

"Thank you, sir."

"Don't mention it, brother."

There was no parking outside the L.A. train station. Meaning, there is no free parking at the L.A. train station. Walter Jr. parked four blocks away and walked it.

The main hall of the station was a large work of art – designs on the walls, floor, and ceiling. The chatter of the people echoed off the high ceilings and marble floors. The décor was Southwestern art deco; straight lines in all directions, muted colors, and images of ancient superior beings, male and female. He found a place where he could sit and watch the entire goings-on, especially the clock and the exits from the landings. The signs told when the trains would arrive. He felt tired; he fell into a daze; however, he knew he needed to remain awake and alert. If he dozed for so much as an instant, he might miss his grandfather. Then all his efforts would be in vain, and there'd be no way of tracking the old man. His only course of action would be to go back home empty-handed. Above all else, he'd hate to do that. He had to stay awake.

****

Trisha's gentle knock on her sleeping compartment door woke Chris.

"Mr. Goodman, Chris, are you decent?"

"It's okay. You can come in."

Chris sat on the edge of the bunk, tying his shoelaces.

"Sorry to wake you, we'll be pulling into L.A., soon."

"That's all right. I needed to get up, anyway."

Trisha began packing; Sara looked out the window, keeping her balance by holding on to Chris' knees. He'd never asked Trisha what was wrong with Sara. He felt he should, except it saddened him too much to do so. He purposely changed the subject in his own mind for his own sake.

"So, what does Bill, your husband, do?"

"He's a welder."

"Really, I used to weld when I was in the navy." He fell silent, not being able to think of anything else to say.

"Chris, you said you were going to San Diego to see your girlfriend. When was the last time you saw each other?"

He looked to the ceiling, as he calculated in his mind. "Ah. . .let's see. . .sixty-six years."

She stopped her packing and looked at him. "Sixty-six years! There's got to be a story in there, somewhere."

"More than you can imagine. We got back in touch with each other by a. . .a miracle. Now, it's our. . .dream, you might say. . .to be married."

"Married, that's wonderful! You have a dream, Sara has a dream."

"And what's your dream, Trisha?"

She looked at her daughter and then at Chris. "Can't you guess?" He felt slightly embarrassed for even asking. "Only your dream will come true. You will be married. Sara's dream will come true. Tomorrow we'll both be in Disneyland. The doctor's tell me there's no chance of my dream coming true."

Chris couldn't feel more relieved to see signs of the city outside the window.

"Look, we're coming into L.A.!" he shouted, glad to change the subject.

They all huddled in front of the window.

"America the beautiful," smiled Chris.

"Indeed," said Trisha, and she resumed her packing.

When they came to a stop at the station, Chris went out into the corridor to get a porter to take their luggage. He kept hold of his little black bag.

Stepping off the train and unto the platform, Trisha and Chris smiled at each other.

"Say good-bye to Pawpaw," she told Sara.

He bent low; Sara put her arms around his neck and kissed his cheek.

"Bye-bye, Pawpaw..."

Then her face grew bright, her eyes went wide and she shrieked with delight. Chris stood up and turned to see what caught her attention. A large group of cartoon characters rushed towards them, followed by a large group of news reporters. Flashbulbs went off, floodlights blared into their faces, as news cameras rolled. Trisha kissed Chris' cheek. Before they could say a proper good-bye, she and Sara were surrounded in the hoopla. Chris backed away and waved, as they were swept away into the hall.

In the main hall, the crowd and confusion doubled every few seconds. Walter Jr. stood up and looked to see what all the hubbub was. Other trains were arriving at the same time, contributing to the chaos.

"What's going on?" Walter Jr. asked a young man standing on top of a bench to get a better look.

"Not sure," shouted the lad. "Looks like the media are covering something. Say, wait a minute! I can see Langford in the center of it all."

"Louise Langford," shouted an old woman standing next to Walter Jr., "Where? I'd do anything to get her autograph. She's so beautiful. I've never missed one of her movies."

"You won't even get close enough to wave to her, let alone get an autograph, not without getting crushed to death," cautioned the young man.

Walter Jr. got up on his tiptoes for a better look. As he aimed his sights on the center of the mob, something in his peripheral vision caught his eye – a gray-haired old man. It was only a brief glimpse. He could easily been wrong. He hopped up on the bench for a better view. He looked, yet saw only the multitude of cartoon characters and news reporters encircled around a small inner group working their way to the exit. Then he saw him going out the front door.

"Grandpa!" he shouted at the top of his lungs, except it was like praying at a baseball game – only God heard it. He jumped off the bench, and tried his best to get to the front door; only it was useless. He finally decided to go out one of the side doors. He ran to the corner – just people he didn't know. It was useless on foot. He turned and ran the four blocks back to his car. He drove around the station once, twice, and three times – nothing. It was so frustrating. The rush hour just started. A tortoise could move faster.

He was so upset with himself. He had to find the old man. He couldn't have gone far. He stopped here and there to get a better look. Drivers honked at and cursed him for slowing down. Every gray-haired head was a possibility. He cussed himself along with the other motorists. Why hadn't he called the police once he knew what his grandfather was up to? What if something happened to the old man, he'd never forgive himself. What would he tell his parents? He could hear the laughter of his brother. Everything was upside down. He was still too tired to think straight. He punched the steering wheel in anger.

Finally, at a corner three blocks from the station, he waited at the light. His entire body shook and he began to cry. Then through his tears he saw him – his grandfather, standing at the corner, holding his little black bag, waiting for the walking green. Walter Jr. honked his horn.

"Hey, old man; need a lift?" Walter Jr. shouted.

Chris bent low and looked into the car. His face grew as luminous as a New England lighthouse.

"Junior…?"

Eleven

When my dreamboat comes home

When my dreamboat comes home
Then my dreams no more will roam
I will meet you and greet you
Hold you closely in my arms

Words and Music by Cliff Friend & Dave Franklin

THE JOURNEY

Say what you like about Beth Bouchard, everyone admits she has a heart as large as all Texas. If a neighbor or church member falls ill and needs a helping hand, she's the first over with a mop and a pail in one hand and a casserole in the other. If you complimented her on one of her recipes, she'll write it out step-by-step, and not leave out one ingredient. At the sewing circle, where gossip runs rampant, she always makes sure to say something good about the person in question. She's on more church and community boards than anyone in town – not to mention her work at the school. And everyone in the county secretly knows it was Beth and Walter who donated all that money when the Haze family had no place to go.

Now, it was that Texas-size heart that was breaking. It was Beth Bouchard who needed help, now; and the church and community were there for her. Not a day went by that someone didn't check in on her to see if she needed anything. And the food: coffee cake, monkey bread, pots of chili, beans and rice, and chicken and dumplings. A woman in her predicament could hardly be expected to feel like cooking and cleaning.

Within the first hour that she knew her father was missing, she became useless to the world. Most of the fight and energy left her body.

When the police called her and told her someone picked up her father hitchhiking, she wondered if they had the right man. He was last seen downtown. They told her some crazy story that her father was on his way to see his girlfriend in San Diego. The only good news was that it meant they would put a tristate lookout for him. That was the same night Walter

Jr. took off. Outside of a single call late that night from her son, something about looking for his grandfather, she never heard back from Junior. Now her heartbreak doubled.

As the days slipped by with no word of either her father or son, Beth's strength began to dwindle. Walter Sr. was worried, too. However, he had his work to keep his mind occupied. He loved his wife; he worried about her state of health. He had Nurse Molly continue her weekly visits, only now it was Beth she examined, and rightfully so.

"Your blood pressure is on the high side," Nurse Molly said to Beth as she took the stethoscope out of her ears and let it hang around her neck.

"I'm losing weight," replied Beth.

"Yes, only you're losing it too fast, and in the wrong way. Have you been taking your vitamins? You haven't, have you?"

"I just don't feel like eating."

Nurse Molly took pity on her and wrote out a prescription. "Here, these will help your nerves. You need to stay calm. Your lungs don't sound clear. How much do you smoke each day?"

"I'm up to two and a half packs a day."

"That's too much. Try to cut down. How are you sleeping?"

"Not at all."

"You still have those sleeping pills I gave your father?"

"Yes."

"Use those, but only one a night; only one." Nurse Molly placed her hand on Beth's. "Don't worry so much, not to the point of making yourself sick. Besides, your father will turn up any day. I'm sure he will. He's a tough old cuss."

****

Pastor Jeffery from the First Baptist Church of Venus came as soon as he had a few hours to spare. Walter Sr. answered the front door.

"Pastor, we weren't expecting you."

"Good to see you, Walter. I came as soon as I could. How is Beth?" he asked as he stepped inside.

"Not good, Pastor. She's in the back. They both walked to the kitchen. "Honey, Pastor Jeffery's here to see you."

"Oh my, oh no," she kept repeating moving her hair with her fingers, trying to make herself look presentable. "I wish I knew you were coming I would have...would have..." Her voice trailed off and she began to cry. "I'm sorry! I'm still in my housecoat!"

Pastor Jeffery turned to Walter Sr., "Could we have some time alone, please." Walter Sr. didn't need to be asked twice, he was gone. Pastor Jeffery walked over and put his arms around Beth. "Now, now, don't be that way. I've seen the face of depression many times, and I know what it does to a person. May I sit down?"

"Please. Would you like some coffee?"

"No, thank you. Sit down and talk with me." He reached across the table and took her hand. "Don't fell ashamed. Tell me what's on your heart."

It was then she realized that of all the good people, with all their good intentions, the pies, cakes, the dinners, and the housework, not one asked how she was. She loved them all; except nothing is more valued and cherished than a sympathetic ear and a shoulder to cry on. And now that someone finally asked, she couldn't speak, she could only cry.

"That's all right. No need to say a word." She cried all the more. "I just want you to know we're praying for you. The entire church is praying for you and your father."

She struggled to speak. "I couldn't ask for more. Tell them all thank you for me."

"You mustn't cry, Beth. It'll all work out. Just remember, your father is in God's hands."

She looked at him through the tears. "Please, Pastor, please tell God if His hands get tired, He can put him back in mine. I wouldn't mind holding him for just a little while longer."

****

The living room was bathed in the moving blue light of the television with its sound turned down soft and low. Walter Sr. slept upright, his feet on the ottoman, reading glasses on the end of his nose, and the evening newspaper covered his stomach. She sat next to him, chain-smoking. Whenever he began to snore, she'd poke him gently; he'd grunt and stop for a while. She reached to her purse on the coffee table, took one of the sleeping pills and washed it down with the last cold swallow of decaf.

The ten o'clock news started. She'd watch it, alone. When it was over she would wake her husband and guide him to the bedroom, where he'd magically strip, put on his pajamas, and jump into bed, all without opening an eye. His snoring would resume the moment his head touched the pillow.

The news that night was like any other night. She didn't understand why she watched the ten o'clock news every night. She had a head full of troubles of her own without learning about the trouble of others.

International news as always was biblical – famines, pestilence, wars and rumors of wars. The national news was a long list of crimes and punishments. The local news gave concern to laws passed and high school football scores. The weather was no more than an educated guess. They always like to end each night on a high note. The news anchorman and woman smiled, as if what they delivered over the course of the last hour was of no real consequence.

"Tonight, we end with a story from L.A. California."

A photo of Louise Langford appeared on the screen.

"Who says Hollywood has no heart? Well-known star of stage and screen, Louise Langford, best known for her roles in such hits as *Tomorrow Again*, *Peaches and Scream*, and everybody's once a year favorite, *Christmas at 102 degrees*, leads a double life. When she's not in front of the movie cameras, she's working hard on the board of directors of *Dream Makers*. Dream Makers is a charity organization whose mission it is to see that young children with fatal illnesses get a chance at having their dreams come true."

The on-screen photo turned to one of a small child and her mother.

"Little Sara Millwood has Leukemia, and her two loves are trains and Disneyland. Dream Makers gave Sara and her mother, Trisha, shown here, an all expense paid train ride from their home of Denver, Colorado to California, where a Disneyland vacation awaits.

"When the mother and daughter arrived today at the L.A. train station, actress Louise Langford met them with a big surprise. She brought Disneyland with her to greet little Sara. The Disney Corporation, who has always worked closely with Langford and the Dream Makers team, sent down some of their costumed characters with Ms. Langford to the station. And now we know why Louise Langford does what she does. One look at the surprised face of little Sara Millwood tells you it's all well worth it."

The scene changed to footage of the small child being greeted by all her favorite cartoon characters. It was heartwarming to see a child so happy. However, something caught Beth's eye. In the confusion, she saw the mother kissing someone good-bye. She recognized him immediately.

"Daddy!" she cried, jumping up from the couch. She turned off the television and turned all the living room lights on. She shook her husband, frantically. "Walter, wake up! It's Daddy!"

He sat up, groggy. The newspaper fell to the floor. His reading glasses fell off his nose. "What are you talking about?"

"I've just seen Daddy on the TV, on the ten o'clock news!"

"Are you sure?"

"I ought to know my own father!"

She ran into the kitchen, turned on all the lights, and put on a pot of coffee. “I just took a sleeping pill. It ain’t no time for sleeping. I got things to do.”

After an hour explaining to the police what happened, they told her that a full-state alarm would be sent throughout California, in the morning. For the first time in a long time she felt something was finally being done. There was hope. She could finally get some sleep. Perhaps God’s hands *were* getting tired?

Twelve

My dream lives on

You're so long ago and so far away
But my dream lives on forever
I guess I believe that I'll see you one day
For without it there is no dream

Words and Music by Todd Rundgren

THE JOURNEY

Before the light turned green, Chris was in the front seat.

"Junior, I don't believe it. I don't understand."

"To make a long story short, I figured you were on your way to see Irene. And knowing you, I knew you'd take the long roundabout way, especially if it had anything to do with trains."

"That's my boy, smart as a whip," he said with pride. "What time is it?"

Walter Jr. pointed to the clock on the dash.

"It's still early. I've got to get to a…." Chris stopped midsentence when he realized what just happened. "The clock's working!" he shouted, inspecting the rest of the car. "Junior, this isn't the same car!"

"That's another long story, Grandpa."

He told him all about Megan, the hitchhiker, and the deal he made with his brother.

"David was like that, even as a kid. He was always getting something over on you."

"That's because he's smarter."

"No, that's because he's a selfish backstabbing brat. It's not brains he has over you; it's something he lacks that you don't."

"What's that, Grandpa?"

"I'm not going to tell you about it. Because if I point it out, you'll think about it, and then you may lose it."

Walter Jr. could make no sense of what his grandfather said.

"So, tell me about this Megan. Was she pretty?"

"It wasn't like that, Grandpa. I was just trying to help her out."

"See, that's what I mean."

"About what?"

"That thing you have."

"What thing?"

"That thing, I don't want to talk about."

Walter Jr. realized that they had had a discussion, only he wasn't sure what it was about or how it ended, only that it ended. It confused him completely. He changed to a new subject in hopes of getting back on a reality track.

"So, Grandpa, you were saying you needed to go somewhere?"

"The library."

"For what?"

"I want to look up some books on how to make a raft from natural resources found on an island."

"Your island?"

"Yeah, either Irene or I or both of us must leave the island. A raft is the only thing I can think of."

"That reminds me of another story, Grandpa," he said timidly.

"What's that?"

"You're going to think I'm crazy; but I swear it happened. I stopped at a diner for something to eat. When I finished, the waitress told me some guy already paid for it. And she handed me. . . ."

Chris broken in, "A handwritten note saying your grandfather needs to leave the island."

Walter Jr. nearly lost control of the car. "Yeah, that's right; how did you know?"

"I'll tell you in a minute; first finish your story."

"Well, that's pretty much what the note said, only a little different. I remember it word for word.

It said: *Your grandfather has been warned. Leave the island or else. The stakes are high.* I was scared stiff. Now, here's the spooky part, as if that wasn't spooky enough. When I was walking back to the counter, to ask the waitress something. . ."

"Let me see if I can finish this," said Chris. "She didn't remember any note."

"She didn't even remember any man paying my tab. She didn't even remember me eating anything. And when I went to read the note again. . . ."

"It was blank."

"Exactly! There's something unnatural about all this. What's it all about, Grandpa?"

"I don't know, Junior. I just know you're not crazy. The same thing happened to me on the train in the dining car, the note and all. Then I tried to find him. I looked up and down that train, he was nowhere to be found. He'd vanished. Then one day he spoke to me from the seat behind me on the train, the same warning; his voice was cold. When I turned around to look at him, he was gone; the seat was empty."

"Whoa, that's too creepy. Who do you think he is?"

"I have no idea. I do know he has more power over my situation than I do; so I think it's wise to take him at his word. There'll be Hades to pay if one of us doesn't leave the island. And I've decided that someone will be me."

"You're not going to take Irene?"

"I don't want her to have to go through that. Out at sea, on a raft, in a dream, I don't know what will happen. I do know she's safe on the island."

"Have you told her your decision?"

"Not yet. I'll wait till the raft's finished, and then spring it on her."

"Then why are we going to San Diego, if you two are going to separate?"

"So we can be married. And because, once I'm out to sea, I'm going to look for another island. Somewhere we can live together without a sword hanging over our heads. Then I'll return to the island to collect my bride."

****

It was a small, one-story branch library, yet it held three times as many books as the library back home in Venus. It was nearly empty except for the stout middle-aged woman behind the information counter.

"Excuse us, miss," whispered Chris. "I'm looking for any books that show how to build a raft."

She took her reading glasses off and let them dangle from a string around her neck. She seemed to be looking down her nose at the vagabonds. Then, like an instant sunrise, she exploded into a welcoming smile. She rubbed her hands together, palm to palm, in anticipation.

"How wonderful," she announced. "See, that's why I became a librarian. You get to meet the most interesting people, each with a different problem to be solved." She put her glasses back on, turned the computer on and began to type. "Now, we're talking water raft, right?"

"Yes, miss."

"White-water?"

"No, miss. It needs to be made only with materials found on a desert island."

"Interesting. Is this a hobby of yours?"

"No, miss. It's life-or-death."

"Of course it's life-or-death. Desert Island, natural materials, what else could it be?" She laughed at her own shortcomings. "Just bear with me, please," she whispered as she continued to search. "Let's see…rafts…raft riding…rubber rafts…George Raft…Ah, here we are…raft building."

She wrote down the titles on a slip of paper and handed it to Chris. She pointed at it with the tip of her pencil. "You've got three choices. Tell me, does your island have any bamboo?"

"There's a large patch of it on the north side."

"Good, because they all prefer a bamboo frame. Now, these first two books I'll have to order. I can have them here, tomorrow or the next day."

"Thank you, but I'd rather not wait."

"That's right; you did say it was a matter of life-and-death, didn't you? Well then, that leaves us with the only choice we have here at this branch. She circled the title with her pencil; Chris read it out loud.

IF ROBINSON CRUSOE HAD HALF A BRAIN
By
Jacobi Linton Dupree

"That would be on aisle twenty-seven, in the mechanics section." She pointed with her pencil.

"Can you show us, please?"

"My pleasure."

At the end of aisle twenty-seven, she took the book down and handed it to Chris.

"Would you like to check it out for a few days?"

"If you don't mind, I'd like to sit at this table and read it here."

"That's right, life-or-death, how silly of me. There's paper and pencils at each table, you're welcome to them. We close in half an hour. I'll call you when it's time."

"Thank you very much, miss…?"

"Ms. Buckstein."

"Thank you again, Ms. Buckstein; you've been very helpful. If you don't mind me asking, what is your first name?"

"You promise not to laugh?"

"I promise."

"It's Marion, you know like the song?"

Walter Jr. was completely lost. "I don't get it? What song is that?"

She shook her head in disbelief. "Sometimes I wonder about this younger generation. Marion the librarian, of course."

****

For the next half hour, Chris buried his face in the book.

"Aren't you going to take notes?" suggested Walter Jr., holding up paper and pencil.

"Won't do no good. I can't take it into a dream. I need to put this to memory. Just be patient and quiet for a few more minutes."

Marion's voice echoed down the aisle. "It's time, gentlemen."

****

Chris and Walter Jr. stood and watched Marion lock the doors of the library.

"I've told you my name; however, I don't know your names."

"I'm Chris and this is Walter Jr., my grandson."

"Very nice to meet both of you, now, if you'll excuse me, I have to get home."

"You've been so kind, Ms. Buckstein. Do you mind if I ask one more favor?" Walter Jr. said. He felt tired, dead on his feet. He knew his grandfather couldn't be too far behind. He didn't mind sleeping in the car. But it was no place for an eighty-five year old. She smiled at the young man, waiting for the question. "Is there an inexpensive place around here, where we can spend the night?"

She pointed in the direction behind them. "There's the *La Casa de Oro Motel*, two blocks in that direction. It's clean. There's Wang's right next door to it; if you like Chinese."

"Would you care to join us for dinner?" asked a smiling Chris. Walter Jr. scrunched his face, wishing his grandfather wasn't so generous with what little funds they had.

"That's very kind of you, except Androcles would be furious with me."

"Your husband?"

"No, my cat, if he's not fed at exactly six o'clock he gets as mad as a lion."

"Well, then, maybe we could drive you home?" smiled Chris. Again, Walter Jr. scrunched his face.

"No, thank you. Ricardo, that's the bus driver, if I'm not waiting on the corner for the five-thirty, he gets sick with worry. Thank you, perhaps another time?" She was just about to walk away when she looked curiously at Chris. "I thought you said it was life or death? Why are you going to a motel, instead of your island?"

"I'll go tonight. I go there every night in my dreams. I live there on the island with my fiancée."

Walter Jr. looked at the ground and shook his head. He wished his grandfather wouldn't say such things in front of strangers.

"Really, I do the same thing every night in my dreams, too!"

"You go to an island?"

"No, I go to my Swiss chalet in the alps. Gilbert, that's my boyfriend, he's always there waiting for me. Some nights we go ice-skating, or go skiing, in some dreams we just sit in front of the fire and cuddle."

"I know just what you mean," agreed Chris. "Small world, isn't it? We need to compare notes, someday."

"That would be nice." She looked at her wristwatch. "Oh my, I must be going. I'll miss the five-thirty. Ricardo will hold the bus for up to ten minutes, if I'm late."

****

La Casa de Oro Motel was clean looking from a distance. The room had a musky damp smell about it. The bedsheets were stained and torn. Still, at least they were off the streets. Chris sat on the edge of his bed; pointing the remote control at the TV, channel surfing. Walter Jr. called from the bathroom.

"You getting hungry yet, Grandpa? You know, Chinese food doesn't sound so bad."

Chris was too occupied in thought to answer. "Can you imagine? That librarian dreams a continuous dream every night, just like I do. She spends her nights with the love of her life, just like I do. I wished I'd asked her where her boyfriend lives. Who knows, maybe he lives on the other side of the world. It makes you wonder how many other people have a dream-life. I should like to speak with that woman again, someday."

"How's that?" Walter Jr. shouted from the bathroom, brushing his teeth with his bare finger. He walked out. "So, what do you think. . .Chinese food?"

"Maybe later, Junior, after I take my shower."

****

It was dark outside. Sitting up in bed, watching TV, their stomachs started growling.

"What sounds good?" Walter Jr. asked, walking towards the door.

"I can't finish an entire Chinese meal. Just get me an eggroll and I'll have a taste of whatever you get."

Just then, loud crashes and screams sounded from the back of the motel. Walter Jr. ran into the bathroom to look out the window that faced the back of the building. He went flying out of the bathroom and was out the door in a flash. "Someone's getting beat-up," he hollered. Chris followed as fast as his old legs allowed.

Around back was a large green dumpster. A motionless body lay beside it. Two teenage boys kicked and slammed their feet down on his head.

"What are you doing?" Walter Jr. demanded.

They stopped and quickly ran away. Not that Walter Jr. posed any threat. They'd gotten what they wanted and didn't want to contend with anyone else. Walter Jr. fell to his knees and turned the man over.

He was a large, stocky old man, somewhere in his sixties. His skin was dark reddish brown. His long black hair was split down the middle, leading to two long hair-braids, one on each side of his head. He was unmistakably an American Indian. He wore a black suit with a matching vest. It was hard to tell how badly hurt he was. There was a large deep gash over his left eye. Blood dripped down the side of his face.

"Are you okay?" Walter Jr. asked.

"I'll be fine. Just help me to my feet."

Walter Jr. did just that; but the man almost fell down, again.

"Come on, I'm taking you inside."

Chris finally arrived.

"I'm taking him to our room," Walter Jr. said.

"Is there anything I can do?"

"Get my hat!" the man mumbled in pain.

He looked around on the ground till he found it next to the dumpster. The strangest hat Chris ever saw. It was black with a tall round bowl. The brim was flat and wide, reaching out evenly in every direction. There were three feathers tucked in the black satin headband. Around that was a leather cord that ran six inches down the back of the hat. Tied on the cord were more feathers and bright colored beads. Chris carried it in both hands.

When Chris returned to the room, he found the stranger sitting on the edge of his bed and Walter Jr. dabbing the wound over his eye with a wet towel.

"We should take you to a hospital. You may need stitches."

"No, no doctors," grunted the stranger.

"Why did they beat you up?"

"They took all my money. Thank you for your kindness. Now, if you'd please give me my hat, I won't bother you anymore."

"Where will you spend the night?"

"That's why I was round back. I was trying to get into the dumpster for the night, when those two hoodlums jumped me."

"Well, you can stay with us."

"No thank you. I have my pride."

"But you're not too proud to sleep in a dumpster?" laughed Chris. "We're not any better-off than you. In fact, I'd say we're all in the same boat. You ain't been here five minutes and you're making waves. Now, my bighearted grandson just offered you a place to stay. If you've got any sense, you'll say yes and thank him."

The stranger looked at Walter Jr. and bowed his head. "I accept. Thank you."

"Now, what's your name?" added Chris.

"Jimmy…Jimmy Gray Horse. I'm from North Dakota, the Hidatsa Tribe, right in the middle of the state."

"Long way from home, ain't you?"

"I hitched all the way. I'm going to Oregon to reunite with my son."

"So why don't we just call your son. He can come and get you, or he can wire the money and we'll put you on a bus," Walter Jr. said.

"I said I was going to reunite with my son. We haven't seen or spoken to each other in years. I can't just call out of the blue with my hand out. There are things I must do first."

"Like what?"

"First, I must apologize to him. I was never a good father. I drank all the time. He never disrespected me. When he was old enough he ran away. I have thrown our lives out of balance; we are living backwards."

"What do you mean?"

"The father must be the man in his son's life, and teach him to be a man. My son has a wife, two young sons of his own, and runs his own business. The son must never become a man before the father does. We are living out of balance; we live backwards. I must apologize to him and put our worlds right, again."

****

Walter Jr. came back to the room holding two bags. He handed out the dinners.

"That's eggroll all the way around, a small chicken rice bowl for Grandpa, almond chicken for Jimmy, and Buddha Delight for yours truly."

Jimmy held his hands over his food for a minute. When he noticed the others watching, he explained.

"I'm asking the spirits to take any poison out of the food."

"That's if you call cat meat poison," laughed Chris. "I kind of like it."

"Say, Jimmy," said Walter Jr., "Please don't take offense. I've lived in Texas all my life and I ain't never met an Indian like you. The way you dress, look, and talk. It's like you're straight out of a....I don't know...straight out of a western movie."

"I take that as a compliment. I like western movies, especially John Wayne."

"John Wayne?" But he was always killing Indians."

"Only bad ones; I don't blame him. I would have done the same, myself."

****

Jimmy insisted on sleeping on the floor. Chris was in one bed, closest to the bathroom, in case he needed to go during the night. Walter Jr. was in the bed near the window. He reached over and shut off the light. In less than five minutes, Jimmy was snoring like a buzz saw.

"Junior?" whispered Chris.

"What is it, Grandpa?"

"I was thinking. What would it take for us to get Jimmy to his son in Oregon?"

"Only a few hundred miles out of our way, a few hundred dollars, which we don't have, for gas, and a few extra days, which I'm not sure we can spare. You do have an enemy out there somewhere, if you remember?"

"I got that all under control. I'm going to start building the raft, tonight. I should be off the island by tomorrow night. Irene will be safe. As for money, we could spare it, if we cut down on some items."

"Like what?"

"Well, for one, we can stop eating in restaurants. We can go to the supermarket and stock up on stuff. You know – cans of tuna, peanut butter, a couple of loaves of bread, and plenty of baloney."

Thirteen

My Isle of Golden Dreams

Drifting in dreams
Drifting it seems
Back to the shore
Back to your Isle of Dreams

Music by Walter Blufuss
Words by Gus Kahn

THE JOURNEY

That night, the first thing Chris began doing when he woke in his dream on the island was to start collecting materials for the raft.

With a sharp rock he cut long pieces of bamboo, tore the greenery from them, and placed them on the beach. He gathered as many straight sections of wood he could find, as many vines as he could pull down, and as many coconuts he found on the ground that fell from the trees. He placed all these bits and pieces in an exact order on the beach.

"What are you doing?"

Chris nearly jumped out of his skin. He spun around to see Irene smiling at him.

"Irene, sweetheart, don't ever sneak up on me like that again. You nearly gave me a heart attack."

"Nonsense! You're too young and strong to have a heart attack. Now, in the waking world, a good strong *Boo* would probably do us both in."

He laughed, stood up, and hugged her.

"You're determined to build this raft, aren't you?" she asked.

"I don't know what else to do. He keeps warning me that one or both of us must leave."

"What makes you think this mysterious villain has any real power?"

"He told me he caused the storm and he could do worse." Still holding her, he looked at her. "He's never tried to contact you, has he?"

"Not once."

"That's strange. He even got in touch with my grandson."

"He did? What did he want?"

"He told him to warn me. I haven't told you I'm traveling with my grandson. Crazy kid drove all the way to L.A. to drive me to San Diego."

"Chris, I still wish you'd give up this foolishness and go back to Texas."

"Just try to stop me! I'm coming to marry my best gal. But…um…it may take a little longer than I planned. We picked up some poor old guy who needs a lift to Oregon. We couldn't just leave him."

"I understand, and that's one of the reasons I love you." She eased out of his arms and looked at what he'd gathered on the beach. "So, this is to be the new improved raft? What makes you think this one will be any better?"

"I read a book on it. We did everything wrong the last time. You don't just slap pieces of wood together. First you build a frame with the bamboo, and then you tie the wood on. You have to braid the vines for strength."

"What are the coconuts for?"

"You put them underneath for buoyancy."

"Clever! What do you need me to do?"

"It would be a big help, if you'd gather food and water. Launch time is in eight hours."

Gleefully, she ran off into the bush.

He followed the blueprint in his head. In a short time, it began to look like a raft – a reliable one.

Every hour, Irene would appear with an armful of different foods: nuts and berries wrapped in large leaves, along with coconuts, and bananas. Using spare pieces of wood, she made a makeshift box to hold everything in.

Late that afternoon, they both completed their tasks. The raft was solid and seaworthy, resting in the sand a few yards from the waves. The food bin was overflowing.

Irene walked around the raft, admiring it.

"Not bad, if I say so myself. But don't you think it's a bit small?"

"Not for what I've got planned," said Chris.

"Well, I think this calls for a christening." She walked to the edge of the shore and came back with a handful of seawater. She poured it over the raft. "I christen thee the S.S. Woodrow Wilson."

"Woodrow Wilson?"

"Our old alma mater. Don't you remember the high school where we first dated?"

He took her in his arms and kissed her.

"There are one or two things I've left to do," he said. "Why don't you gather some more bananas? This time get some green ones, so they'll last."

Again, she ran into the bush.

"I love you!" he cried out to her.

"Love you, too," she called back, her voice muffled from the distance.

He knew he only had a few minutes. He got behind the raft, and using all his strength he pushed it across the sand to the water. It was a struggle, although as soon as it touched the first wave, the sea took hold of it, lifting it from the shore and taking possession of it.

When it was well afloat, he jumped onboard. Using a flat piece of wood, he began paddling away from the island. A few hundred yards out, he heard Irene calling out to him.

"Chris! Chris!"

He called back, "You'll be safe with me gone."

She ran out into the waves. "Chris, no, wait for me!"

"Don't worry! When I find a safe place, I'll come back for you. I swear!"

"Chris! No!" She fell to her knees. The waves pushed her back to shore.

"I'll be back! I swear!" His voice was fading with the distance. "Besides, I'm coming to San Diego to marry you."

She stood on the shore, crying, watching till the raft was just a speck in the distance, and then it disappeared over the horizon.

****

When the island faded from sight, Chris stopped rowing. Not knowing which direction he should go, he may as well let the current carry him.

The weather was perfect, the sky was clear and the sun was dipping slowly in the west. Since this was not necessarily reality, he only guessed it was the west.

Remembering the great storm on the island worried him. On such a small raft, even a storm half as big, he'd be a goner. Then again, if this was your run-of-the-mill dream, how much danger could there be? He'd read an article once by a professor who claimed that if you die in your dream, you die in real life. This is why if you dream of falling from a tall building, you wake up before you hit the ground. If you did hit the ground, your true body couldn't take the shock, and you'd die in both worlds.

He knew he'd miss Irene. He felt terrible about deceiving her; however, he believed he'd done what was right. He'd never take a chance when it came to his beloved Irene. Perhaps there is no pain or death in this dream world; if there was and something happened to her, who's to say what he'd do or feel? A high-sea's voyage was too great a risk.

The dark stranger warned at least one needed to leave the island. Whoever he was, he held great knowledge and power. Hopefully, he'd keep his word and leave Irene alone. She'd lived on the other side of the island from him for who knows how long. She'd done it before and she could do it again. She'd survive.

Anyways, when they meet in real life, in San Diego, and marry, everything would work itself out. He felt sure of it.

Besides, the odds of him finding another island, returning for Irene and taking her back with him were good. After all, anything can happen in a dream.

****

When she could no longer see the raft, Irene stopped crying and went into action. She took her few belongings from her hut atop of the hill and moved into Chris' hut on the beach. She built a fire in the sand and gathered large amounts of wood. Her plan was to remain vigil on the beach, keeping a fire going constantly, something to guide him back to her.

Sitting by the fire, she watched the sunset. The same sunset he watched from the raft. Somehow this made her feel close to him. Her eyes followed the lines in the wet sand – the lines made by Chris when he pushed the raft into the sea. Next to that something was scrawled. She got up to inspect what someone wrote in the wet sand.

Don't cry; he will return.
This is not how you leave the island.

A wave rushed up and washed the message away. Odd, there was power in those words and it comforted her. They assured her that he would return, although, the second part was clearly a warning. How else do you leave an island? Surely, the method must be something unconventional, yet still possible. Who can say? Anything can happen in a dream.

Fourteen

I had too much to dream last night

I had too much to dream last night
Too much to dream
I'm not ready to face the light
I had too much to dream
Last night

Music and Words by Annette Tucker & Nancie Mantz

THE JOURNEY

Walter Jr. felt relieved when at the supermarket there were pressed ham slices that cost the same as the baloney. There was a slight disagreement over the peanut butter – smooth or crunchy. White bread won hands down because of the lower price. They splurged by buying mustard for the ham and grape jelly for the peanut butter.

Traveling north at their rate of speed, Walter Jr. figured it would be a two-day journey. San Francisco was near the halfway point where they'd spend the night, and then another day's ride to their destination.

Walter Jr. and Chris sat up front, Jimmy sat in the back. His tall black hat scrunched into the car's low roof; so he held the hat in his lap. He sat in the middle of the seat so he could look out both windows, and hear what either his traveling companions said just by leaning forward.

They drove in silence with the rising sun to their right as they traveled north. From the corner of his eye, Walter Jr. saw Chris take something from his pocket.

"What'cha got there, Grandpa?"

"My fortune cookie from last night's meal."

"Well, why don't you open it?"

"I'm afraid to. It might be another warning from you-know-who."

Jimmy leaned forward. "I flushed mine down the toilet last night."

"Why'd you do that?" asked Chris.

"I don't believe in such things. It's like the Indians say in those old B-westerns, 'That 'um be big bad medicine', and I agree. I wouldn't open it, if I were you."

Chris stared at the cookie covered with pocket lint in his hand, wondering what to do. Without warning, Jimmy snatched it from his hand and tossed it out of the window.

"I'm sorry, Chris. Sometimes a friend must do unfriendly things to show his friendship."

"Who can argue with that? Thanks."

****

They were off to Coos Bay, Oregon, a thriving city on the Oregon seacoast.

With time on their hands, Jimmy Gray Horse told his tale, in short, it goes like this.

Jimmy was born and raised on an Indian reservation in North Dakota. He lived with his parents till he married at twenty-one. His bride was a local beauty, named Annie Little Crow. She was also of the Hidatsa tribe. They lived in a small trailer on the reservation; but they were happy and very much in love.

Jimmy found work wherever he could – local farms and ranches. When Annie became pregnant, he struggled all the more to bring in money. When the bills began piling up, Jimmy Gray Horse made the biggest mistake of his life. He robbed a convenience store. He'd gotten away with less than seventy-five dollars. It took the police less than eight hours to figure out who did it and arrest him. He received a three-year sentence at the State Penitentiary. For good behavior, he served only two.

His son and only child, Tom Gray Horse, was born while he was away. The joyous occasion was overshadowed by the death of his wife who died in childbirth. Custody of the infant was granted to Jimmy's parents.

On his release from prison, Jimmy returned to his trailer on the reservation. It was another year before he mustered up enough of what it takes to visit his son.

Jimmy slid into a deep depression. He worked little, socialized less, and drank too much, only seeing his son on rare occasions.

Despite so many disadvantages, Tom grew into a well-adjusted young man. He fell in love with a young woman of the tribe, Mary Smiling Feather.

Like so many other young men of the tribe, Tom's dream was to find work and leave the reservation. Through word of mouth from a friend of a friend, he received an offer of work on a fishing boat in Coos Bay, Oregon. His plan was to work hard, save his money till he could afford a house, send for Mary and marry her. He succeeded.

After years of working on fishing boats, Tom saved enough money and got enough knowledge to buy his own boat. It wasn't long before he bought another boat and then another. Eventually, he owned and managed a small fleet of five fishing boats and crews.

They fished the April through November season for Pacific salmon, halibut, albacore, lingcod, rockfish, and flatfish. The rest of the year, the off-season, they got by with clam-digging along the shore and crabbing close to shore.

For business reasons, Tom dropped his last name and adopted what he thought to be a good Anglo name – Tom Jones. Unaware the name was the title of a famous book, a well-loved movie, and the name of a well-known singer from the 60s. He became famed in the fishing business, which caused his company to flourish.

During these years, Mary and Tom had two strong sons. There was Sam II, to honor his father-in-law, and Jimmy II, to honor his own father – though Tom seldom thought about him.

Meanwhile, Jimmy Gray Horse the first, sunk to new lows with each passing year. Except…there is a final bottoming out point that life offers. There are only two alternatives for those who sink this far down – die or bounce back up. Thank God, Jimmy chose the latter. It wasn't easy; he couldn't have done it alone. It took all his strength and the help of his parents, other tribe members, a missionary on the reservation and years of A.A. before he rejoined the human race.

Muslims pilgrim to Mecca, while others, to Jerusalem, Rome, or Lourdes; for Jimmy Gray Horse salvation lay in forgiveness from his son.

After hearing Jimmy's story, it didn't surprise Walter Jr. when his grandfather told his story. Jimmy was a good listener who listened with respect and without judgment. The complete story of the continuing dream, the island, Irene, the forthcoming San Diego wedding, and the threat of the dark stranger, Jimmy heard and accepted it all without question.

"I might be able to help," said Jimmy. "My people have many ways to deal with such evil. I know many ancient remedies."

"I'd be grateful for any help you can offer."

"I'll see what I can do. I can at least try."

****

There must be a secret society of old men that Walter Jr. never knew about that he now was becoming more aware of with each passing mile. Chris and Jimmy could agree on most topics. They saw things the same and offered similar solutions for many of world's problems. Their likes and dislikes often matched, and what excited them and connected them as well.

When they entered San Francisco, both old men voiced an overpowering desire to go to the Golden Gate Bridge and look out at Alcatraz. Staring out at the island prison, they could not contain their excitement. Walter Jr. was sure that if not for their age the two old men would have competed in a swim against the menacing currents to the secluded island in the center of the bay. However, his main concern was finding an affordable place to spend the night. He found this in the *Alcatraz Motel.* The rates were low, and the name appealed to the two old men. Walter Jr. slept in one bed, Chris in the other, and again Jimmy insisted he sleep on the floor.

****

"Grandpa…! Grandpa…! Wake up! Wake up!" Walter Jr. shouted, shaking Chris' bed. The old man woke to confusion.

"What's wrong?"

Walter Jr. pointed to the floor where Jimmy spent the night. Chris looked over the edge of the bed. Jimmy's clothes were laid out flat: his shoes and socks, pants, shirt, vest, jacket, all of it toped by his black hat.

"He's disappeared right out of his clothes!" declared a mystified Chris.

"I don't think so, Grandpa. I think we've got a crazy old man running around somewhere naked."

They dressed quickly and ran out of the motel room. They didn't need to go far. In the parking lot was Jimmy singing and dancing. It was obviously some kind of Indian ceremonial dance. He danced in a circle, his body first bending forward and then reaching up to the sky, his hands raised high, palms up. The singing was repetitious, without words, a three-note ancient sounding chant. Luckily, it was early and there was no one else around, and Jimmy wasn't completely naked; he had on underwear.

This went on for a few more minutes. Jimmy acted unaware of them or the world, fully engrossed with the ceremony. Chris watched on, smiling like a child watching a Wild West show. Water Jr. watched the doors to the other rooms, waiting for someone to complain; he watched the entrance to the motel, figuring any minute a police car would appear.

Finally, Jimmy finished. Walter Jr. grabbed him by the arm and pulled him back into the motel room; Chris followed close behind, laughing all the way.

"Dang, if that wasn't the greatest thing I've seen in years," declared Chris as he closed the door.

"I hope no one else saw it," Walter Jr. said. He turned to Jimmy for an answer. Jimmy was sitting on the bed, out of breath, huffing and puffing.

"What was that all about, old man?"

"I did it for your grandfather. It is an ancient Hidatsa ceremonial dance...the Sun-Dance, given to us by Lodge-Boy and Spring-Boy, to fight off every evil."

"Lodge-Boy and Spring-Boy, who are they?" asked Chris, wide-eyed with enthusiasm.

"Atutish and Mahaash, twin brothers...ancestors of our tribe. A monster killed their mother; after that they vowed to fight monsters, giants, and all forms of evil wherever they found it. Yet no one lives forever. So, before they left this world, they gave us the Sun-Dance, a way of fighting off evil. Since I'm alone, I did the best I could. There is much more to it than what you saw. There should be fasting and prayers, incense, drums, sacrifices, body-paint, medicine-bundles, animal skins, priests, and much more. I did what I could."

"And did you destroy the evil?" asked Chris with anticipation.

"No, I did not, yet not because the medicine of the Sun-Dance was missing. It is because of two reasons. For one, the dark stranger you fear is more powerful than you can imagine. No one can stop him. The other reason the medicine cannot stop him is because they gave us the Sun-Dance to stop evil and he is not evil. He is not your enemy."

"What about those harsh warnings?"

"Sometimes a friend must do unfriendly things to show his friendship."

****

"America the Beautiful," sighed Chris, looking to the mountains at his right and the ocean on his left as they drove north on the Coastal Highway.

"That is true," agreed Jimmy. "But it was not always so. We Hidatsa believe the earth was once formless."

Chris turned in his seat to look at Jimmy. "Go ahead."

"Hidatsa legend says once the earth was nothing but sand. The ancient one we call Only-Man walked the earth singing his song: *Where did I come from? How did I come to this place?*" Since the world was nothing other than wet sand, he turned and saw his own tracks. He decided to follow them back to find out where he came from.

"As he traveled, he came upon another man. The two argued about which of them was oldest. They decided they would lie down in the sand, and the first to get up was the youngest. The other man lay down in the sand; Only-Man placed his cane down to take his place and walked away, singing his song: *Where did I come from? How did I come to this place?*

"Only-Man walked the entire earth for many years. When he returned he found his cane where he left it. Next to it was a patch of grass where the other man had lain down. He took up his cane, and suddenly the other man sprung up from the ground. 'I told you I was older than you' he proclaimed.

"They walked the earth together, creating it anew. They made the earth beautiful. They created plants, and animals. They did this for many years. Then one day, Grandmother Frog said to them, 'In your zeal you have created too much, there are too many plants and animals in the world. You must create death so the old can make way for the new. They agreed and created death. The child of Grandmother Frog was the first to die. She came crying to them, 'No, I was wrong. Take death away!' but they said it was too late, death was here to stay."

Chris turned forward and looked out the car window. "Well, they sure did a great job. Only I have to agree with Grandmother Frog, death is a high price to pay for beauty. Tell me, whatever happened to Only-Man and the other man?"

"After they recreated the world, Only-Man vanished and was never seen or heard from again. The other man turned into a coyote. That is why to this day, every night you can hear the coyotes howl. What they are howling is: *Where did I come from? How did I come to this place?*"

****

The people of the state of Oregon know what they have, a little piece of heaven on earth, and they would prefer not to let the rest of the world know. An overpopulated slice of the Garden of Eden is a little slice of you-know-where. So they never blow their own horn, keeping it to themselves. Coos Bay is a small part of that paradise.

The threesome drove into town just as the sun kissed the horizon; there was less light with each passing moment. They toured the town, the bay, driving alongside the pier; they came to a small group of fishing boats. Overhead was a sign that read, "Tom Jones Inc.". Jimmy looked out the window and cried. No one said a word, giving him his privacy.

"We can't just drop in on Jimmy's son in the middle of the night," said Chris. "We need to do it in the morning."

Both Jimmy and Walter Jr. agreed, which meant food and lodging for the night – cheap food and lodging. Seeing how arriving at their destination gave an air of celebration to the night, they decided to skip the usual ham sandwich or peanut butter and jelly, and eat out. So close to the ocean, seafood would be in order.

They found an out-of-the-way restaurant called *Shark Bait*.

"I'll have the Fisherman's Fantasy Fry," Chris told the waitress.

"That's a lot of fried food, Grandpa," Walter Jr. said.

"That's the one good thing about growing old, Junior, and that it's too late to die young, so don't sweat it."

Jimmy ordered the fish and chips. "The English love this stuff. Let's see if it's all that it's cracked up to be."

The beer was warm, the fish was greasy, and still, all in all it was great.

Later they found a motel, *The Sailor's Wharf Motel*, not quite the gem of the ocean.

With Jimmy in his usual place on the floor, and Walter Jr. in his bed and Chris in his, in the dark, Chris sighed.

"You all right, Grandpa?" Walter Jr. asked.

"I'm scared, Junior."

"About what? Once you fall asleep, you'll be with your Irene."

"Not really. I left her on the island. I built a raft and sailed away."

"Why would you do that?"

"I wanted to make sure she was safe."

"Don't do that, Grandpa. If I had someone to love, I'd stick by them no matter what. And I'd expect them to do the same. Together you can conquer anything."

"Out of the mouths of babes," sighed Chris. "Goodnight, Junior."

"Goodnight, Grandpa."

Fifteen

You dreamer you

I fell in love like one, two, three
Oh, what a dream
I asked the angel to marry me
Oh, what a dream
She said, "Sir, I can't marry you,
But I'm a dream that can come true
There are dreams of much my worth
That live upon the earth, sir
Live upon the earth
You dreamer you

Music and Words by Johnny Cash

THE JOURNEY

Chris' face grated across the wood of the raft. He wasn't sure how long he'd slept. It was becoming confusing. This so-called dream seemed just as real as his wakened state. Perhaps, Irene, the island, and the raft were just as real. Another thought was that both were dreams. Maybe his travels with Junior and Jimmy were only dreams he dreamed while he slept on the raft. And the raft was the dream he dreamed while he slept in the motel. Which was the dream and which was real was becoming difficult to tell; the line between the two worlds was becoming thin.

Sitting up, he felt stinging pain rush across his naked back. He'd slept with his back to the tropical sun; now it had a beet-red sunburn. He followed his first instinct and jumped in the water to cool off. This was a mistake. In the water, holding onto the raft, the sea-salt ripped at his pores like thousands of small knives. He hopped back onto the raft.

Looking in all directions, flat ocean leading to the horizons was all he saw. The sea was calm, uncommonly still, not a wave in sight, as smooth as a frozen lake. The raft moved not an inch in any direction. The water was clear as glass; he could see the sandy bottom. There were ruins of an ancient city below. Saltwater or not, he had to explore. He took a deep breath and dove into the sea.

It was amazing. A sunken city, untouched and in excellent condition; he couldn't tell how old it was or what civilization had lived in it. It was all made of stone; the arches looked Roman, the pillars looked Greek, with a touch of Aztec. One large building caught his eye. A temple with two high columns in front with massive capitals on top, all connected by carvings of vines decorated with pomegranates. In front stood what looked to be a great bronze altar resting on the backs of twelve bronze bulls, four facing each main point of the compass. He held his breath, staying down as long as possible to take as much of it in as he could.

Suddenly, something or someone hit him hard in the back. All the wind was knocked out of him; the bubbles rose to the surface. He panicked and frantically swam up. When he hit the surface, he howled as he filled his lungs once more with sweet air. Fearing what was in the water with him, he jumped back onto the raft in a blink of an eye.

Twenty feet out, a fine line in the water circled the raft. It was a group of fish surrounding him. He could only believe that it was sharks closing in. What would he do? What could he do? Out on the open sea, he was helpless.

The next instant, something rose from the sea and stood on the surface of the water. It was a dolphin. He realized they were all dolphins encircling the raft. The one dolphin gave that cackling sound that dolphins do. It sounded so friendly, yet still sounded like a reprimand.

It dove back into the water. All the dolphins, maybe six or more, gathered on one end of the raft. To his surprise, they butted their heads against the raft and began to push it through the water. In no time, the raft was moving at high-speed, the dolphins acting like an outboard motor. There was nothing for Chris to do other than sit back and enjoy the ride.

After an hour, an island appeared on the horizon; it came closer and became larger with each passing moment. It didn't take long before Chris realized he was returning to his original island, back to Irene.

A few yards from shore, the dolphins stopped pushing. The head dolphin jumped to the surface and cackled his friendly warning to Chris, who took it as gospel. In a flash, they were gone. The raft bobbed a few feet forward till it stuck in the sand. Chris jumped in the water and walked the rest of the way onto shore. Irene stood silently on the beach watching him. He stopped just before her.

"I'm sorry. I made a mistake. I never should have left the island without you; and the way I did it was deceitful and wrong. Please, forgive me."

"I forgive you. But don't ever treat me like that again. You say you want to marry me. . .fine. People marry for better or for worse; we make decisions together."

"I know. I didn't realize what I'd done till it was too late. It will never happen again. I'm sorry. Please, forgive me."

"Of course and I will never mention this again. Now. . . are you hungry?"

"I could use something other than fruit."

"I have some crab and lobster I caught today. I've a fire going just up ahead on the shore."

As they sat and ate they caught up with each other.

"That fellow I told you we were taking to Oregon, he's an American Indian. I told him all about us, and our predicament. He performed an ancient tribal ceremony to free us of this dark stranger. I don't know how much stock to put in such things; although he did say something incredibly strange. He said the stranger was too powerful to stop, and that he wasn't an enemy, but a friend."

"I can believe that, somehow," said Irene. "The day you went away he left a message in the sand for me."

"What did it read? Where was it?"

They rose; Irene guided him roughly to where the message was.

"It was there." She pointed at a spot in the wet sand. "It was a warning, all right. Only there was friendliness to it, too. It told me not to cry, that you would return. It also said going off on a raft was not the way to leave the island."

"What happened to it?"

"As soon as I finished reading, the waves washed it away."

"Not the way to leave the island?" Chris thought out loud. "What other way could there be?"

"This is a dream, as you know. Anything is possible."

"You're telling me! I found an ancient sunken city out there," he said, looking out to the sea. "Then dolphins pushed me and the raft back here and up to the shoreline. You're telling me *anything* is possible."

"There's something we're not seeing when we look at this," said Irene.

"I met a woman who dreams every night about being with someone she loves in the wilderness of the Alps, in a chalet."

"Really. . .! Similar, but not the same. . . What else did she say?"

"Her name is Marion; she works at the library where I read the book on raft building."

"Marion the librarian? You're kidding?"

"No, that was her name. Foolish me, I was too busy learning about raft building that I didn't ask any questions. Before I knew it, it was time to close the library and she was gone. As soon as we drop this fellow at his Oregon destination, we'll be heading south once more. I think I'll look her up again and see what I can learn from her."

"We need to look at the big picture," said Irene. "Whenever we sleep, we dream. Whenever we dream, we're here together on this island. Leaving the island on a raft doesn't change a thing. We remain in the dream."

"Then, what you're saying is we need to stop dreaming. Except, how do you stop dreaming?"

"You have to stop sleeping."

"That's impossible. You can't stop sleeping."

"There is one way."

Sixteen

You're innocent when you dream

It's such a sad old feeling
The fields are soft and green
It's memories that I'm stealing
But you're innocent when you dream
When you dream
You're innocent when you dream

Words and Music by Tom Waits

THE JOURNEY

Hemingway was no saint or prophet; he made mistakes like any other man. However, he was truly blessed when he proclaimed *The Sun Also Rises*. For it does rise and shine equally on the great and the small, and the rich and the poor.

It was Saturday morning in Coos Bay. The sun shined clear and golden on the *Fisherman's Warf Motel* as it does on the Great Wall of China, the Great Pyramids, the peaks of the Himalayans, the backstreets of Saigon, and the main thoroughfares of Hoboken, New Jersey, without decimation.

They all woke early and at the same time.

"Today's the day," proclaimed Chris to Jimmy.

"It's early," said Jimmy. "We should find a place to have breakfast, first."

"You're just trying to put off the inevitable," Walter Jr. said.

Jimmy thought for a moment. "You're right. Let's go."

****

The home of Tom Jones was a modest two-story house. It had steel-gray shingles all around, white painted wooden trim, and a widow's walk along the pitched roof, facing the sea. It rested on a high hill overlooking the harbor.

Walter Jr. parked the car just below the steps leading to the front door.

"We'll wait here," he said.

Jimmy got out slowly and started up the steps like a mountain climber examines Mount Everest before the ascent.

"I just thought of something," Walter Jr. said.

"What's that," asked Chris.

"If Jimmy's son rejects him, we're stuck with Jimmy."

"We'll cross that bridge when and if we have to," said Chris. "Although honestly, I don't think that will happen. They don't say blood is thicker than water for nothing."

"You're trying to tell me better days with my father have yet to come?"

"You both need to grow a little more. Take my word for it. In a few years, you'll have a much better relationship than you do now; I hope you will remember you heard it from me first."

"I hope you're right."

"I know I am."

They watched Jimmy reach the front door and knock. A moment later the door opened and a young man in pajamas and robe appeared – presumably his son, Tom. There was much talk between the two; Chris and Walter Jr. were too far to hear a word.

"What could they be talking about? Why is it taking so long?" Walter Jr. moaned.

"Give them time," said Chris. "They've put an ocean between them; you don't swim it in two minutes."

The quiet of the morning was broken by the rushing sound of seagulls flying overhead, going west. Then the father and son were in each others arms.

"I told you they'd come to terms." Chris turned and smiled at Walter Jr., "Junior, are you crying?"

"No, it's just the cold morning air."

"Don't give me that; you're crying. Now, why would you want to hide a thing like that? Only a real man can cry, at the right times, of course. All the elements of a person's life are held together with tears, both joyous and sorrowful."

Jimmy waved for them to come up to the house.

"Well, here we go," said Walter Jr., turning off the engine.

Everyone felt a bit awkward, standing in the living room. No one knew what to say. Father and son hadn't spoken in years. Tom's wife, Mary, had never met her father-in-law. Chris and Walter Jr. felt out of place. The two sons, Sam and Jimmy, seven and six, ran around in their pajamas.

"Boys, boys, stop running around," said Tom. "I want you to meet someone."

They stood still, close to their mother.

"Boys, I want you to meet your grandfather."

"We already have a grandfather, Grandpa Sam," said Sam the oldest.

"That's true, but everyone has two grandfathers. Grandpa Sam is momma's father. We named you after him, Sam. That makes you Sam the second. This is my father. Jimmy, we named you after him. That makes you Jimmy the second. Come, say hello to your grandfather."

Little Jimmy stepped forward, took his grandfather's hand and shook it.

"Pleased to meet you Jimmy the first."

"Pleased to meet you Jimmy the second."

Much needed relief filled the room as everyone laughed.

"That's no way to say hello to your grandfather," said Mary. "Both of you give him a kiss."

Jimmy took his young grandson Sam's hand and shook it. "No, that's all right. A handshake is a good place to start. Kisses must be earned." He then stood before Mary. "I owe you an apology, too. Please forgive a foolish old man."

She reached up and kissed him. "There's no need. My love and respect for your son is as wide and deep as the sea. How can I not love and respect the river that gave it life."

Jimmy pointed to his traveling companions. "These are my friends, Christopher Goodman, and his grandson, Walter Bouchard. They were kind enough to drive me here."

"We thank you for bringing my father to us, safely," said Tom. "You are both welcome in our home."

Walter Jr. shook little Jimmy's hand. "My father's name is Walter, also. I'm a second, too."

The boys just laughed.

"Come, everyone, into the kitchen for breakfast." Mary guided them before her.

"My wife is a good cook, you will see," Tom said to his father. "We have much to talk about. If we are to be in each other's lives again, you must stay with us a long time." He turned to Chris and Walter Jr., "We have plenty of room. Your friends are welcome to stay as long as they like."

"Thank you. We may bother you for one night; but we must be on our way," said Chris. Walter Jr. nodded in agreement.

After a hardy breakfast, everyone sat in the living room to get acquainted.

"What is this?" announced Jimmy. "Your sons never heard of Lodge-Boy and Spring-Boy!"

"I'm afraid much of our old tribal ways are forgotten here in the white-man's world. It is my fault, forgive me, father?" said Tom.

"That will be your responsibility, Poppa," said Mary.

Jimmy reached over and took Mary's hand. To be called *Poppa* in his son's house was a dear and wonderful thing.

"Sam, Jimmy, upstairs, wash up and get dressed, we're going to take Grandpa Jimmy to see our ships and take one of the boats out to sea. Show off a bit," declared Tom.

The boys were off in a flash; Jimmy smiled with pride, Walter Jr. smiled with anticipation, although Chris looked a bit worn for the journey.

"If you don't mind, I'll back out," said Chris. "I feel too tired."

"I'll stay with you," Walter Jr. said.

"Nonsense, how often do you get to take to the high seas? Go, have fun. I just want to relax."

"Don't worry, I'll be here," said Mary. "I don't need to play pirate for a day, like my husband and sons do. I'll have dinner waiting when you get home."

When the others left, Chris relaxed on the living room couch, while Mary went about her usual routine of cleaning, laundry, and cooking. She came downstairs carrying a laundry basket, the phone rang, she put down the basket and answered it.

"Yes, hello, yes he's here." She covered the mouthpiece with her hand and offered it to Chris. "Mr. Goodman, it's for you."

"Is it my grandson?"

"It didn't sound like him. He just asked for Mr. Goodman."

"That's strange," said Chris, taking hold of the receiver. "Hello?"

"Chris?"

He didn't need to hear another word. He knew the voice immediately. It was the same voice he'd heard on the train – the dark stranger.

"How did you find me? What do you want?"

"Chris, you know I have the power to find you wherever you are; you know what I want."

"Then you know I built a raft. I tried to leave, except I came right back."

Not feeling it was her place to hear anymore, Mary took the laundry basket and left the room.

"Chris, you're not listening. Irene understands what to do."

"You mean leave the dream! How do you leave a dream if every time you fall asleep you dream?"

"Then stop sleeping!"

"That's impossible. You can only stay awake so long before sleep takes over and you dream. You can't stop dreaming because you can't stop sleeping."

"Of course you can, Chris. Thousands of people do it everyday."

"I don't understand."

"Ask Irene about it, tonight. Either you do something about it soon, or I'll come and do it for you. Goodnight, Chris, pleasant dreams."

Chris placed the receiver down.

"Is everything all right?" asked Mary. Chris turned to see her standing in the doorway.

"Yes, everything's just…no, everything's not fine."

"Is there anything I can do?"

"You're very kind. There is one thing you can do. If I'm not imposing too much, may I lie on a bed and take a nap. I'm awfully tired and there's someone I need to see."

****

Chris looked up and down the beach, except he saw no sign of Irene. Perhaps she hadn't gone to sleep, yet; it was early. Then he saw her collecting shells. He ran to her.

"Okay, tell me straight, have you been in contact with the stranger?" he asked.

"What are you talking about?"

"He called me this afternoon."

"Called you? Where are you?"

"It's a long story. He phoned me and there was no way he could have known where I was, but he did. He said if we didn't sort this out, he'd come and do it for us. He said to ask you about all this, that you understood what needs doing. I told him I didn't understand. How can a person stop sleeping and dreaming. He said thousands of people do it everyday. I just don't understand."

"My sweet, innocent darling, don't you see the thousands who don't sleep or dream are those who die everyday. There's no sleeping or dreaming for the dead."

"But I won't let you die for my sake."

"Why not, at my age, another year, another day, what does it matter?"

"It does matter, even if we have only a day as one, it's more than I could hope for. I love you so much. I'll take whatever time there is."

"I feel the same," said Irene. "Then it's we two against the world, in life or against death, agreed?"

"Agreed."

The two fell into each other's arms and then to the ground, kissing and hugging.

"This is only an afternoon nap, I need to get back."

"Just a little longer, darling; everyone knows an old man needs his rest."

****

All during dinner, Walter Jr. couldn't stop relaying what a great time he'd had that day.

"I'd never been in anything bigger or faster than a rowboat. How many miles an hour were we going?"

"On the sea we don't go by miles, we go by knots. I'm glad you enjoyed it, it actually wasn't that fast," laughed Tom.

"This is great fish," said Chris. "Is it yours?"

"Fresh caught this morning."

"Eat, everybody, there's plenty," announced Mary. "Anyone for hushpuppies?"

"Me! Me!" cried little Sam and Jimmy in unison.

Jimmy Sr. scrunched his face. "Hushpuppy? You eat dog?"

They couldn't stop little Sam and Jimmy from laughing.

After dinner, the children went to watch television in the living room. The adults stayed in the dining room and talked.

"Congratulations, Mr. Goodman. My father tells me you're on your way to get married," said Tom.

"Just call me Chris. Yes, I'm very excited."

"He also tells me, outside of your grandson, your family doesn't know where you are. If they did, there'd probably be no wedding."

Chris looked at Jimmy, as if to say, "Did you have to tell him everything?"

"It's all right, Chris. Your secret is good with us," Tom pledged.

Mary reached over and placed her hand on her husband's. "Yes, we believe very much in love in this house."

Tom continued, "He tells me you are having spirit troubles, too."

"I don't know if you can call it spirit troubles."

"Don't you worry; my father knows all the old ways. He'll figure something out."

****

Later, they retired to the living room.

"Bedtime!" announced Mary to her sons. Surprisingly, there was no dispute about going to bed. "Say goodnight to Papa, and Grandpapa."

They hugged and kissed their father and grandfather.

"Say goodnight to Mr. Goodman and Mr. Bouchard."

"Just call me Walter," Walter Jr. said.

"No, Mr. Bouchard," said Mary. "They are too young to be on a first name basis with an elder. They must show respect."

"Goodnight Mr. Goodman, Goodnight Mr. Bouchard," the boys said in harmony. They were off with their mother to their upstairs bedroom.

"If you don't mind," said Tom, changing the TV channel. "I need to watch the news and see what tomorrow's weather will be like. Please, sit down."

The weathercaster declared the following day to be one of clear sunny skies and warm soft breezes, all to the approval and relief of Tom. The camera returned to the anchorman and anchorwoman.

"One last item, before we sign off," said the anchorman. "If you remember the other night we reported a story how actress Louise Langford with the Dream Makers Organization greeted a sweet young lady, Sara Millwood and her mother, at the L.A. train station. Then, Ms. Langford treated them to a fun filled week at Disneyland. After examining the footage of the event, as you see here, Trisha Millwood, Sara's mother, is saying good-bye to an elderly gentleman. The man has been identified as Christopher Goodman from Venus, Texas. Christopher is a senior citizen who has run off from his family to, get this, meet and marry the woman of his dreams in San Diego, California."

The anchorman and woman, as well as the studio film crew, all got a chuckle over the story. The screen switched to a close-up photo of Chris; the anchorwoman took over the story.

"Mr. Goodman is eighty-five years old. His family is extremely worried about his well-being. If anyone in our audience knows of Mr. Goodman's whereabouts, please contact the local police."

The anchorman took over.

"And that ends another addition of Freedom News. Have a goodnight and a pleasant tomorrow."

Tom shut off the TV.

"It looks like you'll need eyes in the back of your head," said Tom.

"I'll think of something," said Jimmy.

Chris and Walter Jr. shared a bed in the guestroom.

"Are you going to be all right, Grandpa?" asked Walter Jr., before turning out the light.

"I'll be fine," said Chris. "I'm going to see my best gal, tonight. I'm going to tell her, I don't want to speak a word. I just want to hold her all-night, till I wake in the morning, or I have to go to the bathroom, whichever comes first."

****

Early the next morning, just before sunrise, and before the children woke, everyone else gathered in the living room to say good-bye to Walter Jr. and Chris.

Mary handed Walter Jr. a large paper sack. "I made you some sandwiches, no baloney, and some other things you'll enjoy."

"Thank you," he said, placing the bag under his arm.

"You sure I can't give you any money for all you've done?" asked Tom.

"No, you've been most kind, as it is. We should thank you," said Chris.

Jimmy stepped in front of Chris and placed his hands on Chris' shoulders. "My dear brother, I can't thank you enough. Last night, I prayed before sleeping for a way of helping you. I dreamed I was in paradise and I asked the White Buffalo how I could help my friend Christopher Goodman. He told me I'd find the answer in the river nearby. I walked to the river and fell to my knees to gaze at my reflection in the water. When I looked at the reflection it was not mine, it was yours. Then I knew what to do."

Jimmy walked to the front door. He took down his great black hat that hung next to the door. He came back and placed it on Chris' head.

"They are looking for a white man from Venus, Texas, not a Hidatsa tribe member from North Dakota."

Each person felt inclined to laugh, however when the hat rested on Chris' head, no one laughed. It was an amazing transformation. He no longer looked like himself, yet he looked natural. The hat changed his appearance, entirely.

"Thank you," said Chris. "I will wear it with honor."

****

With heavy hearts they drove off. Chris sat slightly slouched to allow the tall hat not to crunch into the car roof.

An hour later, well in route, Walter Jr. confined in his grandfather.

"Don't look now, Grandpa. I don't want you to worry. When we traveled north to bring Jimmy to his family, I was just suspicious. Now that we're traveling south, I'm sure. We're being followed."

Seventeen

Dream Police

The dream police, they live inside of my head
The dream police, they come to me in my bed
The dream police, they're coming to arrest me, oh no

Music and Words by Rick Nielsen

THE JOURNEY

In Ancient times, travelers kept to the well-known and well-worn trails throughout Europe, the Far and Middle East. The trails were passageways used by merchants journeying across the globe, bringing goods from one land to another and back. It was wise to keep to these pathways. Though not always the most direct route, they proved to be the safest and easiest way with plenty of food, water, and lodging. It was not uncommon to meet a traveling merchant and his caravan at an oasis in far-off Persia. Then meet the same man, six months later, peddling his goods in Venice or Paris, or as far east as the coast of Portugal, or points farther north, England and Scotland.

In 1926 the Mother Road, the Main Street of America, Route 66, was completed. It started in Chicago, Illinois and ran through Missouri, Kansas, Oklahoma, Texas, New Mexico, Arizona, and ended in California, after 2,448 miles. People drove this highway west to east and east to west. It was not unusual to see the same cars driving at your side for days on end. It was not out of the ordinary to meet someone on the same course at a motel in Kansas, and then meet them again days later at a diner in New Mexico.

Knowing such things, Walter Jr. found nothing strange about seeing the same tan convertible behind them, as they traveled north up the Coastal Highway. It always seemed to be there. Now and then it'd disappear, only to return behind them a few minutes later. Even when they stopped in San Francisco for the night, the car was behind them in the morning when they left. Why not, San Francisco was a logical place to spend the night; the tan convertible probably did the same. When they stopped their journey at Coos Bay, he still shook off any suspicion. Coos Bay was a common destination, especially for professionals in the fishing, boating, or railway industries.

Traveling south along the same roads they came from, all doubts were gone. The morning they left, they walked down to where they parked the car. Jimmy remained standing at the front door, waving them good-bye. It was still early and the sun was just barely peaking over the horizon. The streets of Coos Bay were silent, except for a few early birds off to work at early jobs or night owls just getting home. Leaving Coos Bay city limits, they got on the highway. Walter Jr. adjusted his rearview mirror. That's when he saw it, the tan convertible.

He slowed down to get a better look. It was the same car that trailed them all those miles. He'd memorized the California license plate. He slowed down a little bit more to get a look at the man behind the wheel. It was him, a black man in his midthirties, bald – shaven head, wearing a suit and tie. At first, Walter Jr. thought he was a traveling businessman – the suit and tie gave that impression. Now he knew different.

The man's dark handsome face was always without expression, staring a hole in the back of their heads, constantly right behind them, matching their speed, be it fast or slow.

Unable to fight the temptation, Chris turned to get a good look at the man and the car.

"Are you sure?" asked Chris.

"Absolutely, no question in my mind." Walter Jr. sped up, the tan convertible kept pace. "You never got a good look at him. Do you think he might be the stranger?"

"It's possible. Although he's never been shy about telling me what's on his mind. Following us and not saying anything is so unlike him. I suspect this man works for him, or he's following us for some other reason. Either way it doesn't add up."

"Well, whoever he is, my vote is we try to lose him."

"I second the motion."

****

Farther up the road, Walter Jr. quickly entered a rest-stop on the side of the road. The *Posse*, the nickname they gave the man tailing them, had no time to react. They watched him drive quickly by.

Other than a couple of truckers catching some Zs, they had the rest stop to themselves. They sat at a picnic bench and rummaged through the sack Mary gave them. There were all kinds of sandwiches, chips, snacks, cookies and...

"Will you look at this!" said Walter Jr., shaking his head as he took out a one-hundred dollar bill from the bottom of the sack. "We can ship it to them when we get back to Texas."

"I wouldn't do that, Junior. They're the type of folks who take pleasure in giving, and I'd be afraid that might insult them. When we get back we'll send them a thank you card."

As they ate, Walter Jr. spread a map across the picnic table.

"Ten to one, our friend, the Posse, is waiting for us somewhere up the road. There's a two-lane road, a mile back, we can take that, make a big loop and come back here on this highway, some ten miles south. Altogether, it'll take us thirty miles out of our way, it should get you-know-who off our trail."

"Sounds like a plan."

****

The twenty mile scenic route was just that. The mountains, valleys, trees, and steams captivated them. They felt like intruders in a world few people ever see or know. The route emptied onto the highway, and they were again traveling south with the glorious ocean to their right.

An hour later, Walter Jr. looked into the rearview mirror. "I don't believe it! It's him; Posse is back on our trail. How did he do it?"

"If he's in cahoots with my stranger from my dreams, he might have strange powers," said Chris.

"I don't believe such things," said Walter Jr., "I refuse to believe such things. But I'll tell you this. He's a professional."

"What's his purpose?" asked Chris. "Why doesn't he tell us what he wants?"

****

Entering San Francisco, Walter Jr. drove directly to the Golden Gate Bridge, and then down to the pier.

"Where are we going?" asked Chris.

"I've got a plan to get rid of the Posse. You're going to like this. You're going to get to see Alcatraz."

****

A tour of Alcatraz, of course, starts with a ferry ride to the lone island in the middle of San Francisco Bay. Chris and Walter Jr. stood up at the bow of the ferry; they turned around and saw Posse leaning against the railing at the stern.

"This is ridiculous; I'm going to go talk with him," Walter Jr. said.

"No, don't," warned Chris, except he was too late, Walter Jr. was walking to the stern.

He stood next to Posse. "So, who are you? And what do you want from us?"

"Excuse me?"

"Don't play games. You've been in my rearview mirror for days, now. What do you want?"

"I don't want anything. Do you ask your guardian angel what he wants? He wants what's best for you. Now, go back up front and let me do my job."

"And what is your job?"

"To make sure you're safe. Now, go back before I complain and have you arrested."

"I don't understand."

"You're not supposed to. Now, get away from me."

"I'm going to do what I can to get rid of you."

"I understand; you must do what you must do."

Walter Jr. walked back to Chris.

"What did he say?" asked Chris.

"I can't figure it out," said Walter Jr., "He tells me he's our friend; yet he won't say how or why. We need to lose him."

"I second that motion."

****

"From 1934 to 1963 Alcatraz housed some of the most notorious and dangerous criminals of the past one hundred years," the tour guide bellowed, "Al Capone and Robert Stroud – the Birdman of Alcatraz – being the most well-known. Once called *Isla de los Alcatraces* by the Spaniards – Island of the Pelicans, the island has a history that could fill a library with stories. Nowadays, Alcatraz is a home for wild flowers, tall grass, marine wildlife and seabirds"

For the next two and a half hours they were guided throughout the island. Chris and Walter Jr. remained at the front of a group of thirty. Posse remained at the tail of the group, biding his time. They moved from building to building, listening to the tour guide describe every nuance of each building. As they approached the end of the tour, Walter Jr. grabbed hold of Chris' arm and guided him away from the tour to the prison cells of solitary confinement.

"What are we doing here?" asked Chris.

"It's all part of my plan," said Walter Jr., "We spend the night here, and Posse continues with the tour and heads back to the mainland. When the tours start again tomorrow, we get in line and head back, with Posse just a memory."

"Sounds like a plan."

They lay on separate beds in different cells. Chris relaxed with his hands folded behind his head.

"I hope these mattresses don't have bedbugs."

"I doubt it," replied Walter Jr., "No one's slept on them in years. If there were bedbugs, they've all died a long time ago from starvation."

"I hope you're right," said Chris. "I can hardly wait to fall asleep and tell Irene where I'm sleeping. She won't believe it."

"Say hello for me."

"I will. Say, Junior, I just thought of something."

"What's that, Grandpa?"

'We're spending the night in Alcatraz to give Posse the slip. But all he has to do is wait by the car for us when we return in the morning."

Walter Jr. thought long and hard, and realized the flaw in his plan. "That's true. Only think of the money were saving by not staying at a motel."

****

"You'll never guess where I'm spending the night," Chris said to Irene as soon as he appeared on the shore.

"The orchestra pit at the Hollywood Bowl…no…the dugout at Dodger Stadium…no…how about front row center at Grauman's Chinese Theater?"

"Stop it! Be serious."

"Okay, I give up. Where are you sleeping?"

"In a cell, in solitary, in Alcatraz."

"I thought you said, be serious?"

"I am being serious."

"So, tell me, how did you wind up there?"

"It was Junior's idea. You see, there's this man following us."

"Whoa! What man?"

"We don't know who he is. He's been following us for days."

"Is he the stranger who's been warning us?"

"I don't think so. Anyway, we took the tour of Alcatraz, lost the man in the shuffle and we're spending the night there."

"Chris, if your car is in the parking lot, all the man has to do is wait till you return in the morning."

"That's where the plan falls apart. Junior meant well. At least the boy's thinking."

Suddenly, Chris' body began to shake violently; a white light shone in his eyes, blinding him.

"Chris, what's happening? Are you all right?"

"Someone's waking me. I'm sorry, Irene. I'll be back soon."

****

A security guard stood at the foot of Chris' prison bed, alternating shining the light of his flashlight in Chris' eyes and then hammering it on the metal bed frame.

"Time to get up old-timer; show's over."

Walter Jr. came running in.

"Oh, there are two of you," said the guard. "What do you think this is, the YMCA?" A bleep sounded from his walkie-talkie; he answered. "Stan, here... We've got a couple of bums trying to spend the night in solitary."

"We're not bums!" protested Walter Jr., "We were on the tour. My grandfather is old, he's tired, and so I told him to lie down. I figured we'd get a ride on the last ferry out."

"The evening tour left twenty minutes ago."

"Listen, mister, we didn't mean any harm."

The guard shined his light on both their faces. "I suppose, if I call the police, that's the story you'll hand them; and I'll spend the night answering questions and filling out forms." He thought for a moment. "Okay, there's a small ship with equipment leaving for the mainland in five minutes. You two are on it."

****

Back onshore, their car was one of three still in the parking lot. They looked around. There was no sign of Posse.

"He's not here," Walter Jr. said.

Chris smiled. "He figured what we were up to, and decided to get some sleep in comfort at one of the hotels. He'll be back in the morning after the first tour."

Walter Jr. drove them to the *Alcatraz Motel.*

"We've stayed here before, and Posse knows it," warned Chris.

"He knows that we know that he knows. That's why he won't think of looking for us here. Besides, he thinks we're still on Alcatraz."

"Smart thinking, Junior."

****

Once in their motel room, in their separate beds, Chris turned off the light.

"You did it, Junior; you outsmarted Posse."

"I wish I did, Grandpa. It was all just dumb luck."

"Don't let them kid you, Junior. All luck is dumb."

"Goodnight, Grandpa."

"Goodnight, Junior. I can hardly wait to tell Irene what happened."

****

Early the next morning, Posse woke, drove to the nearest drive-through and ordered a double latte. He drove to the pier. The sun was just illuminating the world. In the parking lot for the Alcatraz Tours he found no sign of their car. If possible, he would have kicked himself. What would he tell his boss?

At the same time, Walter Jr. and Chris got in their car and headed south on the highway.

"When we get to L.A., I need to stop and talk to that librarian, Marion the librarian."

"Whatever you say, Grandpa…"

Eighteen

Dream on

Every time that I look in the mirror
All these lines in my face getting clearer
The past is gone
It went by like dusk to dawn
Isn't that the way
Everybody's got the dues in life to play

Words and Music by Steven Tyler

THE JOURNEY

Lying on their beds in the *La Casa de Oro Motel* was like coming home. After being on the road in unfamiliar territory, anything familiar was comforting.

Later, they started down the street towards the library.

Chris was excited. "I should have questioned her in depth, once she told me about her dream-life. Maybe, if we can compare notes, we can help each other."

Entering the library, they saw Marion standing at the information booth with her back to the door. Chris thought he'd be cute and make a joke of it.

"You know anyone with a Swiss chalet for rent?" he spoke out loud.

The woman turned around. It wasn't Marion. It was a woman half as kind, half as helpful, and not nearly as sweet as Marion.

"Excuse me, may I help you?" she said, the words slid down her nose.

"Yes, I'm looking for Marion. . .I can't remember her last name."

"Are you referring to Ms. Buckstein?"

"Yes, that's the name."

"Well, I'm sorry; Ms. Marion Buckstein no longer works here."

"But we were just here a couple of days ago."

"I understand," said the woman. "Nonetheless, I'm afraid she no longer works here."

"We need to speak with her," Walter Jr. said.

"Then I'm afraid I can't help you."

"Why's that?"

"She no longer works here. I'm sorry, I can't say anything more, nor can I tell you how to contact her."

"So, you're saying it's useless," said Chris.

"In this circumstance, I'm afraid so."

They walked away disillusioned.

There was a hissing sound coming from behind an aisle of books. They scurried down the isle to the informant.

"She was a great lady," said a gray-haired old woman. "I work here part-time, and I can tell you that no one ever understood what was going on here as much as she."

"So, what happened?" Walter Jr. asked.

"She freaked out. She received a phone call and she started throwing books around; she tossed over whole aisles of books. There were books everywhere on the floor. It scared Ms. Bridges, that's the woman you spoke with; she fired Ms Buckstein right there on the spot, no questions asked."

"Do you know where we can find her?"

"I'm afraid I don't."

"Thanks and bless you for your help," said Chris. He meant it.

They stood outside the library, thinking.

"What do we do now, Grandpa?"

Chris pointed down the street. "There, the bus stop."

They didn't have to wait long. A bus stopped; they got on. The bus driver was a squatty little Spanish man with black hair and a pencil-thin mustache.

"Are you Roberto?"

The question caught him off guard. "Yes, I am."

"We're friends of Marion Buckstein. Do you know where we can find her?'

"Marion the librarian?" he asked.

"Yes, she's our friend. We need to find her. We think she's in trouble. We can help her."

He pointed to the seat just behind him. "Sit, I will take you to her." As they drove slowly on, he told them what he knew. "She is not well. She lost her job; I don't know how. I went to see her, I knocked on her door, but she wouldn't answer. She refuses to see anyone. She is my friend. If you can help her, I'd be extremely grateful."

A few miles down the road, he stopped at a corner and pointed down the street. "Half a block down, the Alpine Apartments, number 313. Vaya con Dios."

They knocked – no answer. Again – still no answer.

"Maybe, she's not home?" Walter Jr. said.

Chris framed his hand over his eyes and pressed his face to the window. He could see through the darkened apartment to a bright kitchen. Marion sat at the table near a window.

"She's in; I see her."

They knocked again, this time much harder.

Chris looked inside, again. She didn't move. Her body slumped in the chair, her head hung, and her motionless hand held a coffee mug.

This time Chris pounded on the window. He shouted, "Marion, it's Chris Goodman; you know, the old guy who wanted to build a raft? What's wrong? Let us in, maybe we can help you?"

Still she didn't stir.

"Marion, please open up. To be honest, I need your help. You're the only other person I know who has a dream-life like mine. Only I dream about being on an island with my love, Irene. You said you dream about living in a chalet in the Swiss Alps with your boyfriend. What was his name, Gilbert? Please, let us in. Things are getting bad. I need your help."

He could see her turn and look towards him.

"Please, open up, Marion. I don't know who to turn to. Remember, life-and-death, it's a matter of life-and-death."

With that she rose from her chair, walked across the apartment and opened the door.

"Come in," she said sounding cheerless.

They followed her to the kitchen. That once vibrant, life-loving woman was now an empty shell moving slowly and painfully through the world. In the light from the kitchen window, it was clear to see she had lost weight, her appearance was ill kempt, and her eyes were dark, sunken and red from crying.

"Would you like some coffee?"

"Marion," said Chris. "What happened?"

She paused for a moment and then spoke. "Gil is dead."

"Your boyfriend, Gilbert, how did it happen?"

She paused for a moment. Realizing they needed to hear the full story, she started from the beginning.

"It was less than a year ago; I started dreaming the same dream every night. I dreamed I lived in a Swiss chalet in the Alps. I thought nothing of it, since I'd always loved the cold and snow. It was a continuous dream, starting up where I last ended. I thought I was in paradise. There was always enough food in the kitchen cabinets, and a fire in the fireplace kept the cold at bay. I spent my days skiing and ice-skating, it was wonderful, except I was lonely.

"Then I started seeing signs that I wasn't alone – footprints in the snow, ski lines on the sides of the mountains, missing food at the chalet. Finally, I came face-to-face with the man; I didn't recognize him at first. After days of talking, we realized we'd known each other long ago.

"His name was Gilbert Summers; I called him Gil. After much investigation, I realized he was my first love, a boyfriend from my youth, the seventh grade to be exact. His father became a government ambassador, they moved to London when he was thirteen. We wrote to each other at first, and in time we moved on with our lives and forgot each other.

"I didn't think much about it, at first. Sure, it seemed strange to have a continuing dream every night, although it seemed like something an aging person might do. And of course, having your first love in the dream played into that. Then after a time, we both realized it wasn't my dream and it wasn't his dream; it was our dream. In our day-lives, we spoke on the phone to confirm this. Yet, we hardly ever spoke on the phone. We spent hours with each other every night, hours that seem like days. Each night, we spent more time together than most married couples spent together in a week.

"In the dream-world, we were both young, beautiful, and soon we fell in love, again. I began taking sleeping pills so I'd fall asleep sooner, faster, and longer. We were so happy; then he came."

"He…who?" asked Chris, sounding exceedingly interested.

"I don't know who he is; other than he's powerful. He caused heavy snowstorms in our little winter wonderland, countless earthquakes and avalanches. He turned our paradise into a living hell.

"He first got in touch with me. He'd leave messages for me between the pages of the books at the library. He called Gil more than a few times. He even left messages in the snow in our dream-world. They were all warnings, telling us that one or both would have to leave. We didn't know what he meant. How do you leave a dream? Somehow, recently, Gil figured out what needed to be done."

"How'd he do that?"

"The building on top of the far mountain, that's what we called it. Somehow, Gil knew the answer was there."

"Did the building look like a temple?" asked Chris.

"I don't know; it was too far to see clearly. It took Gil days to reach it. When he returned, he had an ancient manuscript he found there. He studied it for days. He said it told the full story, and what to do about our situation. A few days later, I learned he took his own life. The threats stopped. I'm safe in my dream-world; but that's not what matters. I've lost my whole world."

She stopped and began to cry deeply.

Chris waited a moment. "Marion, anywhere in your dream-world, were there two lines of figure drawings?"

She stopped crying and sniffled. "Yes, how did you know? We found drawings in a cave. At first they made no sense. Then we realized the two lines represented our lives. Someone chiseled away the last part of our lives and in place of it was a primitive drawing of our chalet, as if the dream-world conquered the real-world."

Chris stood up. "You've been a great help, Marion. If we can be of any help, I'll let you know what I find out."

"Any help?" cried Marion. "It's too late. Gil's dead and nothing else matters."

"I don't know if that's the end of it," said Chris. "I'll do what I can. I won't ever give up and neither should you. Anything can happen in dreams."

****

Before retiring to their room back at La Casa de Oro, they stopped off at Wang's for supper. The two men, both in deep thought, ate in silence. Somewhere between the wonton soup and egg roll and the main course, Walter Jr. began asking questions.

"So, what do you think?"

Chris shook his head, "I honestly don't know. I feel so sorry for the woman. I do know one thing; I need to learn what Gil learned."

"How will you do that?"

"He found a manuscript that explained everything in a building that sat on a mountain top. Well, there's a building in my world, too – a temple. Only it's underwater, far out at sea. Irene and I need to take the raft out again, and try to find that temple. I don't know how we can; just that we've got to try. It may be our only chance. I've just got to know what Gil knew. I need to understand what's happening."

"Grandpa, you once told me you loved Irene. How much do you love her?"

"Junior, if this is a roundabout way of asking me if I'm going to kill myself to save Irene, don't you worry. I'd die for her, sure, but not when there's still some fight left in me. Besides, where there's life, there's hope."

When they finished, the waiter brought the check and two fortune cookies. Walter Jr. took one, opened it and read it as he ate the cookie. His hands began to shake.

"Junior, what's wrong?"

"You're not going to believe what it says, Grandpa."

"Go ahead, Junior, read it out loud."

"*Where there's life, there's hope.*"

Chris took up his cookie. "Where's Jimmy Gray Horse when you need him?"

"Go on, Grandpa, read it."

"*That's it. No more chances. I'm coming to the island.*"

"What are you going to do, Grandpa?"

"Let's get to our room. I want to go to sleep, immediately. I need to speak with Irene."

Nineteen

Sweet dreams

Some of them want to use you
Some of them want to get used by you
Some of them want to abuse you
Some of them want to be abused

Sweet dreams are made of these
Who am I to disagree?
I traveled the world and the seven seas
Everybody's looking for something

Words and Music by Annie Lennox & David A. Stewart

THE JOURNEY

Chris walked across the shoreline towards Irene. He wore a serious look.

"Chris, darling, what's the matter?"

"He's coming, the stranger is coming. I don't know what he may do; but we should prepare for him."

"How?"

"Today, Junior and I went to visit a woman we met the last time we were in L.A. She and her boyfriend have been sharing a dream, just like us, only they're in a snow-filed world. Her boyfriend learned what this is all about from a manuscript he found in a building on top of a high snowcapped mountain. The description of the building reminded me of the temple I saw in the middle of the ocean. If he found the answer in his world, maybe we can find the answer in ours."

"If he found the answer, why didn't she share it with you?"

He hesitated for a moment. "Because he's dead; he killed himself."

"Oh, Chris, I'm so frightened."

"Don't be. We can lick this, together. That was what he did wrong; he did it alone. We have each other."

"I hope you're right. So, now, what do we do?"

"We fix up the raft, collect food and water, and head out to sea."

"Do you think you can find it again?"

"I don't know if we can; but we've got to try."

The raft needed little renovating; a few new vines were enough. They gathered food and water, this time enough for two. They walked the raft out into the ocean till the waves hit their chests, and then got on and paddled with all their might, till they were in open water.

"Now which way?" asked Irene.

"The last time I did nothing; I just let the currents take me. May as well do the same, sit back and wait and watch."

Hours passed. The lovers fell asleep in each other's arms. When they woke it was impossible to tell how much time – hours, days, or weeks – had passed. Both their backs were crimson red from the sun.

"Oh, darling, you're as red as a lobster," exclaimed Irene.

"That's what happened the last time. Maybe we're there."

Chris walked to the edge of the raft, looking down into the water's depths.

"No, I don't think this is the place."

"Maybe I can see it," said Irene, looking over the other side.

Suddenly, bubbles rose to the surface. Something was coming up from the deep. She backed away. The next moment, a beautiful gray dolphin was dancing on the surface of the water.

"Don't be afraid," said Chris, "They helped me the last time; maybe they can help us, now?" The dolphin's head bobbed on the surface, seemingly smiling at them. "I need to get to the spot you first found me; I need to get to the underwater temple. Can you please help us?"

"Chris you're talking to a fish!"

The dolphin reared up out of the water, cackling at her.

"I think you've insulted him."

"I'm sorry," shouted Irene. "I didn't mean to call you a fish; I know you're not a fish. I'm sorry."

"Can you please help us?" repeated Chris.

The dolphin submerged; a group of six dolphins came around back, pressed their noses against the side of the raft and began to swim faster and faster.

"Ha, ha," laughed Chris, sounding like a well-seasoned salty-dog pirate. "That's what they did the last time. We'll be there in no time."

"I'm scared, Chris, hold me."

The raft moved so swiftly their hair blew in the breeze, away from their faces. Fifteen minutes later, they stopped.

"We're here!" shouted Chris, pointing down in the water.

Irene looked over the edge. "It is; it's an entire sunken city."

"Do you see the temple?"

"Yes, I can see it right there. It's magnificent!"

The main dolphin appeared on the water.

"I know you've done so much for us, and we're very grateful," said Chris. "If I may ask one more favor? Could you stay and return us to the island, when we're done?"

The dolphin's reply sounded like laughter and then he nose-dived out of sight.

Chris stepped to the edge of the raft. "Well, here goes nothing." He took in a deep breath and jumped headfirst into the water.

As he swam down, the pressure filled his ears. He made it to the temple; its stone was smooth and cold. He could see the altar before him, although as he began running out of air, the distance became farther away. He started to feel panic set in. All he could think of was making it to the surface. He rose out of the water, gasping for air.

"Chris, are you all right?" asked Irene.

"I'm fine; I just need to get more air into my lungs."

He began to take deep quick breaths, till he felt light-headed. He went back down. This time he made it to the altar; he could see the parchment under the bottom stone. His fingers were just inches away from grabbing it when again he began running out of air. He rushed to the surface. He frantically huffed and puffed, filling his lungs with life-giving air.

Irene sat on the raft, her arms wrapped around her knees. He jumped back onto the raft. He lay at her feet, trying to catch his breath.

"It's useless; I can't do it," he mumbled between breaths.

"Sweetheart," said Irene, ever so gently. "Can I make a suggestion?"

"What is it?"

"Let me try it."

"You?"

"I was the captain of the woman's swim team in high school."

"You were?"

"You don't remember, do you? It's no wonder why I dumped you."

"You dumped me? As I remember it, I dumped you."

"Senile old man," she laughed as she stood up. She walked to the edge. "Stay here I'll be right back." Taking a deep breath, she leaped off the raft, looking incredibly professional.

Once he regained himself, he sat up and looked down into the water. He couldn't see her. He waited one, two, two and a half minutes. He began to worry. Finally, after he'd counted for three minutes, he was about to dive in after her, when she exploded to the surface. She tossed the manuscript onto the raft, and then jumped up after it. Now, she lay flat, breathing heavily.

"Are you all right?" he asked.

"I'll be fine. Just give me a minute."

When she was feeling better, they hugged and kissed.

"I got worried there for a minute," he whispered in her ear.

"I was the captain, remember."

"To be honest, I don't." He took hold of her hand. "What's this you have in your hand?"

She held her hand out and opened it, palm up. There were two black pieces of charcoal.

"Charcoal? Where did you get charcoal?" he asked.

"It was strange. In front of the temple was an altar. I found the manuscript below it. When I was about to rise back up, I noticed remains of a sacrifice – burnt offerings. All that was left was charcoal. So I grabbed a couple pieces."

"But, why?"

"Don't you remember in the cave, the writings on the wall?"

"How can I ever forget them?"

"Well, they were written and drawn in charcoal. Have you ever seen any charcoal on the island?"

"Only what we've made."

"Exactly, this is the only charcoal I've seen in our dream-world. Perhaps, it will come in handy?"

"Good thinking," said Chris.

Irene looked around. "It looks like our friends abandoned us. We'll have to paddle back."

Just then, a force slammed into the side of the raft, knocking them down. It was the dolphins guiding them back to the island.

Just a few yards from shore, the dolphins stopped, letting the raft drift forward on its own. The lead dolphin appeared at the side of the raft.

"We can't thank you enough. You've been most kind," said Chris.

"Yes," agreed Irene. "You are very...very...very regal."

This sent waves of joy through the creature. It shot out of the water, and came down splashing them. The group of dolphins turned and swam away. Irene and Chris stood on the raft, waving, and watching their fins glide through the waves and out of sight.

As much as they were in a hurry to see what was on the manuscript, they took their time preparing. They gathered food and water, and then dry wood for a fire. Chris boasted about his days as a Boy Scout, as he got a fire going. Irene arranged the fruit in large shells, which they used for plates.

Once settled, together they unfurled the manuscript. There was hardly an inch of space not taken up with either a drawing of symbols, numbers, or letters. Thankfully, the letters made words, however it was not English. It was difficult to decipher. After hours of examination, they knew no more than they did without it.

"There's something we're not seeing," said Chris.

"Yeah, but what?" said Irene. "From the looks of it, only a combination of architect, archeologist, lawyer, safecracker, code-breaker, and crossword enthusiast could make sense of this."

Chris' body began to tremble. "I'm sorry, my love, I'm waking up. I have to go."

"I understand," she said. "See you tomorrow night."

Twenty

Daydream Believer

Oh, I could hide 'neath the wings
Of the bluebird as she sings
The six o'clock alarm will never ring
But six rings and I rise
Wipe the sleep out of my eyes
My shavin' razor's cold and it stings

Cheer up, Sleepy Jean
Oh, what can it mean
To a daydream believer
And a homecoming queen

Music and Words by John Stewart

THE JOURNEY

Chris woke early. The room was starting to fill with sunlight creeping in from behind the curtains. He looked to the other bed and saw Walter Jr. in deep sleep, motionless, and snoring heavily. Not wanting to wake his grandson, he lay in bed, staring at the ceiling, wondering about the manuscript.

"What do people do in motel rooms beside sleep," he thought. He laughed at such a silly question. Things like that skip your mind when you pass eighty. Then he remembered there's always a Gideon Bible in the top drawer next to every bed in every motel and hotel room. Why not start the day with the good book? He reached over and, not wanting to wake Junior, he opened the nightstand drawer ever so carefully and slowly. He took the Bible out. Obviously, no one had ever touched it; it was in mint condition.

"Where do you start?" he questioned himself. Then he remembered "Bible Roulette". Close your eyes, open the Bible, and place your finger down. Wherever it lands, that's what you need to know; and he did just that. When he opened his eyes, he read softly to himself, moving his fingers over the words, "*Solomon's Temple.*"

He was amazed at what he read. The description of Solomon's Temple was exactly like that of the undersea temple where Irene retrieved the manuscript from the depths, right down to the pomegranates. It couldn't be the same temple; Solomon's was destroyed. Yet isn't everything in dreams a replica, a reproduction of what is real? The temple in Marion and Gil's dream, had it been the same? Too bad Gil was gone; Chris had so many unanswered questions. Gil figured out what the manuscript said. Was that why he killed himself? Chris shivered at the thought. What did this all mean?

"Morning, Grandpa," murmured Walter Jr. from the other bed, smacking his lips, his eyes opened to slits. "I'm hungry. You think we could splurge and have breakfast somewhere?"

"Why not?" said Chris. "I could do with a short stack, some grits, and a cup of Joe."

****

They decided their prospects of a cheaper and better breakfast waited for them somewhere outside Los Angeles. Once out of town and on the highway, they kept their eyes peeled for a diner with plenty of trucks and cop cars – always a good sign.

An hour later, they hadn't found what they were looking for. Then, like magic, just coming out of a turn was a truck stop with dozens of trucks and a half dozen cop cars.

"This must be the place," said Walter Jr. as he turned into the lot and found a parking space close to the diner.

Inside, they stood in a long line, waiting to be seated. Chris wore Jimmy's hat low over his eyes, hoping to hide his identity.

"The food must be good here," said Walter Jr., "I've never had to wait in a line so long just for breakfast."

Finally, they were escorted to a booth next to a window. After two cups of coffee and reading the menu several times, Walter Jr. ordered. Chris knew what he wanted hours ago.

The food was good and plentiful. They lingered long and joyfully over every bite. In his bliss, Walter Jr. looked out the window, surprised to see a familiar vehicle, an old International Harvester with household items, a bed, crib, and stuff tied down in the back.

It was the truck belonging to the Wilkins family, Travis, Felicia, and their infant son Tyrone. The family he met, helped, and dined with on the road. The family on the run, Felicia long AWOL, Baby Tyrone wanted by Family Services, and Travis wanted for burning his parents' home down to the ground. What made matters worse is a Highway

Patrolman was examining the truck. He wrote down the license plate number and called it in. Walter Jr. knew what the patrolman learned.

Walter Jr. looked around for a sign of the Wilkins family; there was none. The truck stop diner was large with more rooms. Walter Jr. looked into a mirror. He could see the Wilkins family dining in another room, feeling happy and safe. As the patrolman entered the diner, Walter Jr. knew he needed to do something – warn the Wilkins family or sidetrack the patrolman.

"Grandpa, you remember that family I told you about, the ones on the run. Well, they're here in this diner and I think there's a highway patrolman who's wise to them. We need to help them."

Chris thought for a moment, not knowing what to say.

The highway patrolman started walking across the room.

"That's him, that's the cop," said Walter Jr. to Chris. "We need to do something or they'll all be arrested."

"I know just what to do," said Chris, standing up and adjusting Jimmy Gray Horse's hat on his head.

Chris turned and started across the room. Without warning, Chris toddled across the area; Jimmy's hat no longer square on his head. In the middle of the room, he went into a tailspin, bumping into customers and waitresses. He slammed into tables, spilling drinks and knocking plates to the floor. Finally, he tumbled to the floor, hitting his head, hard, on the edge of a table. Jimmy's hat fell from his head and became a symbol of things not yet seen.

The entire room went bonkers. Everyone ran to help, including the patrolman investigating the Wilkins' vehicle, hoping to lend a hand. In no time there was a crowd around the old man lying motionless on the floor. In the confusion, the Wilkins family left the diner and drove off.

"Somebody call an ambulance!" hollered a waitress. The patrolman called it in on his walkie-talkie, as he checked Chris' breathing.

"Let me through!" shouted Walter Jr., "He's with me."

"You know this guy?" asked the patrolman. "He a friend of yours?"

"He's a hitchhiker. I was giving him a ride."

"Well, he's still alive." The patrolman moved in closer. "He's still breathing, barely."

The next instant, two paramedics carrying a gurney, rushed in and up to Chris. One of them got down on one knee and checked his vitals, as the other hooked him up to oxygen.

One of the paramedics looked at the patrolman. “I can’t say what’s wrong. We need to take him to County.”

“I’ll give you an escort,” said the patrolman.

“Can I go, too?” Walter Jr. asked.

“The old guy was hitching a ride with him,” said the patrolman.

“I guess so,” said the paramedic. “Just don’t get in the way.”

“I won’t.”

They placed Chris on the gurney; Walter Jr. took up his hat and placed it on his chest. He wished he hadn’t; it made him look dead.

Sliding the gurney into the ambulance, Walter Jr. got in and sat to the side. The paramedics were outside, talking to the patrolman.

Walter Jr. moved in close to Chris. “Quick thinking, Grandpa.”

Chris did not respond. Fear took hold of Walter Jr.; this was real. A thought entered his mind. He needed to get his grandfather’s wallet. His driver’s license may have expired but it was still identification. If they knew who he was, they’d ship him back to Texas; and his dream would go unfulfilled. Walter Jr. slid his hand into his grandfather’s pocket and grabbed his wallet, slipping it in his pocket just as one of the paramedics got in and slammed the doors shut.

Walter Jr. looked out the back window of the ambulance. He could see his car in the parking lot. He saw the old International carrying off the Wilkins family. They looked at him with clear recognition and waved good-bye.

At the hospital, they wheeled Chris away and directed Walter Jr. to sit in the waiting room. He looked around the room at all the other worried people, thumbing through magazines, never reading a word – their faces troubled and anxious. He couldn’t say how long he waited; when you’re fearful, time moves slowly. Finally, a doctor entered and approached him.

“You the guy with the old man; can you tell me anything about him?”

“He hitched a ride with me; that’s all I can say.”

“Not even his name?”

“I couldn’t say. Is he going to be all right?”

“That’s hard to say. Technically, there’s nothing wrong with him; he’s just suffering from exhaustion. Normally, a few days rest and you’re back on your feet. However, someone as old as he, it’s hard to say; it can go either way. He came in with a hat that looked Native American Indian in style, but from the looks of him, I doubt he is.”

“Can I see him?”

"Not right now. I think it's best he rests. We put him on the third floor, room 313; you can visit him tomorrow."

"Thank you, doctor."

The doctor smiled, turned and walked away. Walter Jr. sat back down, unsure of what to do next. Just then, the patrolman from the restaurant and the paramedic from the ambulance appeared at the doorway. The paramedic pointed at Walter Jr. with his chin.

"That's him. He snatched the old guy's wallet when he was in the ambulance."

"Are you sure?" asked the patrolman.

"Sure, I'm sure."

The patrolman walked over to Walter Jr., eyeing him.

"Excuse me, sir, could you please follow me?"

"Why, officer, is there something wrong?"

"Maybe, maybe not; I've got a few things to ask you."

Walter Jr. followed the patrolman out of the room and into a room marked *Security*. It was a small room with two desks, two file cabinets, and four chairs. There was another door at the back wall; the patrolman checked it to make sure it was locked.

"I have some questions I'd like to ask you, except I'd like another officer present when I ask them. I'm sorry for this; please be patient and wait."

He left, the door clicked behind him. Walter Jr. checked the front door, it was locked; he checked the backdoor, locked also. He sat down and waited.

He heard a clicking sound. The doorknob of the backdoor turned, clicked open, the door remained ajar six inches. He ran to the door, opened it fully. There was no one there. It was an empty hallway. Mistake or not, Walter Jr. ran down the hall and out of the hospital. Five minutes later the patrolman and another officer, to their surprise, entered an empty office.

Outside, Walter Jr. walked around the hospital over and over, wondering what to do. He came to the decision he needed to get to his grandfather at any cost. Entering a side door into the building, he walked down an empty hall to the elevators. Once in an elevator, he pressed floor three. The elevator door opened to an information booth, he walked to the nurse behind it.

"Excuse me, the old man they brought in this afternoon, I wonder if could visit him?"

"I'm sorry, sir. Visiting hours are over; they'll start up again tomorrow at 11am."

"Yeah, but, you see, it's kind of important I see him now, even for a minute."

"I'm sorry, sir. Rules are rules."

Thinking fast he looked around. He pointed to the restroom. "Mind if I use the restroom, before I go back down?"

"No, go right ahead."

In the men's room, he huddled behind the door, peaking out now and then. It seemed she either forgot about him or thought he went down in the elevator when she wasn't looking.

"She can't stay there forever. Everyone needs to go sometime."

His patience paid off. She left her post and entered the lady's room.

Walter Jr. hustled down the hall till he got to his grandfather's room, he ran in, closing the door behind him.

"Junior, how'd you get here?"

"It's a long story, Grandpa. First, we've got to get you out of here."

"That's impossible. They've got my clothes."

Walter Jr. let out a long sigh. "I hate to say this, Grandpa. We may have come to the end of the road. Maybe I should call Mom?"

"You do and I write you out of my will."

"That wouldn't matter; Dave gets everything of mine, remember?"

"Just don't do it, Junior. There's got to be a way."

The doorknob began to turn slowly. Walter Jr. panicked; there was nowhere to hide.

The door opened, in walked an attendant pushing a wheelchair. Chris' clothes were in the chair. They looked at the attendant, shocked. They knew him, instantly. He was a tall black man with a shaved head. It was Posse.

"You!" said Walter Jr., pointing at him. "You again, what are you doing here? Who are you, anyway?"

"I'm your gift horse and I'd advise you not to look in my mouth, let alone jump down my throat." He tossed the clothes onto the bed. "Here, put these on." He handed Jimmy Gray Horse's hat to Walter Jr., "Here, you hold this."

Once dressed and seated in the wheelchair, they wheeled Chris out into the hall.

"What about the nurse?" Walter Jr. whispered.

"We don't have to go that way," said Posse. "There are some elevators down this hall."

On the first floor, they moved passed the front desk towards the exit. They were just a few feet away from escaping when a nurse stopped them.

"Whoa, where are you three going? I need to see some release forms."

Posse took a clipboard hanging on the back of the wheelchair and handed it to her.

"These are not the right forms," she said.

"Are you sure? What about here?" Posse played dumb, pointing at the pages.

"No, this won't do. Come with me." She pointed at Walter Jr., then at Chris, and then at Walter Jr., again. "And you two, don't you move an inch."

As they walked away, Posse held his hand behind his back, waving them on. Walter Jr. quickly rolled Chris through the electronic doors and onto the street. Once there, he had no idea where to go. Where do you go with an eighty-five year old man in a wheelchair? They'd left the car in the parking lot of the restaurant, miles away.

As if an answer to a prayer, the old International Harvester screeched to a halt in front of them – it was the Wilkins family – Travis behind the wheel, Felicia holding Baby Tyrone. She moved closer to her husband.

"Quick, get in!"

Without a second thought, they were all squashed in the front seat of the International. Chris held his hat, so not to crunch it into the ceiling.

"We appreciate you doing this for us," commented Walter Jr., "What were you folks doing by the hospital?"

"We just came to thank you. We know what you did in the diner. It saved our necks," said Travis. He pointed to the bandage above Chris' right eyebrow. "But that couldn't have been what you had planned."

"I wanted to create a diversion," said Chris. He rubbed the bump on the top of his head. "And I did. And you're right; the way it all turned out wasn't part of my original plan."

Felicia reached over and placed her hand on the bump. She was gentle; still it made him flinch. "You poor baby," she sighed. "It feels like you're growing a new head."

"I only hope it works better than the old one. It ain't been much good to me for a long time," chuckled the old man.

"Oh, I wouldn't say that," she smiled.

"Say, if you two guys don't have a place to stay the night, we've got ourselves a motel room just up the road. The wife and I would be honored if you'd be our guests. It ain't much; but we can all get some sleep."

Walter Jr. leaned forward. "Well, I don't think…"

"That's right kindly of you, Travis. We'd be honored," interjected Chris.

Walter Jr. looked to his grandfather who just smiled. Chris whispered in his grandson's ear. "These are good folks. We'd only embarrass and insult them by not letting them give what little they have to offer."

The car was near the diner, where they left it earlier that day. Travis let them out. There was an orange colored sticker on the windshield; Walter Jr. tore it off and read it.

"It seems we're scheduled to be towed."

"Then it's good we got back when we did," said Chris.

"Not necessarily," said Walter Jr., "That means the police have this license plate number. It won't take them long to track down who it belongs to – me. And when they finally figure out at the hospital who you are, they'll put two and two together and know we're traveling together. I can just hear my mother screaming my name."

"I'll go slowly," said Travis. "Just follow me."

The motel room was small; still it would do. They set up a foldaway bed in the middle of the room, and then took turns using the bathroom.

Travis pointed to one bed. "Felicia and the baby will sleep here." He pointed to the other bed. "Grandpa and I will take the other. Walter you're stuck on the foldaway. You don't snore, do you, Grandpa?"

"I don't know," said Chris. "Do I, Junior?"

"Like a buzz saw, Grandpa."

"Sorry," said Chris, shrugging his shoulders.

Travis was just about to turn off the TV, when the news story came on, catching their attention.

"If you remember, we reported that the stranger at the L.A. train station, the other day with the award-winning actress Louise Langford, was Christopher Goodman, a runaway senior from Venus, Texas. His family, who reported him missing, saw him on the news report. Well, there's another twist to this story. It's possible Mr. Goodman is not alone, and is traveling with Walter Bouchard Jr., his grandson Here is a picture of Mr. Bouchard."

A portrait photo of Walter Jr. filled the screen.

"That's my high school yearbook photo; I hate that picture!" Walter Jr. shouted at the screen.

"If any of our viewers have any information to the whereabouts of either one or both of these gentleman, please contact state authorities."

Travis switched the TV off. "Well, it looks like we're all fugitives, now. I guess there's nothing else left to do other than forget it for now and try to get some shuteye." Once his wife and child were in bed, he walked over and kissed her. "Goodnight, sweetheart; I love you." Then he kissed his son. "Goodnight, Tiger; pleasant dreams."

Walter Jr. was having a difficult time with the foldaway. More of his body parts hung off the edges than were on it.

"You look like you're having a hard time there, cowboy," laughed Travis. "You want to switch with me and sleep with your grandpa?"

"What…and miss one of the opportunities of adventure offered a wanted man?" said Walter Jr., "I wouldn't think of it."

Travis looked at Chris. "Well, Grandpa, it's just you and me left. Which side of the bed do you want?"

"This one here; the one closest to the bathroom, when you get my age…"

"Understood," said Travis. "I'm looking forward to it myself."

"What, going to the bathroom?"

"No, getting old."

Chris laughed. "It ain't all they make it out to be. I'd skip it, if I had my choice."

Once in bed Travis pulled up the covers and turned off the light.

"Travis," whispered Chris.

"What's that, Grandpa? What cha' need?"

"If I snore during the night, I'm sorry. Just shake me a little. Only please, don't try to wake me. And if I talk in my sleep, don't wake me, no matter what I say, even if it sounds like I'm in trouble. I've got to try to get as much sleep as possible. I've got a lot to do in my dream, tonight."

"Got yourself a dream girl, do you, Grandpa?"

"Yeah, how'd you know?"

"When I was little, my mother took me to the Ice-Skating Show. I never forgot it. That night I dreamed the most beautiful girl in the world ice-skated through my window and all around my room. I dreamed about her every night for years. She'd do tricks for me, dance for me, sing to me, all the time smiling."

"Then what happened?" asked Chris.

"When I grew up, the dream stopped."

"That's a shame."

"Not really. Years later I got to meet her in the flesh."

"Really! What did you do?"

"What could I do? I married her."

"You mean…."

"That's right; Felicia is the same ice-skating beauty from the dreams of my youth, though I doubt she knows it."

"Travis, answer me one last thing. Was she ice-skating when you first saw her?"

"Not quite, but close. She was on roller skates at the *Dreamland Roller Rink*, downtown King's Corner, Nebraska."

Twenty-One

I have dreamed

I have dreamed that your arms are lovely
I have dreamed what a joy you'll be
I have dreamed every word you'll whisper
When you're close
Close to me
How you look in the glow of evening
I have dreamed and enjoyed the view

In these dreams I've loved you so
That by now I think I know
What it's like to be loved by you
I will love being loved by you

Music by Richard Rodgers
Words by Oscar Hammerstein II

THE JOURNEY

When Chris woke in his dream on the island, he found Irene kneeling on the beach, the temple manuscript sprawled out on the sand before her.

"Figured it out yet?" asked Chris.

She smiled up at him in greeting. "Hello, my darling. No, I'm not having much luck. It all looks like a bunch of gibberish to me, a lot of symbols written upside-down and backwards."

"Well, you got part of it right."

"What?"

He fell to his knees, next to her, and kissed her. He smoothed out the manuscript and ran his finger across the writing. "The backwards part, you got that right. Though I'm sure the guy who wrote it didn't think it was backwards, at least it wasn't to him."

"What are you talking about?"

He smiled. "The reason you can't read this is because of the way they raised you."

"Now you've lost me," she said.

"If I remember correctly your family was Baptist."

"What's that got to do with anything?"

"Well, if you were raised in a Jewish family, you'd know this is in Hebrew."

"Hebrew, how'd you figure that out?"

"By accident, I read a passage in the Bible describing Solomon's Temple. It was an exact description of the temple we found out at sea. So, I figured if that was a dream-replica of a Jewish temple, then this is a dream-replica of Hebrew writing."

"My genius," she cried, kissing him. "Now, what do we do?"

"We've got to figure it out. Gil, the English guy from that other dream world, he figured it out; if he could do it, so can we. Even if we have to memorize it, and then look up its meaning in the waking-world, we can do it."

She lifted the manuscript and handed it to him. "Here, be my guest. While you're memorizing, I'm going to look for food. I'll be right back." She kissed him and ran off.

Chris stared at the manuscript, trying to memorize every line. He made a game of it. Looking at the first symbol, he closed his eyes, and then wrote it in the wet sand. Then he erased what he wrote, memorized the next symbol, and then tried to write it and the previous symbol. It was slow going; however he couldn't think of any other way.

He turned to see Irene standing with an armful of picked fruit.

"You want me to help you with that, sweetheart?" he asked.

She remained motionless, staring out to sea. Her mouth dropped open, as did her arms, letting the fruit fall. He turned to see what it was that caught her full attention.

Sitting in the water, a quarter mile out, was a ship. Not just any ship, an old-time wooden sailing ship of middle-eastern design. It looked like something straight out of the Arabian Night's saga – perhaps the great ship of Sinbad the Sailor, himself. They could see movement on the deck, the sails were folded down, and the anchor dropped, causing the ship to come to a standstill.

"I know we've said that anything can happen in a dream; only this is taking it to the limit," said Chris.

"Look," shouted Irene, pointing out to the ship.

They lowered a small boat from the side of the ship. The oars of the boat rose and fell like the wings of birds, as the sailors rowed to shore. A tall dark figure of a man stood in the bow. Chris and Irene stood silently watching. When the small boat was a few feet from shore, the sailors got out of the boat and stood in the water. Some held the boat steady while others carried the man over the water and onto dry land. The sailors dressed in keeping with the ship's motif. They wore gold, silken puffed pants and large gold turbans. Their chests were bare, hairless, and muscular. They placed their leader on the beach, in front of Irene and Chris.

He was a tall, dark, slender man with a thin mustache and a long pointed goatee. He wore all black with the same puffed pants, a silk shirt, a long black cape and a matching turban with a large silver diamond in the center of it. There was a silver sword at his side that raised his cape as he bowed at the waist to them. He stood with one hand on the hilt of his blade, the other he held out in greeting. There was an air of royalty about him, mixed with just a touch of arrogance. His smile was bright and large, although lacked friendliness.

"My name is Mortalitas Decessus, at your service."

"Who are you?" demanded Chris.

"A friend."

"I recognize your voice. Friends don't go around threatening their friends."

"I never thought of it as threatening you; I'd say I was warning you. I was trying to help you, as I'm trying to do, now."

Irene stepped forward. "Before we go any further, why don't you come clean and tell us who you really are."

"What do you mean?" he said, becoming more erect, and sounding insulted.

"I mean, I took Latin one and two in high school," said Irene. "Mortalitas Decessus, indeed; those are two Latin words that mean death!"

He smiled, seemingly relaxed. "You have me at the quick, My Lady. It's true, I am he; I am Death."

"I don't understand," said Chris. "If you're Death, how are you here to help us?"

"You obviously have the wrong idea who Death is." He walked to a large rock and pointed to it. "Do you mind?" Neither spoke; he leaned against the rock. He pointed to the sand at his feet. "Please, sit. This may take some time."

Slowly and cautiously, they sat down on the ground at his feet.

"Why am I called the *Grim Reaper*? What is so grim about something so natural?"

"Come to the point; why are you here?" asked Chris.

"My job is not only to collect souls who've died and deliver them to their next life. I do so much more."

By the questioning look on Irene and Chris' faces, he knew he needed to go slow.

"Allow me to explain. You see, the universe is very large. Oh, you're nodding your heads in agreement; however you truly don't understand what you're agreeing to. You have no idea how vast it really is. Even though it's unbelievably immeasurable, for the most part everything runs rather smoothly. Nevertheless, because of its size, now and then things slip through the cracks."

"Mistakes?" questioned Chris.

"I wouldn't call them mistakes. Let's call them oddities due the large amount of possibilities."

"Slip through the crack, you say," added Chris. "Are you trying to tell us that we're one of those oddities, and that we've slipped through the cracks?

"In so many words. . .yes. These things happen and it's my job to see they're corrected."

"And how would you propose that?" asked Irene.

"Well, there are several ways. You must admit, both of you are extremely old. You both could die or maybe only one of you."

"Old or not, few people want to die," said Irene.

"What if I sweetened the pot," added Death. "What if I made you a deal?"

"Go ahead, we're listening."

"Here's the deal. If one of you agrees to die, the other will be allowed to live many more years, without pain, and die in their sleep. And that's not all. The one who agrees to die will be whisked off to a paradise where their former mate waits for them. Now, is that a honey of a deal, or what?"

"You're saying I'd get to be with Phyllis, again," said Chris.

"And I'd be with my husband, Mark?"

"Just sign on the dotted line, and it could be true."

As if out of nowhere or perhaps it was out of nowhere, he presented them with two contracts and two pens.

"Nothing dramatic, there's no need to sign in blood or anything like that."

They each took their contract and pen.

"That's right, take your time and read them; there's no hurry."

Surprisingly, it was short, clearly written and easy to understand.

"No tricks, no small print; it says what it says. We just want this matter cleared up," he said.

Irene looked Death square in the eye, something few people ever do and live to tell about it.

"Mark Cooper was my husband; I loved him very much. We vowed to be together till death do us part; as you know *that* contract is null and void. I thank you; but no thank you."

She handed back the contract.

"That goes for me, too," said Chris, handing back his contract.

Death looked startled only for a moment; he quickly regained his smile and calm manner. He handed back their contracts.

"No need to be so hasty; there's no rush. Hold on to these for a while. Take your time. Sleep on it, if you'll forgive the pun." He laughed; Irene and Chris didn't. He began slowly backing away. "I'll be in touch.'

"Wait," said Irene. "I've something to ask you…a favor."

"What's that, My Lady?"

"Are you the captain of that ship?" she asked, pointing out to sea.

"None other," he said proudly.

"As I've always understood it, a ship's captain can perform a marriage?"

"That's true," he said with pride. "If you're asking me to marry the two of you, I couldn't think of a greater honor. I'd be glad to marry you."

Irene looked to Chris for confirmation. He smiled and reached out to her. "I couldn't think of anything that would make me happier."

They both looked to Death for further instructions.

"There is one stipulation," said Death. "A ship's captain only has the authority out at sea. So, if you both would please follow me."

He waved four of the sailors from their posts. "I want you to carry these good people to the boat."

The next moment, they took Irene and Chris up on their shoulders and gently placed them in the boat. The four returned to shore to take back their captain to the boat.

As they rowed back to the ship, Death commented, "I've done some interesting things in my line of work; this is a first. I'm actually excited." He looked at Irene. "Believe it or not, we have flowers on board. I will personally make a bouquet for you." He smiled at both of them. "After the ceremony, please be my guest in my cabin for a celebration. The ship's galley is well stocked with best of food and wine."

"That's kind of you," said Irene.

"It's my pleasure."

On board ship, Death gave the order, "All hands on deck, raise the anchor, we set sail," he bellowed, pointing out to the horizon.

When they were a mile from land, the crew lined up in two lines, one port and one starboard. Death magically produced a lovely bouquet of white orchards and handed them to Irene.

"Now, if you two will take your place in front of the mast, please." They stood before the mast, holding hands.

"Dearly beloved, we're gathered here today in the presence of these witnesses, to join Irene and Christopher in matrimony. Do you, Irene, take Christopher, to be your husband, from this day forward, until death do you part?"

"I do."

"And do you Christopher take Irene, to be your wife, from this day forward, until death do you part?"

"I do"

"By the power vested in me, I now pronounce you husband and wife. You may now kiss the bride."

The two fell into each other's arms and kissed, as they'd never done before. The sailors broke rank and returned to their work, as if nothing of any great importance happened.

The three of them sat at a large table in the captain's quarters; Death poured three glass of wine. "A toast, to the loving couple, may they love as long as they live, and live as long as they love." His toast sounded more like a threat.

Minutes later, the table was filled with delicacies. They ate and drank till they could no more.

"It was all very nice. Thank you," said Chris, leaning back in his chair.

"Yes, thank you very much," added Irene.

"My pleasure, I'm glad you enjoyed it. Now, I'm afraid there will be no honeymoon."

"What do you mean?"

"Your vows were until death. This is a death ship."

"You promised us time to think it over!" demanded Chris.

"That was on the island. We are miles away, now." He pointed to the three windows in the room at the ship's stern. It was true; the island was now a small dark dot on the horizon.

Chris jumped to his feet and tossing his chair, shattering one of the windows.

"Quick, Irene, follow me," he shouted as he leaped out the window. Irene followed right behind him. They began swimming for the island. They could hear Death hollering at them from the window.

"You're making a grave mistake! You can't get away, you know! This isn't the end of it!" He hesitated for a moment, and then laughed. "Actually. . .it is!"

Twenty-Two

Dream Operator

Hard to forget
Hard to go on
When you fall asleep
You're out on your own

Let go of your life
Grab on to my hand
Here in the clouds
Where we'll understand

And you dreamed it all
And this is your story
Do you know who you are?
You're the dream operator

Music and Words by David Byrne

THE JOURNEY

Walter Jr. gently shook his grandfather. "Wake up, Grandpa." The old man grunted and turned on his side. "Come on, Grandpa, it's nearly check out time."

Chris opened one eye, then the other; it took some time to focus.

"Ay, Junior, why did you wake me? I was having the best dream of my life."

"Oh?"

The old man slowly sat up and smiled. "I was on my honeymoon."

"Do you mean that you and Irene…?"

"Sure did. We tied the knot."

Just then Travis came in holding a large paper bag.

"I'll tell you about it, later in the car," Chris whispered to Walter Jr., ever so softly.

"Coffee and Danish for all," announced Travis.

Chris got out of bed and walked to the bathroom, only to find the door locked.

"If you could hold it for just a little while," Travis said to Chris, sounding a bit embarrassed. "I'm afraid it's Baby Tyrone's breakfast time."

"Oh, I see," said Chris.

Chris reached over, opened the nightstand drawer, and found paper and pen. He thought long and hard. He wrote down as many characters he could remember from the manuscript. It was only twelve, still, he was surprised he remembered that much. This made him feel hopeful he could do it.

Just then the bathroom door opened, Felicia stepped out, holding the baby. "Sorry to make you gentleman wait; a mother's work is…well, you understand."

"Excuse me," said Chris, rushing into the bathroom.

Later, Baby Tyrone played on the floor while everyone enjoyed their breakfast.

"He sure is a handsome little fella," said Chris.

"Takes after his daddy," smiled Felicia. She looked at Chris. "Sorry for being nosy; I couldn't help overhearing. You said you dreamed you were on your honeymoon?"

Chris laughed. "I'm not sure it's a dream, anymore."

"I understand what you mean," said Felicia. "That happens to me sometimes, too. There are times in a person's life that are so remarkable that it feels like a dream."

"Something like that," said Chris. "Except I think this is something more."

"When I was nine years old," said Travis, "I dreamed I had this BB gun, see. I was hunting bad guys with it and shooting squirrels and birds for dinner. When I woke up, I ran to my bedroom closet. My mother said, 'What you looking for?' I said, 'My BB gun.' She said, 'You ain't got no BB gun'. She thought I was crazy. I looked in that closet for that BB gun for three days, never found a thing. I could have sworn I had one. It seemed so real."

"I once dreamed I was milking a cow," Walter Jr. said.

They all waited for the other shoe to drop.

"And…?" said Travis.

"Well, I woke up to find my hands pulling on the bedposts."

Everyone laughed; Chris spilled some of his coffee.

"I think I understand what Mr. Goodman is going through," said Felicia. "There is a fine line between the dream-world and the waking-world. When you're dreaming, it seems real, and you have no clue you're dreaming. With that in mind, who's to say what a dream is or is not? Maybe, this is a dream. I only know that if my life with my husband and baby turned out to be a dream, I would still have enjoyed it, and been glad I dreamed it."

Just then the phone rang; Travis answered it.

"Wendell, it's you, finally." He cupped his hand over the receiver and turned to his wife. "It's Wendell." He returned to the line. "Wendell, thank you for getting back with us."

Felicia looked at Chris and Walter Jr., "Wendell is Travis' brother. He and his wife live in Alaska."

Travis spoke into the phone. "That's right. Then, you've heard. I hate to ask you like this." He went silent and listened, and then spoke. "We can never thank you and Nellie enough for this."

"Nellie is Wendell's wife," Felicia told Walter Jr. and Chris. They nodded. Travis continued.

"Wendell, I hate to do this, only I'm short on cash. Could you wire me some money? That's right, anything you can spare. No, wait, don't wire it to me; my name is probably on a list." Travis looked at Chris.

"Don't look at me," said Chris. "I'm wanted, too; and I've had TV coverage."

"No one's looking for me; I don't think, even if they did mention my name on the news," Walter Jr. said.

Travis covered the receiver. "You don't mind?"

"No, not at all."

He returned to his brother on the line. "Write this down, Wendell. Wire whatever you can to Walter Bouchard Junior. That's right. Give Nellie our love. Thanks again, Wendell; see you in a few days." He hung up and looked at Chris and Walter Jr., "That was my brother, Wendell. He's invited us to stay with him and his wife in Alaska for a while." He looked directly at Walter Jr., "You don't mind doing this for us, do you?"

"I told you, I didn't."

"Great, you're a true friend. Okay, it's off to the telegraph office."

****

In front of the telegraph office, Travis slowed to let Walter Jr. out of the truck. The others let out a sigh of relief for the extra room in the cab. They could see no parking spaces.

"I'll keep driving around the block," Travis told Walter Jr., making a circular motion with his hand with one finger up.

A lean gray-haired man stood behind the counter. He smiled as Walter Jr. approached.

"May I help you, sir?"

"Yes, I have some cash waiting for me. Walter Bouchard Jr. is my name."

The man punched a few keys on his computer and read what was on the screen.

"Yes, Mr. Bouchard, two hundred dollars. How would you like it?"

"In twenties, please."

The clerk counted out the money. "May I see some identification, please, and could you sign this form for me?" The clerk placed a slip of paper and pen down.

Walter Jr. went for his wallet, when the clerk noticed something on the computer screen he hadn't seen before.

"Excuse me, sir, I'll be right back." The clerk placed the two hundred dollars down and walked away. He returned a moment later with another man.

"May I see some identification, please?" asked the man.

"Is there something wrong?" asked Walter Jr., handing over his driver's license.

"Not a thing, Mr.... Bouchard, just routine; if you could please fill out the form, I'll be right back with your driver's license." The two men went into a small office. Walter Jr. could see the one man dialing the phone. Something was wrong.

Walter Jr. waited till his patience began to wear thin.

"Excuse me," shouted Walter Jr., "May I have my money and driver's license, please?"

"One moment," replied the man in the office. "I'm afraid our computers are down."

Walter Jr. leaned forward and looked at the computer screen. There was nothing wrong with their connection. There was a mirror on the back wall of the office. Walter Jr. saw the reflection of a police squad car stopping out front; two officers got out and started for the front door.

Without thinking, Walter Jr. grabbed the two hundred dollars, jumped over the counter and ran out the backdoor. He was in an alleyway; there was no one in sight. He ran down the alley to the street where he waited for the truck to pass by.

"Come on, come on!" he moaned, his fists balled in his pockets, his eyes peeled for the truck.

Finally, it came down the street, slowly. Walter Jr. jumped in front of it. Travis slammed on the brakes. Walter Jr. hopped in.

"Just start driving, fast!" ordered Walter Jr., handing the cash to Felicia.

"What are you doin' here?" asked Travis.

"Just drive! I'll explain as we go."

****

Back at the hotel, they all stood in the parking lot between their two vehicles, to say good-bye.

"I can't tell you what you've meant to us," said Travis, shaking both their hands.

"You've helped us, too," Walter Jr. said.

Felicia kissed both their cheeks. "Walter, you're going to make some woman very happy someday. And Chris, I hope your honeymoon never ends."

Travis nudged his wife and child into the cab of the truck. "Come on, before everybody gets too mushy and starts crying. Take care, you two. If you're ever in Alaska, look us up...the third igloo on the right."

The next moment, the truck was gone, Chris and Walter Jr. stood alone, looking at each other.

"Well, Grandpa, I guess it's just you and me, again."

"I'm still game, if you are?" said Chris.

"Ready when you are, Grandpa."

****

Traveling south on the California Coastal Highway, Walter Jr. found it near impossible to keep his eyes on the road. The Pacific Ocean always at their right, only a few yards away. The sky and sea the same sapphire blue, making it difficult to tell where one started and the other one ended. The waves crashing against rock formations, sending white foam into the air and across the cream and coffee colored sand.

Now and then, they came on seaside communities, so unique, they had to stop and check them out. There were people on roller blades and skateboards. Muscle-bound men and woman lifting weights and spotting one another, while children flew kites, as others played basketball or volleyball. However, nothing compared with the surfers. Those death-defying acrobats performing gyrations that most folk would find impossible to do on solid dry land, let alone atop planks of wood sailing over six foot waves. Their long youthful bodies sun-kissed to a rich toffee brown and their windblown hair crowned them masters of the beach.

Chris and Walter Jr. walked to the end of a long pier. They bought a bag of popcorn and tossed the kernels into the air, not one fell into the water as seagulls gobbled them up in midair.

Low funds or not, they found it hard not to splurge. They ate hot dogs with everything on them, later a slice of pizza each, and the ice-cream could not be passed over.

Chris chuckled, as they got back in the car. "Your mother would have my head if she saw what I let you eat, today. You'd think we spent the day at the circus."

"Well, it is kind of like a circus," Walter Jr. commented.

"I guess your right," laughed Chris, taking one last look as they drove off.

Hours later, they still hadn't driven very far south. The sun was beginning to set.

"Grandpa?"

"Yeah, Junior?"

"Grandpa, I know we haven't gone far, today, but do you think we could stop for a while? I've never seen a sunset over the ocean."

"Neither have I, come to think about it. Yeah, sure, we can stop. I guess it's just one of those kinds of days when time just slips through your fingers. Don't worry about it; we can make up for lost time, tomorrow."

Walter Jr. pulled the car over to the shoulder of the road and parked. He helped his grandfather down the slope to the shore, where they found a large, dry smooth rock to sit on, facing the ocean, facing west.

As the sun sank low, it appeared unnaturally larger than normal. It turned from a harsh hot-white glare into a friendly golden disk that was easy to stare into. When the sun just barely touched the horizon, Chris gently pushed his elbow into his grandson's ribs.

"Do you hear it?" he asked.

"What's that, Grandpa?"

"If you listen really hard, you can hear the hiss of the ocean as the sun sinks into it."

Walter Jr. closed his eyes and concentrated. "Yeah, I can hear it; I can also hear the blub, blub, blub of the water boiling from the sun's heat."

Chris placed his hand on his grandson's shoulder. "You know, Junior, when you were little, I used to pull your leg like that all the time, and you used to believe me."

"I remember," said Walter Jr., "To be honest, it was fun having my leg pulled."

The sky became a panorama of color, reds, pinks, purples, blues, of every shade. They watched till the sun was below the horizon, its rays shooting to the sky and reflected off the ocean. Then without warning, the sky and world went black. All they could see before them were black waves bobbing up and down like velvet blankets waving on unseen clotheslines hundreds of miles long.

"Well, that was well-worth the price of admission," said Chris.

"Come on, Grandpa, I'll help you back to the car.

Seated back in the front seat of the car, Walter Jr. tried the ignition. The engine rumbled, choked, and coughed, yet did not turn over. He turned the key again; it whined once or twice and then not a sound.

"We out of gas?" asked Chris.

Walter Jr. looked at the dial. "No, we've got more than half a tank."

"The battery could be dead."

"The guy who sold it to me showed me a bill saying the battery was almost new."

"Maybe you flooded it. Give it a rest."

"Yeah, that's possible. Maybe I flooded it. Let's just sit here for a minute."

They sat in the dark car on the side of the road, in silence, counting in their heads.

"That should be long enough," Walter Jr. said. He tried again; this time the sound of metal ripping against metal filled the air, like a lion roaring. Then smoke started spewing from the sides of the hood.

"Quick, Grandpa, we need to get out!"

Outside, Walter Jr. forced the car hood up. There was a small fire starting at the carburetor, getting bigger and bigger. Walter Jr. bent down, picked up two handfuls of sand and tossed them onto the flames. He did this over and over, till the fire was out.

They stood with their mouths open, sulking, watching the smoke rise.

"Any hope?" asked Chris.

"If I had a bugle, I'd blow taps."

"So, now what do we do?"

"Nothing we can do, other than wait here for the police."

"The police," whispered Chris. "That means back to Texas."

"Sorry, Grandpa, I don't know what else to do."

"What if we pushed it into the sea; kind of gave it a Viking funeral. Then we hoof it on foot."

"Grandpa, you must not be feeling your age, lately. The two of us could hardly budge this monster. And be honest, how far do you think we'd make it on foot? We'll just have to wait and see what happens."

So wait they did. Few cars passed by, and none stopped to help. Suddenly, two headlights appeared about a half mile down the road. When it came close, it stopped. They recognized it. It was a two-tone tan convertible. Posse got out and walked over.

"You two amaze me," he laughed, shaking his head. He pulled out a cell phone and put it to his ear.

"Gabe here…what do you think happened? Just what I said would happen. The old jalopy finally broke down. No, it's useless; you better send a tow truck. Okay, I'll tell them." He turned to Walter Jr. and Chris. "They're sending a tow truck for the car, and they're sending a car for you."

"A car for us…?" Walter Jr. asked.

"Well, not actually a car; they're sending the limousine."

"A limousine…?" Chris questioned.

"Who are you, anyway?" Walter Jr. asked.

"There you go again; looking a gift-horse in the mouth."

"Well, at least tell us why you're trying to be so nice to us."

"Oh, it's not me," said Posse. "I couldn't care less. You'd rot out here, if it were up to me. I'm just doing my job. It's my boss who wants your dreams to come true, not me."

"And who is your boss?" demanded Chris.

"Why, you haven't figured that out, yet? It's your fairy godmother."

He laughed hard and long; he laughed till the tan stretch-limo pulled up. Another man got out of the limo and handed Posse the keys. Posse tossed his set of car keys to the man. "Here, take my car back in. I'll take care of Hansel and Gretel, here, and bring them to the Gingerbread Castle." He looked at the two of them. "If you're waiting for me to hold the door for you, you've got me mixed up with Amos from Amos and Andy." They looked questioningly at him "Amos was a taxi driver." He pulled a card out of his wallet and held it for them to read. "Gabriel Angelis, private investigator, with a license to carry a canceled weapon. Now, get in the back of the limo." They hesitated. "Now!" he shouted, frightening them into action; they hopped into the backseat.

"You know, some people would consider this kidnapping," said Chris.

"You want me to take you back to where I found you?" said Posse. "You can wait for the police who will ship you back to Texas faster than you can blink. Then your dream will never come true."

"How do you know about that?" asked Chris.

"A little bird told me."

"Where are you taking us?" Walter Jr. demanded.

"Seems the apple didn't fall far from the tree, you two are two peas in a pod. What's the matter, don't you like surprises? Ever heard of going with the flow? Why don't you relax, enjoy the ride, and be glad you're not in a police station." Posse looked at them in the rearview mirror and smiled. "Listen, nothing bad is going to happen. Every good story has some tension and mystery to it. It's a long hard road to a happy ending."

****

They rode north on the Coastal Highway for thirty minutes, then Posse took a turn up a winding road to the top of a high hill overlooking the ocean. They came to a towering gate with a guardhouse. When the security guard saw who was driving, he opened the gate and waved him on.

After a quarter mile drive, they came to a massive two-story mansion – as large as a hotel and as luxurious as a palace. It was lit up like the fairgrounds at the State Fair; off to one side was a guesthouse that could easily house a family of six; to the other side was an Olympic-size pool, a pool house and patio. Posse parked at the front entrance.

"All ashore who's going ashore!" announced Posse.

They stood next to the car, admiring the building.

"It's enormous," Walter Jr. exclaimed.

"There are twelve bedrooms, sixteen bathrooms, two living rooms, a dining room, a ballroom, and a library. There's also a game room, a small movie theater, a two-lane bowling alley, and that's not counting the kitchen and servant's quarters," said Posse as he walked up the front steps. "Follow me."

The inside was as impressive as the outside. Posse led them to a large living room. They stood looking and waiting. Suddenly, there came the cry of a small familiar voice.

"Pawpaw!"

Little Sara Millwood came running into the room towards Chris. He wished he was only ten years younger; he would have lifted her up in his arms. All he could do was place his hands on her head, as she wrapped her arms around his legs. Sara's mother, Trisha, was right behind her, and behind Trisha was that star of the stage and the silver screen, Louise Langford.

"Good to see you again, Chris," said Trisha, kissing his cheek.

"Trisha, what's this all about?"

"We are all under the wings of our patroness, Ms. Louise Langford."

The movie star offered her hand to Chris. "It's an honor to meet you, Mr. Goodman. Please, call me Louise."

"And you can call me Chris."

"Very well, Chris," she said, and then turned to Walter Jr., "And you must be Junior?"

"Just call me Walter."

"Please, sit down." She pointed to the two couches facing each out. "Are you hungry?"

Chris and Walter Jr. bit their lips, feeling uneasy about saying yes and coming across as rude.

"Silly me, of course you're hungry." She turned to Posse. "Gabe, be a sweetheart, and tell Rodolfo to make some sandwiches and iced tea, enough for all of us, including yourself." He nodded and left the room. Louise smiled at Chris. "So you want to know what this is all about. Actually, I think it would be better if Trisha starts the story off, and then I can finish it."

Sara got up on the couch and got comfortable in Chris' lap, and laid her head on his chest.

Trisha started the story.

"It all started with my husband, Bill. Sara always loved the Disney movies, and we decorated her bedroom with everything imaginable from Disney. Bill realized how happy these things made Sara, which made him very unhappy. He wanted so much to give Sara everything; however our financial situation made that impossible. If I remember correctly, he read a magazine article about all the wonderful things *Dream Makers* were doing for ill children. That night he sat down and wrote a letter to the foundation. Within three weeks we were contacted, and here we are." She looked to Louise to continue the story.

All eyes were on the actress, although none stared as razor-sharp as Walter Jr., captivated by her beauty. He'd seen all her films, and could not believe his good fortune; to not only meet her, but to be in her home, sitting inches away from her. She was a star in every sense, with an ageless beauty that made it difficult to tell her true age. Only Chris had a memory of Hollywood that did not contain Louise Langford.

Her shoulder-length hair was not exactly blonde, although not dark enough to call her a true brunette, with specks of red thrown in. Her eyes were blue, yet slightly gray when the light hit them just so, with flecks of green. Her skin was milk. Her figure was that of a dancer, thin, muscular, and willowy. Her voice filled the room like a song. Walter Jr. purposely looked away from her, afraid his gawking would offend.

"We were all moved by Bill's letter," said Louise. "Dream Makers is such a great organization. It didn't take us long to get the ball rolling." She placed her hand lovingly on Sara's head. "We've spent the last few days at Disneyland. It was great, wasn't it, Sara?"

The child smiled and nodded her head.

"Tomorrow we leave for Helsinki," said Louise.

"What for…?" Walter Jr. asked.

"There's a doctor there with some new and hopeful methods. Louise is kind enough to pay for it all," answered Trisha.

"That's beautiful…I mean, wonderful," said Walter Jr., shy and tongue-tied, staring at Louise.

Just then, Posse entered the room. "Dinner is served," he announced in a thick English accent. "Gee, I always wanted to say that."

They all sat at the long dining room table. Walter Jr. was starving; he dug right in, although Chris continued with his questions.

"That is a fabulous story, and I commend you on the great work you do." He pointed to Walter Jr. and himself. "But how do we work into all this?"

Louise smiled at Chris. "When I met Sara and Trisha at the train station, you were hard not to notice. I asked her about you. She told me your whole story. Gabe, here, is head of my security." She gestured to Posse. "I told him to get in his car and take you anywhere you wanted to go. Then what happened, Gabe?"

Posse put down his sandwich and swallowed. "Well, I drove around looking for you," he said to Chris. "You were standing at the corner. I was just about to stop and give you a lift, when your grandson came along. You got in his car, and I followed you."

"But why all the secrecy?" asked Chris.

"You are a wanted man, Mr. Goodman," said Posse. "Ms. Langford does not need any bad publicity darkening her good image, so I made the call to stay in the shadows and do whatever I could to help."

Louise continued the story. "So now you two are my guests. Eat up, when you're ready I'll show you to your rooms." She looked at Walter Jr., "They're working on your car, as we speak. They'll deliver in the morning and you can resume your quest."

****

Later, everyone, except Posse, gathered at the top of the stairs on the second floor.

"Say goodnight to Pawpaw," said Trisha.

"Goodnight, Pawpaw," said Sara, yawning as she walked towards her room, too tired to make any real effort.

"We'll be gone early in the morning, before you get up," Trisha told Chris. "I wish you all the best."

"Good luck in Helsinki," said Chris, reaching over and kissing her.

"Goodnight, everyone," she smiled at Louise and Walter Jr., and then turned and entered the bedroom.

"Walter, this will be your room," Louise said, guiding him to the door. "There is a robe on the bed. Leave your clothes on the floor outside your door; I'll have my people clean them."

"Thank you so very much," said Walter Jr., bowing slightly as he entered the room.

"And your room is at the end of the hall," she said, leading Chris by the arm. She opened the door and turned on the light. They both entered. "It's one of my favorite rooms; it has a great view of the ocean."

"It is beautiful," said Chris, walking to the window.

"I'm going with Sara and Trisha in the morning, so I won't be seeing you again. Gabe will be here. If there's anything you need, he'll get it for you. You have a good night, Chris." She turned and started out the door.

"Ms. Langford?"

"Yes, Chris."

"Why are you doing this?"

She thought for a moment and smiled.

"Growing up, we were dirt poor. I've been blessed; most of my dreams have come true. Now I find great joy in making dreams come true for others. And it isn't just sick little girls who have dreams. Everyone has a dream and everyone deserves to at least have a chance at making them come true."

"Ms. Langford?"

"Louise."

"Louise…" He couldn't say another word. There were tears in his eyes.

"Goodnight, Mr. Goodman."

****

When Chris woke in his dream on the island, he sat down in the sand and went right to work trying to memorize the symbols on the manuscript. Irene approached him, seemingly from nowhere.

"Darling," she asked, "what are you doing?"

He was writing the symbols in the wet sand. "I find that if I write out each caricature, I have a better chance of remembering them. I've memorized twelve already."

"What will you do with them when you've memorized them all?"

"Find someone who can translate it, I guess."

Irene went silent for a moment, and then cried out. "Chris, look!" He looked up at her. She was pointing out to sea. He followed the direction of her finger out over the waves. There, two hundred yards from shore, was a large wooden ship, not the same ship as before, an old-fashioned sailing ship, European in style. A black flag with a skull and crossed bones waved from the top of the mast – it was a pirate ship.

They recognized Death standing at the stern next to the helm. He raised his arms, while giving orders. The heads of the sailors bobbed up and down, as they made ready; they raised the wooden covers from small windows in the side of the ship. Dark black cannons appeared, one in each window. Death's arm went down. They could hear his command from far off, "Fire!"

Cannonballs began raining on the island. Sand and stone flew into the air, and trees fell. Irene and Chris ran for higher ground. The sailors immediately changed to higher aim.

"We should try to make it to the other side of the island," Irene shouted to Chris. "We can hide in the cave."

"Good idea," hollered Chris.

As if Death could read their minds, they began to open fire on the path leading to the other side of the island. There was no escape. Chris grabbed Irene and tossed her to the ground, covering her with his body. The sound of the shelling was deafening. Chris couldn't hear her, although by the way she trembled in his arms, he knew she was crying. Suddenly, the barrage stopped, all was silent. Chris let go of Irene; the two stood up and looked around. To their amazement, there was no damage. Everything was as it was before. There was no sign of an attack. Looking out to sea, there was no ship, not even a ripple in the water.

"I don't understand," said Chris.

"Anything can happen in a dream," Irene said softly.

Chris started down the hill to the beach.

"Where are you going?" asked Irene.

"This has got to stop. We can't go on living in fear. I'm going to read that manuscript and memorize it, if it's the last thing I do."

Twenty-Three

I'll see you in my dreams

Though the days are long, twilight sings a song
Of the happiness that used to be
Soon my eyes will close, soon I'll find repose
And in dreams, you're always near to me

I'll see you in my dreams
And I'll hold you in my dreams
Someone took you right out of my arms
Still I feel the thrill of your charms

Lips that once were mine
Tender eyes that shine
They will light my way tonight
I'll see you in my dreams

Music by Isham Jones
Words by Gus Kahn

THE JOURNEY

In the morning, Chris woke to a gentle tapping on his door.

"Chris, it's Gabe, your clean clothes are hanging out here on the doorknob. Breakfast is in the kitchen. Come on down, when you're ready."

After a shower and shave, it felt good to put on clean clothes. It surprised Chris to find Walter Jr. leaving his room just when he was leaving his.

"Good morning, Grandpa. Did you sleep well?"

"Good morning, Junior; don't ask."

"Where do you think the kitchen is?" Walter Jr. asked.

"I guess downstairs. Just follow the smell of coffee."

Posse sat at a large round kitchen table, while a small elderly woman stood at the stove, cooking. Posse placed down his coffee cup.

"Sit down gentlemen. Breakfast is the most important meal of the day, and Maria can sure cook. Here, Chris, sit here; she's already made you your favorite, grits and maple syrup."

"You certainly are thorough," said Chris, sitting down.

"It's my job, and my nature," laughed Posse.

Walter Jr. sat down. Maria smiled at him; he smiled back. She spoke softly in Spanish.

Posse smiled at the confused looking Walter Jr., "She wants to know what you want for breakfast."

"Oh, I don't know, whatever, I'm easy," Walter Jr. replied.

Maria nodded with a beaming grin. Two minutes later she placed in front of Walter Jr. a large plate. On it were two eggs over-easy, sausage, bacon, fried potatoes, toast, and a short stack of buttermilk pancakes. Walter Jr. looked at the plate apprehensively.

"That's what you get when you don't tell Maria exactly what you want," said Posse.

"I don't think I can eat all this."

"You'll offend her, if you don't."

Walter Jr. smiled and nodded at Maria; she smiled and nodded back, seemingly pleased with herself. Walter Jr. got down to the task of cleaning his plate.

"Ms. Langford sends her greeting and apologizes for not being here this morning. She, the mother and the kid, were off to the airport before sunup. She left orders for me to see to your needs."

"She's quite a lady," remarked Chris.

"She's a peach," exclaimed Posse.

"So, what's next, might I ask?" said Chris. "That is if I'm not looking the gift-horse in the mouth, again."

"Still in a hurry," said Posse, smiling and shaking his head. "First, we finish breakfast, and then I have a surprise for you."

"I don't think I can finish all this," Walter Jr. said.

Maria was grinning from ear to ear at Walter Jr., "You like?" she asked, looking for approval.

"Se, mochas gracias," replied Walter Jr., returning to his plate, starting on his pancakes.

"De nada," sang a thrilled and contented Maria.

****

After breakfast, Posse guided them to the front door and outside into the morning sunlight. There, parked at the foot of the front steps was a new silver two-door sedan.

"Hop in, guys, it's all yours," said Posse.

"What do you mean?" Walter Jr. asked.

"Just what I said; it's all yours. We tried to get that old bomb of yours fixed, but it gave up the ghost before reaching the garage. Ms. Langford ordered it last night. I told you she was a peach."

"But we can't accept this," Walter Jr. said.

"First you try to insult Maria's cooking, now you tell your fairy godmother to get lost. You don't just look a gift-horse in the mouth; you wring its neck. Now, thank your lucky stars, and get in the car. All the paperwork is in the glove compartment. There's a week's worth of groceries in the trunk, plus a set of new clothes for the both of you. It's got a full tank of gas. Oh, I nearly forgot. Here…" He handed Walter Jr. five one-hundred dollar bills.

Walter Jr. looked at the money, looked at the car, looked at his grandfather, and looked at Posse. "But…"

"No, buts! Just take it all and go. Do me that favor."

"Do *you* a favor?" remarked Chris.

"Yeah, me a favor; you think I've nothing better to do than follow you two around all-day and night? I've got a life, too, you know."

Before either of them could say another word, Posse turned, walked up the stairs, and went back inside, leaving them bewildered.

Chris looked at Walter Jr., "Go knock on the door."

"Please don't," they heard Posse's voice holler from behind the door. "Adios, Auf Wiedersehen, Ciao, Au Revoir, so long and good-bye!"

There seemed nothing left to do other than do as they were told.

"Thank you!" Chris shouted at the door. There was no answer. "Tell Ms. Langford, thank you!"

Posse's voice was muffled by the door. "I will; now, good-bye."

The keys were in the ignition. The motor purred like a thousand kittens. They drove down the lane, back to the Coastal Highway, heading south.

Chris' body stiffened when he saw the sign that read "San Diego – 68 Miles".

"Nervous?" Walter Jr. asked.

"A little," answered Chris. "No, I take that back; I'm very nervous."

"Well, that's understandable," Walter Jr. said.

"What do you mean?"

"Well, it's not everyday a guy gets married, goes on a honeymoon, and then gets to meet his wife a week later. There's something…different…about the whole situation. I'd be nervous, too."

"You think she'll like me?"

"No, I think she'll love you. She married you, didn't she?"

"It's just that I look so different from how I do in our dream."

"Would you love her if she looked nothing like what she does in your dream?"

"Of course, I would."

"Why?"

"Because she's Irene; because she's the sweetest thing this side of heaven."

"There you go. I'm sure she feels the same about you. If love is blind, that covers everything, including wrinkles and gray hair."

Chris thought about this for a moment.

"Say, Junior, how old are you? That's pretty profound for a young man, your age."

"I had a good teacher."

****

Ten miles out from San Diego, they stopped at a diner for something to eat. Sitting in a booth by the window, the waitress handed them menus and stood over them doing what waitress do, holding her pad and pencil.

Chris handed back his menu. "I'll have a cheeseburger and fries, and a cup of coffee, please."

"I'll have the same," said Walter Jr. as he slid out of the booth. "I'll be right back, Grandpa."

Chris looked out the window, his mind whirling. If only he could see Irene once more in their dream-world before seeing her in the waking-world. If only he'd prepared her better. But it was too late. They'd see each other before the day was over. He looked at his reflection in the napkin holder, and sighed.

The waitress returned and placed their orders down. Walter Jr. was still not back. Finally, he returned and sat down, grabbing his burger.

"What took you so long?" asked Chris.

"I made a phone call. I got directions to the Blue Jay Nursing home."

Chris' appetite vanished.

"You okay, Grandpa?"

Chris shrugged.

"You're not wearing the hat Jimmy Gray Horse gave you."

"I want Irene to see the real me. Besides, I'm tired of hiding." Chris looked thoughtfully out the window, again. "Junior, you think we can stop and buy a bouquet of flowers for Irene?"

****

Drenched in sunlight, downtown San Diego was no different from any other downtown during weekday work hours. Drivers honked their horns as slow lines of cars filled the streets. People going to and fro cluttered the sidewalks.

Walter Jr. drove slowly, watching. When he found what he was looking for, he parked the car. The neon sign flashed in red and white – Starlight One-Hour Cleaners.

"What are we doing here?" asked Chris.

"You've got to look your best for your bride," said Walter Jr., reaching behind his seat and bringing forth Chris' black bag, which the old man always kept close at hand. "Come on, Grandpa."

There was an elderly Asian gentleman behind the counter. Inwardly, Walter Jr. reprimanded himself for stereotyping the man, old movie-images of Chinese laundries. He felt self-conscious even more when the man spoke without a hint of an accent.

"May I help you?"

Walter Jr. opened the bag and placed his grandfather's new suit down – it was waded up. He spread it out on the counter – it was terribly wrinkled. "Yes, we'd like this suit pressed, please."

The man examined the suit, and then took a pen and pad. "Address…?"

"Ah…Venus, Texas."

"Excuse me?"

"We're not from around here. We just got into town."

The man shrugged this off. "Name…?"

"Walter Bouchard."

The man wrote out the ticket, ripped out the copy, and handed it to Walter Jr., "Tomorrow, after nine," said the man.

"Oh, no, that won't do," said Walter Jr., "Your sign says one-hour cleaning."

"That's if you get here before noon. Everything after that is next-day."

"But, I'm going to see Irene, today," explained Chris.

The man looked at him, inquiringly, clearly unimpressed.

"I'm sorry, those are the rules."

"Please, sir," said Walter Jr., "we've come such a long way. My grandfather needs to look his best. He's going to see his wife, today. They haven't seen each other since high school."

The man squinted one of his eye, as the eyebrow over the other went up. "I'm sorry, but…"

A small, elderly Asian woman came up behind the man and took hold of the suit. She smiled at Walter Jr., "No problem. Please sit, we'll have this done in just a few minutes." The smile left her face, as she looked at the man with a cold stare. Having seen that look before, and knowing better, he didn't say a word.

Fifteen minutes later, she returned with the suit, on a hanger, nicely pressed. Chris and Walter Jr. stood up, Walter Jr. took the suit. "Thank you; how much do we owe you?"

"On the house," she smiled, "a wedding gift."

"That's very kind of you," said Walter Jr. as he handed the suit to his grandfather.

"Thank you very much," said Chris. "May I bother you with one last thing? Is there someplace I can change clothes?"

"Yes, of course. Follow me," she said, gesturing with a pointed outstretched hand.

The man slammed the cash register drawer closed, loudly, and walked to the back of the shop.

Later, back in the car, Walter Jr. glanced at his grandfather. "Looking sharp, Grandpa."

"I look all right?"

"Like a million bucks."

"Yeah, all green and wrinkled."

"Cut it out," laughed Walter Jr., "Now, off to the florist."

****

The smell of fresh-cut flowers made them smile the moment they stepped into the Rothenberg Florist. The room was cold to keep the flowers lively. The colors were vibrant, like a living rainbow.

"Smells like church, only more so," Walter Jr. reflected.

A young man walked out from the backroom. He couldn't have been more than fifteen. He was lean and boney with bad a complexion and a long neck with an Adam's apple the size of an apple.

"May I help you?" His voice cracked up and down two octaves, somewhere between boy and man.

"Yes, we'd like a bouquet, please," Walter Jr. said.

“What’s the occasion?” asked the young man. They looked with squinted eyes and question marks over their heads. “Is it for a wedding, a date, a gift, a prom, a birthday?”

“All of the above,” smiled Chris.

Now the question mark settled over the young man’s head.

“My grandfather’s come a long way to see an old sweetheart of his.”

“An old girlfriend?” asked the young man.

“No, my wife,” replied Chris.

“Oh, divorced, ay?”

“No, newlyweds.”

This threw the young man into a tailspin, although after a moment he recovered.

“Roses!” smiled the young man. “All the women like roses.”

“No, too predictable,” said Chris, looking around the store. His eyes moved to the clear glass of a cooler. “That’s what I want,” he declared, pointing to a bouquet of white, blue, and pink.

“But that’s a wedding bouquet,” said the boy.

“It’s perfect! Just cut the ribbons off, and I’ll take it.”

The young man looked to Walter Jr. for support. “Nobody gives wedding bouquets.”

Walter Jr. shrugged. “Don’t look at me; if that’s what he wants, then that’s what he wants. Besides, they’re going to get married.”

“I thought he said they’re already married?”

“Only in his dream; this time it’s for real.”

The boy decided it was safer to not say another word, and went to the cooler.

****

Chris sat in the car, holding the bouquet in front of him. Walter Jr. snickered.

“What’s so funny?” asked Chris.

“You, you look like you belong on top of a wedding cake.”

“Ha, ha, keep your eyes on the road and your comments to yourself.” Chris rested the bouquet in his lap.

After driving ten minutes east of downtown, leveling off after a series of steep hills, they found themselves in a posh section of town. Walter Jr. slowed down.

“What are you slowing down for?” asked Chris.

“We’re close; look for Turtledove Drive.”

Chris read the street names out loud, “Windsor, Country Club Road, Newport, Willow Place, there it is, Turtledove Drive.”

Walter Jr. made a right turn. “Look for number 1160; it should be easy to spot.”

"That must be it, there," said Chris, pointing to a building on the right, nestled on a corner lot, taking up half a block. The sign out front read, *Blue Jay Adult Living.* It was a one-story, red brick building with a green roof, and large windows in a row on all sides. Most windows had an ornament stuck to it, an expression of individuality placed there by the inhabitant of that room. As they pulled into the parking lot, Chris wondered which window, which room was Irene's.

Inside was clean and neat, looking like a combination hotel and hospital, with an atmosphere and antiseptic smell that leaned more towards being a hospital. The lobby was large with plush brown carpet and green ferns all around. The woman behind the front desk greeted them with a smile.

"May I help you?"

"Yes, I'm here to see Irene Cooper," said Chris, holding his bouquet.

"Your name, please?"

"Goodman, Christopher Goodman."

"One moment, please." She lifted the phone to her ear and dialed. "Hello, this is the front desk. There's a Mr. Goodman to see Irene Cooper. Yes...I'll tell him." She placed the phone down. "She'll be here in a minute. Please, take a seat and wait."

"Thank you," said Chris.

Chris and Walter Jr. sat, waiting silently. There was a long hall to their left; Chris stared down it, waiting for his first glimpse of Irene. A minute later, the figure of a woman turned the corner and started down the hall towards them. When she was halfway down the hall, Chris rose to his feet. His body shook and the bouquet fell from his hand to the floor.

"Grandpa, are you okay?" asked Walter Jr. as he picked up the flowers.

Chris remained silent, never taking his eyes from the woman. He recognized her immediately. Her hair might have been different and she wore jeans and a sweatshirt, nevertheless, he knew her – it was Irene, except something was wrong, very wrong. She was young, no more than thirty years old. She walked up to them.

"Mr. Goodman?"

"Irene! I don't understand! You're young again!"

She wore a half-smile. "My name is Olivia; I'm her granddaughter. Follow me; I'll take you to my grandmother."

She walked slowly so Chris could keep up; Walter Jr. followed close behind, carrying the bouquet.

"So, Mr. Goodman, how long have you known my grandmother?"

"We were high school sweethearts."

"Really. . .she never told me about you. Have you kept in touch with each other?"

"Not until recently."

"Really?" she said surprised. "How recently?"

"Well, to be honest, face-to-face, not since high school."

"Then you don't know."

"Know what?" asked Chris.

"Oh, here's my grandmother's room," she said, opening the door.

Chris looked in. It was a small, plain, but bright room, the sunshine pouring in from the two floor-length windows. In the corner near one of the window was a hospital bed with the back portion lifted to an upright position. There lay an elderly Irene, her eyes closed. On both sides of the bed were machines with flashing lights and electronic monitors. Wires ran from different parts of her body to the machines. A thick intravenous tube was stuck in her arm; thin catheter tubing ran from under her blanket to a container on the floor, under the bed.

Olivia entered the room. "That's why I asked you the last time you were in communication with her. My grandmother has been on life support for nearly a year, now."

Chris staggered slowly in and up to the foot of the bed.

"No wonder why I always find her waiting for me on the island. She's always asleep," Chris said softly to himself.

"Excuse me?" asked Olivia.

"I'm sorry; I didn't know," said Chris. "Is there any hope?"

"None, I'm afraid," said the young woman, brushing her hand lovingly across her grandmother's forehead. "I've been in a legal fight with my parents for months to have her disconnected, so she can die in peace and with honor."

"You mustn't; not yet," pleaded Chris.

"My grandmother was a lively and happy woman. She'd never agree to live like this."

"She still has her dreams," Chris said in appeal.

"Then she'll dream," said Olivia with tears forming in her eyes. "Why does a dream have to end, just because a person dies?"

"Do you really think so?" asked Chris, hopefully.

"I'm sure of it," said Olivia. "My grandmother will go on, somewhere. I'm sure of it."

No one spoke for what seemed an overly long time. Chris took the bouquet from Walter Jr., walked forward, gently placing it on the bed.

"May I have a minute alone with Irene?"

"Of course, you may." She walked to the door. Walter Jr. backed out into the hallway with her; she closed the door.

Walter Jr. waited patiently in the hall. He felt so bad for his grandfather; however there was little he could do.

"Please excuse me, I need to call the doctor," said Olivia.

"Of course," Walter Jr. replied.

After a few minutes alone in the hall, his worry for his grandfather grew. He walked to the door and put his ear close to it. He could hear his grandfather's voice – singing.

Irene goodnight, Irene goodnight
Good night Irene, good night Irene
I'll see you in my dreams.

Music and Words by
Huddie 'Lead Belly' Ledbetter

Walter Jr. backed away and leaned against the wall. A minute later, the door opened and Chris came out slowly. He walked over to Walter Jr. and looked at him; there were tears in his eyes.

"Junior, I'm tired, let's go home, let's go back to Texas."

Twenty-Four

I dreamed a dream

I had a dream my life would be
So different from this hell I'm living
So different now from what it seemed
Now life has killed the dream I dreamed

Music by Claude-Michael Schonberg
Words (French) by Alain Boublil
Words (English) by Herbert Kretzmer

THE JOURNEY

The phone in the kitchen rang; Beth ran to get it.

"Mom…?"

She didn't need to hear another word; she knew that voice as well as her own.

"Junior! Where are you? We've been worried sick!"

"I'm in California. Mom…I'm with Grandpa."

"Is he all right? Is he there? Put him on!"

Chris shook his head and waved his hands back and forth in front of his grandson's face.

"He can't talk, now, Mom. He's resting. We're in a motel in San Diego."

Walter Sr. entered the kitchen; he stood close to listen in.

"San Diego…the Bayside Motel!" Beth hollered into the phone. "What are you doing in San Diego? You get yourselves on a plane this instant, today!"

"I can't, Mom. I got a new car; I need to drive it home."

"Where did you get the money for a new car?"

"It's a long story, Mom. It was a gift."

"A gift! From whom?"

"Louise Langford, you know…the movie star."

"Junior…have you been taking drugs?"

"No, Mom. Believe me; I've got to drive the car back to Texas."

"Then you put your grandfather on a plane!"

"I don't think that's a good idea, Mom."

"Junior, you're going to give your mother a coronary. Do what I say!" Walter Jr. said nothing. She handed the phone to her husband. "Here, talk to your son!"

"Junior, this is your father. I'm going to wire you some money. I want you to get your grandfather to the airport and get him on a plane for Dallas. As soon as you get the ticket, I want you to call and tell us the flight number and time. We'll pick him up. Then I want you to get in that car and head home, immediately."

"But, Dad…?"

"I'll *butt* your head for you, if you don't do what I say. What are you trying to do, give your mother a coronary?"

"Okay, I'll call you right back."

Walter Jr. hung up and looked at his grandfather.

"I heard," said Chris, shrugging his shoulders. "I'll get ready."

After showering, Chris combed his hair, put on his clothes, and walked out.

"Bathroom's free," said Chris.

"Thanks, Grandpa."

Before Walter Jr. got up, there was a knock at the door.

"Who could that be?" asked Chris.

"Search me," Walter Jr. said, walking to the door. "Yes, who is it?"

A dark muffled voice came through the door. "Police Department, open up."

Walter Jr. looked to his grandfather for advice, who could only send a questioning look back. He opened the door. Two police officers were there.

"Walter Bouchard?" asked the officer.

"Yes."

"Is there a Christopher Goodman with you?"

"We haven't done anything!" Walter Jr. insisted.

"No one said you did."

Chris walked over. "That's me, officer."

"Mr. Goodman!" The officer's face broke out in a smile. "The entire state police force has been looking for you." He looked at Walter Jr., "Your mother was kind enough to call us and have the hunt called off. She told us where you're staying. We thanked her and promised to make sure Mr. Goodman, here, gets on the next plane to Texas."

"Oh," said Walter Jr., "Just give us a minute to get ready."

"No sweat."

"I'll have to stop at the telegraph office to get some money and then buy my grandfather an airfare ticket."

"That won't be necessary," said the officer. "Your mother said there would be money waiting for you at the telegraph office, and you can get it later. But first we get your grandfather on the next plane out. She's already bought a ticket by phone." The two officers backed away. "We'll just be out here if you need us."

Walter Jr. closed the door and looked to his grandfather. Chris picked up his small black bag in one hand and put Jimmy Gray Horse's hat on.

"Well, I'm ready."

****

The two police officers accompanied Chris and Walter Jr. into the airport terminal and to the boarding area. Camera flashes blinded them; a small group of news reporters crowded around.

"Mr. Goodman, why did you come to California?"

"What's this all about?" asked Chris.

"You're news, Mr. Goodman. You were last seen on a train platform with Louise Langford, and then you disappeared, reported missing; now you're found and on your way back to Texas. You're news, Mr. Goodman; tell us why you came to California."

"I was hoping to see the San Diego Zoo."

"What did you think of it, Mr. Goodman?"

"We never got to it."

"Are you friends with Louise Langford?"

"She's an extraordinarily beautiful and gracious lady; I'd feel privileged to be her friend."

"Mr. Goodman, there's a rumor that you came to California to get married. Is that true?"

"That's impossible, fellows, I'm already married."

"Our records don't show that, Mr. Goodman. Does she live with you in Texas?"

"No, she lives…"

"You'll have to excuse us, gentlemen. My grandfather will be late for his flight, if we don't hurry," said Walter Jr. as he took hold of his grandfather's arm and rushed him away from the reporters.

At the gate, before boarding, Chris and Walter Jr. said their farewells.

"It feels strange continuing the journey without you, Junior."

"It feels weird to me, too, Grandpa. Tell my mom not to worry; I'll be there as soon as I can."

Chris reached out and hugged his grandson. "I love you, Junior."

"I love you, too, Grandpa."

****

It was a small plane. Chris had a window seat. As they pulled away from the terminal, he waved. Chances were Walter Jr. wasn't watching, still, he waved good-bye just to be on the safe side. A large middle-aged man in a wrinkled dark blue suit sat next to him.

"Going to Dallas?" asked the man.

This seemed like an odd question to Chris, since it was a flight to Dallas. He answered politely just to be friendly. "Yes, I am."

"You from Texas?" asked the man.

"Born and bred."

"The name's Wittenberg, Harry T. Wittenberg. I'm in paper."

"Excuse me?"

"I'm in paper products. I fly out to Dallas twice a year to check on my clients, wine them and dine them, you know?"

The plane took off; Chris began swallowing to keep his ears clear, as the plane gained altitude.

"Great party town, Dallas," continued Harry.

"I wouldn't know; I live south of Dallas. I'm from Venus."

"How's that?"

"Venus, Texas, it's a small town just south of Dallas."

"Whew, you had me scared there, for a while. I thought maybe you were a nutcase, and I'd have to ask to be moved to another seat."

"Listen, Harry, I don't want to sound impolite. Maybe we can talk later; but right now I need to see my wife."

Chris closed his eyes and crossed his arms across his chest.

Harry tried to flag down the flight attendant.

****

When Chris woke in his dream on the island, he was alone on the beach. He saw Irene at the highest point on the island, waving for him to come up. He waved his arms for her to come to him. She ran down the path to him, smiling and laughing all the way. When she came close enough to see the stern look on his face, it worried her.

"Chris, what's wrong?"

"Why didn't you tell me?"

"Tell you what?" She thought for a moment, looking into his eyes. "Oh, you mean. . .you're in San Diego."

"Not any more. I'm sleeping on a flight back to Texas."

"Then you've visited me at Blue Jay?"

"Irene, we love each other, we're husband and wife, why didn't you tell me?"

"I tried to warn you. I tried to talk you out of visiting, but you wouldn't listen."

"I wanted to be with the woman I love. Is that so wrong?" He stopped, took hold of her and pulled her close. "I do love you, you know." They kissed gently. "Does that mean you're on this island constantly?"

"It's not so bad. I have you every night. Besides, old men sleep a lot."

They laughed, holding each other tight.

"Forgive me?" she asked.

"There's nothing to forgive." He backed off and took her by the hand. "Hungry? Let's collect some things to eat." They ran head on into waves, laughing.

They spent hours in the water, frolicking, and splashing each other. Now and then they'd feel a clam or an oyster under their feet, take a deep breath, go under to retrieve it, and then toss it onto the beach. When they gathered what they thought was enough, they returned to shore. Irene went to collect fruit, while Chris built a fire in the sand. He placed the shellfish on rocks close to the flames. The heat cooked them, forcing them open.

When Irene returned with her arms full, they sat close to each other and ate without saying a word, just smiling and kissing between bites. When they'd finished, the sun had set. The orange glow of the flames danced over their bodies, as they lay back in each other's arms, content. The waves crashing rhythmically against the shore, the crackle of the fire like castanets played offbeat, and the sound of their breathing filled their ears.

Suddenly, Irene sat up and placed her hand to her forehead.

"Sweetheart, are you all right?" asked Chris as he sat up and placed his hands on her shoulders.

"I feel so strange, weak, like I'm going to faint."

He went to put his arms around her, but they passed through her, as if she were vapor. She was fading away like a puff of smoke.

"Chris, they're disconnecting me from life support!" she cried.

He felt so helpless; there was nothing he could do other than watch her grow fainter till she was nothing more than a whisper.

"Chris, husband, if there is anything beyond this island, I'll be waiting there for you!" It was the last thing she said to him.

"If there is anything beyond this island, I will come to you!" he shouted. He could only hope she heard his words. "Irene! Nooooo!"

****

"Irene! Nooooo!"

"Hey, buddy, are you okay?"

Chris opened his eyes. It took him a moment to remember where he was, seated in a plane bound for Texas.

"You all right, old fellow? You must have been having a nightmare."

Chris looked into the man's eyes, and then remembered his name – Harry.

"What you need is a drink," said Harry, waving at the attendant.

"Just water, please," said Chris.

"You sure you don't want anything stronger? You're shaking like a leaf," said Harry.

Chris gulped his water and handed the cup back. He turned on his side and stared out the window at the clouds.

Harry ordered another drink for himself. Sipping his drink, he gently placed his hand on Chris' shoulder.

"There, there, old-timer, it was only a dream. Nothing to get so upset about; dreams aren't real."

Chris knew Harry meant well, although he knew how wrong he was. "I wish you were right," whispered Chris, mostly to himself. "But you see I know better. . .sadly."

****

Chris' legs felt weak. He had trouble walking; Harry helped him from the plane into the terminal. Chris looked up to see Beth running to him. She wrapped both arms tightly around him and buried her face into the side of his head – she was crying.

"Oh, Daddy, we were so worried." She blubbered all over him.

"Good to have you back, Pop," said Walter Sr., standing behind her.

Beth looked at Harry. "Is he all right?"

"I couldn't say. I assume so."

"Walter, give the man a tip."

"That's not necessary; I don't work for the airlines."

"A measly dollar, Walter? The man takes care of my father, and all you give him is a dollar? How does that make me look?" She looked at Harry, again. "You'll have to forgive my husband; he don't get out much."

Walter handed Harry a twenty. "You really don't have to." Harry realized there was no way out. He stuck it in his top pocket, and stared into Chris' eyes, as he walked away. "You take it easy, now, Chris. Good luck." He said it with deep sincerity, as he took one last glance at Beth, and then walked off, getting lost in the crowd.

"Oh, Daddy, I'm so glad you're home safe!" She took hold of him, again. The flash of a camera brightened the entire area. A reporter holding pen and pad walked with them.

"So, Mr. Goodman, why did you run away from home?"

"I didn't run; I haven't been able to run in thirty years."

"Well, not run, then, why'd you leave home?"

"It was the only way I could get someplace else.

"That someplace else was San Diego. What's in San Diego?"

"They've got one pip of a zoo."

"What did you think of it?"

"Couldn't say; never got around to it."

"Gentlemen, my father has been through a lot for a man his age. He's hungry and tired. So if you'd please excuse us." She shot a glance at her husband. "Walter, get the car; we'll wait right here."

****

It's an hour ride from Dallas Airport to Venus. Chris remained silent all the way. Familiar sights flew past, not registering in his mind.

"We're having your favorite for dinner tonight, honey ham," said Beth.

"That'll be nice, thank you," replied Chris.

"Your room is just the way you left it. It'll be good to be home again, to sleep in your own bed."

"Yes, that would be nice. I need to sleep. I want so much to get plenty of sleep."

"Sleep would be good for you, Daddy; after all you've been through."

"Beth, do you still have my sleeping pills?"

"Yes, of course, why?"

"I just want to sleep as much as I can."

"Well you know what the nurse said; I'm to keep your pills for you. You'll get one pill and one pill only at night when you need it."

Chris said nothing more during the drive home. He spoke little and ate only a few bites at dinner.

"Thank you, Beth, it was very good. Now may I have my sleeping pill? I'm tired and I'd like to go to bed."

"Of course, Daddy." She grabbed her pocketbook, rummaged through it till she came up with a small plastic container. She fished one pill out and handed it to her father. He swallowed it with a gulp of iced tea.

"Thank you, again. Now, if you'll excuse me. I'd like to go to my room."

"Goodnight, Daddy," said Beth.

"Goodnight, Dad," Walter Sr. mumbled.

****

When Chris woke in his dream on the island, he was aware of being alone, more alone than he'd ever felt in his life. He could see her running down the beach in his mind's eye. He could feel her skin against his body, her form in his hands, the taste of her lips, the scent of her hair. except it was all memory, a dream within a dream.

Chris wasted no time and got right down to business. He laid the temple manuscript out and began to reproduce the symbols in the wet sand with his finger. Over and over he did this. Taking a handful of seawater, pouring it over the sand to erase what he had done, and starting again from the beginning. Each night for an entire week, every night in his sleep, till one night he woke, went from his bed to his desk and wrote down what he remembered on a piece of paper. He examined his handiwork, carefully. It was a perfect copy. Now, his next problem was to get it translated. Where would he go; who could do this for him?

****

Saturday morning Walter Jr. pulled up into the driveway. Apart from a hug and a kiss from his mother and a handshake from his father, who both were clearly relieved to have him back safe, there was no fanfare. Inwardly, Chris' spirit soared to see his grandson again. They hugged for a long time.

"Are you all right, Junior?" Chris whispered.

"Fine, Grandpa, just fine. How are you?"

"She's gone, Junior. Irene's gone."

"They did it, didn't they, they disconnected her?"

Chris couldn't speak; he only nodded.

****

That night, after dinner, Chris asked Walter Jr. to his room, to show him something. He took a slip of paper out of his desk and handed it to him.

"What's all this, Grandpa?"

"It's a copy of a manuscript I found in a temple offshore from the island; I copied it from memory. I believe it's the same manuscript Gilbert, Marion's boyfriend, found in their icy world. I believe that hidden somewhere in this writing are the secrets of our dreams."

"But look what happened to Gilbert;" warned Walter Jr., "He killed himself. Whatever it is he found was too much for him to bear. What makes you think you can do any better?"

"I don't; but I have to take that chance. There's got to be a way. It can't end this way, Junior, it just can't" Chris' voice cracked as he spoke.

"It's okay, Grandpa; we'll figure it out." He held the slip of paper to the light. "What kind of writing is this, anyway?"

"Well, we found it in Solomon's temple, or at least a replica of it, you know, the king from the Bible? I can only guess it's ancient Hebrew."

"Where are we going to find someone who knows ancient Hebrew?"

"I don't know; a Rabbi, I guess. Where's the nearest synagogue?"

"I'm not sure; I can look it up on the internet." Chris followed Walter Jr. to his room, where he went to his computer and typed in: "Synagogues in Texas." They were both surprised at the number that came up.

"Wow, I never realized how many Jews must live in Texas," Walter Jr. exclaimed. He scrolled down. "Here you go. Temple Emmanuel in Coal Town, Texas, that's the closest, just thirty miles from here."

"Great," said Chris, patting his grandson on the back. "Let's call them in the morning."

Twenty-Five

I dream too much

I dream too much, but if I dream too much
I can only dream to touch your heart again
I close my eyes to see your hand,
Your smile, your joy in loving me

We dance and sing, we steal a touch of spring
I dream of everything we two have known,
Perhaps I dream too much alone
Um-m-m-m
Perhaps I dream too much alone

Music by Jerome Kern
Words by Dorothy Fields

AFTER THE JOURNEY

Chris waited till everyone in the house was busy and the kitchen was all his. He dialed the number Walter Jr. wrote on a slip of paper for him. It rang four times, and then a message played. The deep gruff voice of an old man announced, "You've reach the Temple Emanuel in Coal Town, Texas. No one is able to take your call at this time. Please leave a message." Chris readied himself, although before he could say a word an electronic woman coldly broadcasted, "Sorry, this mailbox is full."

Twice a day for three days, Chris tried to phone Temple Emanuel only to hear the same two messages.

"If the bear went over the mountain, then the mountain will come to him," said Chris.

"That don't sound right, Grandpa," said Walter Jr., "But you're right; we need to take a ride to Coal Town."

With that they planned a day trip. They packed sandwiches, fried pies – peach, and a thermos of sweet iced tea, and drove off early the next morning. Walter Jr. told his mother he was taking his grandfather with him for a ride in the country. He promised to stay glued to the old man, and told her not to worry; they'd be home before dinner.

****

There is no coal in Coal Town, Texas; there never was. It was a lie, a lie told by a man named Vernon Underwood, a businessman who prayed on the misfortune of others. However, to understand the story of Underwood and Coal Town, Texas, it is important to know the story of Thurber, Texas – the true Texas coal town.

Near the end of the nineteenth century, the two Johnson brothers, William Whipple and Harvey, discovered large coal deposits forty miles west of Fort Worth. They made a deal with the Texas & Pacific Railway Company to supply all their coal needs. The mining got off to a quick start, yet ended abruptly because of labor disputes with the miner's union. By 1888 the mines closed. The Johnson brothers sold the mines to a group of eastern investors, lead by Colonel Robert Dickey, who formed the Texas & Pacific Coal Company. They sealed a new deal with the railway, bypassed the union and hired workers from other states and finally other countries. The population grew quickly, houses sprung up, then shops, schools, and churches. The town of Thurber, Texas was born.

Unfortunately, after the turn of the century, railways switched from coal to oil. Mining slowed and then finally stopped. The town of Thurber died a quick but painful death, becoming a ghost town overnight. The workers left by the droves, seeking work in the oil fields nearby. The last miners to seek employment at the mines of Thurber were Russian Jews, some one hundred families who had scrimped and saved to travel from their Mother Russia to work the mines of Texas. Now they were out of work, broke, and homeless in a strange land – most couldn't speak a word of English. This is where Vernon Underwood enters the picture.

Underwood bought property south of Dallas. He went to Thurber and offered work to the stranded Russian Jewish community. He promised them work in coal mines, which is what they knew. He'd named the area Coal Town, Texas, to make it sound more appealing. He promised them homes, and to sweeten the deal, he pledged they would have a synagogue.

When they arrived, they found small wooden shacks for their homes, a pitiful wooden structure for a synagogue and no mines. Underwood had erected a large building setup for meatpacking with an adjoining slaughterhouse. He knew, if he'd offered them such work they never would have accepted. Now, they had no other choice.

However, Underwood miscalculated and underestimated the competition. The slaughterhouses and meatpacking companies of the Fort Worth Stockyards had far easier access to the railways. Within ten years, Underwood was forced to close. Many of the workers took what little money they'd saved and headed for parts unknown. Yet some stayed and tried their hand at farming and dairy farming. The town never flourished, nevertheless, it has survived. Now, it is a small community of second and third generation Russian Jews. Few know how or why their ancestors came and settled in such a faraway land, and how Coal Town, Texas, the town without a single lump of coal, got its name.

****

Coming off the highway, Walter Jr. drove slowly as they entered downtown Coal Town. It was no more than eight square blocks and the streets were empty, as were many of the storefronts. The wind blew puffs of dust and dirt down the street. A stray dog barked, as he ran after tumbleweed rolling down the main thoroughfare.

Chris looked out the window and sighed. "Not very promising, is it?"

"It's seen better days, that's for sure," Walter Jr. said. "Say, there's somebody; let's ask him."

He stopped the car and rolled down the window. A tall, lanky middle-aged man, in need of a shave, dressed in blue jeans and a ragged old cowboy shirt, no more prosperous looking than his surroundings, looked in the car.

"Excuse, me," said Walter Jr., "Could you tell us where we might find the synagogue?"

"The what?" asked the man in a slow Texas drawl.

"The Jewish temple, Temple Emanuel?"

"Oh, that thing," he said pointing and swinging his arm in a large curve. "That's that building with funny writing on it. You just go right around this here corner, you can't miss it. But it ain't open anymore; been boarded up for years. Say, you wouldn't have any change on you, you could spare?"

Walter Jr. fished fifty cents out of the ashtray and handed it over. Chris gave him a sandwich and a fried pie.

"Much obliged," said the man.

As they pulled away, Walter Jr. could see him in the rearview mirror. He stood on the corner, eating his fried pie.

The building stood on a corner lot. It was old; the gray stone was without luster with smudges of black soot. The windows and doors were boarded shut with faded wooden planks. The stone-carved Star of David above the entrance was barely visible. Weeds shot up through the cracks in the cement walkway. Not one blade of grass remained, only the familiar brown Texas dust. Chris walked to the cornerstone and ran his finger along the engraved date.

"Nineteen-o-eight, before my time," he said, sounding grateful.

Walter Jr. looked at the small two story house, seemingly on the same property.

"Let's see if anybody lives next door."

Walter Jr. held onto his grandfather's arm, when he heard the front steps screech under their feet; the front porch sang the same song. There was no doorbell. He was just about to knock on the door, when the sound of a car coming to a halt made them turn. A middle-aged man with salt and pepper hair, thick black glasses, and a wrinkled gray suit – his tie loosened at the collar – stepped out of the car. He stood with one foot still in the car, the other in the street. He rested one hand on the car roof, the other on the door.

"Can I help you, gentlemen?"

"We were wondering if the person who lives here has anything to do with the synagogue," Walter Jr. replied.

"Wait there," said the man, stepping away from the car, slamming the door. He came up on the porch. "This synagogue's been closed for years."

"We figured that," said Walter Jr., "We were hoping someone here could help us."

"My father was the Rabbi years ago. He still lives here. I just came to check on him." His eyes darted at them. "What do you want with him?"

Chris pulled a piece of paper from his pocket, unfolded it, and handed it to the man. "We were hoping someone could translate this for us." It was a copy of the manuscript.

The man held it, examined it for a moment, and then snickered. "Who do you think I am...Moses? Just because I was born Jewish doesn't mean I can read this junk."

"Well, maybe your father can?" asked Chris.

"My father's old and sickly. I don't want him disturbed." He started to hand the paper back, but Chris pushed it back.

"Please, let your father see it. My name and number is on the bottom. Please, it's important to me."

The man found it hard to deny the old man to his face. He took the slip of paper, entered the house, and slammed the door behind him.

****

That evening when the family was having dinner, the phone rang. Beth rose and answered it.

"Yes...yes...who is this? Who? Yes, he's here...one moment." She held the phone to her chest and looked at Walter Sr., "It's for Daddy," she said, sounding surprised. She looked at her father. "Daddy, it's for you." Chris looked at Walter Jr., then got up and put the phone to his ear.

"Yes...yes, this is Mr. Goodman. Who is this? Oh, thank you for getting back with me. You what? When? Yes, that would be fine. Yes, of course. Whatever time is good for you...ten in the morning? That would be fine. Thank you, again. Goodnight, Rabbi Zaslavsky." Chris hung up.

Beth still stood next to him. "Rabbi...how do you know a Rabbi? He's not an old friend; you have no old friends."

"He's doing a favor for me."

"A favor, what kind of favor?"

"That's between Rabbi Zaslavsky and me."

Beth's eyebrows went up; this did not sit well with her. "And what's all this ten in the morning business?"

"He's invited me to his home, tomorrow. Junior can drive me."

"He can, can he?"

"Sure, Mom; I'd be glad to," Walter Jr. said.

Chris sat down and returned to his dinner. Beth stood looking at her husband for support. His head twisted slightly, his jaw dropped, as his shoulder shrugged up.

"What? What?" he questioned helplessly.

"Oh, never mind," huffed Beth, sitting down again.

****

Their footsteps and the groans of the old dry planks that made up the front porch announced their approach.

"Come in, the door's open," announced a deep gravely voice from inside.

Chris and Walter entered. The house was dark and musky smelling. They stood in a small living room; the furniture was well-worn and old fashioned. An upright piano flanked the far wall. Aged yellowed lace doilies covered nearly every flat surface.

"In here," the voice called out from an adjoining room.

They entered slowly. Sitting up in bed was an elderly gentleman. His hair and long beard were white. His skin was pale and spotted. He was a large man, dressed in flannel pajamas, like a vision of Santa Claus after the sparkle left his eyes. From the smell of the room and the look of him, they knew this was no ordinary bed – this was a deathbed.

"You must be Mr. Goodman?" he said. "I'm Isak Zaslavsky."

"Yes, I'm Chris Goodman," said Chris, moving bedside. The two old men shook hands. "And this is my grandson, Walter." Walter Jr. smiled and nodded.

"Nice looking boy," remarked Isak. "You've met my son, Gregory. I'm sorry for the way he spoke to you. I heard it all from the window. It's just his way. He's angry that I won't move in with him and his wife, he's angry he lives in this town, he's even angry he's a Jew and his father is a Rabbi." He shook his head. "At least I used to be the Rabbi; it's been years."

Chris and Walter Jr. stood silently listening. Isak reached across his bed and grabbed the slip of paper. He examined it slowly and then held it towards Chris.

"About this," he said, shaking his head again, wearing a small whimsical smile. "Amazing. . .amazing."

"Then you've translated it?" asked Chris.

"Yes I have. And first may I thank you for allowing me to see it? It's changed my life. Thank you."

"I don't understand," said Chris.

"You don't understand any of it, do you?" He let the paper rest in his lap; the smile left him. "You see, Mr. Goodman, I'm not a well man; in fact I'm dying. I've always been a man of faith, strong faith. But there isn't a man who sometime in his life has doubts. This manuscript has removed any trace of doubt I may ever have had. It's all so clear, now. I can die in peace. Thank you. Tell me where you got it."

"I know this sounds foolish," Chris said, "but I found it in a dream."

"That doesn't sound foolish at all. In fact, once you know what it says, you'd understand it can only come from a dream."

"And what does it say?" asked Chris shyly and politely.

Isak reached for a slip of paper on his nightstand. "This is a translation of the manuscript. It is yours under one condition."

"What is that?"

"That you never share it with anyone, especially the young man." He pointed at Walter Jr., as he said this. "The world isn't ready for this. It's best the innocent stay innocent. Promise me this."

"I promise."

He handed the paper to Chris, who read it silently. His eyes grew wide. "I see what you mean," he said softly. Walter Jr. felt tempted to look over his grandfather's shoulder. Chris folded the paper and slipped it in his pocket.

"Young man," Isak addressed Walter Jr., "would you be kind enough to fetch me a glass of water from the kitchen?" When Walter Jr. left the room, he whispered to Chris. "I advise you to memorize the manuscript as fast as you can and then destroy it."

"I understand. I will."

Walter Jr. returned and handed the glass to Isak. "Thank you, young man." The old man took one sip and placed it on the nightstand. "Now, if you'll both forgive me; I'm tired, and I'd like to be alone, now."

"Of course," said Chris. "Do you need anything before we go?"

"Thank you; I'll be fine. My son will stop by later. Once more, thank you for the honor."

"The honor is all mine," said Chris.

As they headed for the door, Chris turned one last time and waved good-bye.

"Mr. Goodman," said Isak. "There is one other thing I'd ask of you."

"Anything," said Chris.

"Pray for me."

****

That night when Chris woke in his dream on the island, he was alone. He wanted to cry out for Irene, out of habit, out of desperation. He stood on the beach looking up the shoreline, first right and then left. He looked out at the blue sea, its waves crashing white. He felt the cool spray on his face and smelled the salt in the air, the wind blowing his young man's hair. It felt so real, as real as the waking world or perhaps more so. Indeed, his loneliness was real. Yet he didn't feel hopeless. Everything had changed since reading the translated manuscript. It would take time, except he knew he was no longer helpless.

He looked at his gripped hand. He concentrated. A copy of the translated manuscript appeared in his hand, because he willed it so. He held it firm and smiled. He closed his eyes tightly, concentrated as hard as he could. He disappeared.

****

When Chris opened his eyes again he was standing on the shore of a large lake. It was frozen solid. His bare feet sank into the four inches of snow; shooting pain, near to a burning sensation, engulfed his feet. He wrapped his arms around himself trying to protect his half-naked body from the wintry wind. He laughed at himself for not anticipating the weather and not preparing for it. Yet it didn't bother him. He willed it, and the next moment he was clothed in heavy hiking boots, thick insulated pants and jacket, gloves, hat, earmuffs, and goggles. He folded the manuscript and tucked it in his pocket.

He could see the chalet on a mountainside, far off in the distance. The shortest distance would be to walk straight ahead over the frozen lake. He placed one foot on the ice and pressed all his weight down.

"It could hold an elephant up," he said aloud.

He began walking forward across the ice. The surface was slippery; he nearly fell twice. Then he envisioned spikes on the soles of his boots, and they appeared. He had no trouble walking after that.

At the foot of the mountain, Chris looked up at the chalet. It was only a quarter mile up, however the climb was steep. He willed a walking stick and it materialized in his hand. His dream-world made the ascent easy.

Chris tapped on the front door lightly; there was no sound. He tried again, harder – nothing.

"Marion, open up."

He tried the door handle, it opened easily. Inside was dark, only the light from a window on the far side of the room made the silhouette of Marion visible. He walked over slowly. She sat staring out the window at a far-off mountain. She was younger and more slender than when they meet in the waking world, except she was pale, her hair was unkempt, and her eyes were red from crying.

"Marion, it's me, Chris Goodman, you remember, from the library? I was the old man who wanted to know about raft making; I was there with my grandson. Marion, look at me."

She turned her head slowly, as if in a trance and just obeying orders.

"I know I look a lot different from what you remember, but so do you." He smiled, trying to make her smile, however, she looked right through him. He took the manuscript from his pocket, unfolded it, and tried handing it to her. She made no response. Finally, he took hold of her hand and placed the slip of paper in it.

"Here, take this, Marion. It's what Gil found in the cave not far from here. Death took him before he could learn its meaning and power. Take it, Marion. Read it, memorize it, and use it. It doesn't have to end this way; this isn't the way it has to be. This is your dream, Marion, your dream; only you can change it."

Slowly she looked at the manuscript.

"That's right Marion. It'll tell you everything you need to know. You *will* see your Gil again, if you only believe."

She perked up and paid attention.

"Gil?" she whispered.

"That's right, Marion; you can see Gil, again. Nothing's stopping you. This is your dream; dream it!" He bent low and kissed her forehead. "I've got to go now, Marion. You take care. Remember, this is your dream; dream it."

****

When he opened his eyes, he was back on his island. He laughed because he'd forgotten to transform his clothes; he was still wearing his winter gear. The tropical sun beat down on him. He willed them gone and he was back in his usual loincloth. He built a fire and prepared for the coming night. He was alone, although he knew not for long.

He sprawled out on the sand, his hands interlocked behind his head, and he gazed up at the stars.

"Anything can happen in a dream," he whispered.

Twenty-Six

It's a dream, only a dream

It's a dream
Only a dream
And it's fading now
Fading away
It's only a dream
Just a memory without anywhere to stay

Music and Words by Neil Young

AFTER THE JOURNEY

Walter Jr. pulled up the driveway and parked in front of the garage. His mother was on her knees planting Sweet Williams in her garden. She looked up at him, and still holding the spade, she ran her hand across her forehead to wipe away the sweat.

"Your Grandpa's inside; he wants to see you," she said in a matter-of-fact tone.

"Thanks," said Walter Jr., taking two steps at a time up the back stoop.

When the screened door slammed, she called out after him. "And don't go running off. Your father will be home soon. We're fixin' to eat as soon as he gets here."

Inside, Walter Jr. found his grandfather and a middle-aged man in a suit seated in the kitchen. There were official looking papers sprawled all over the table.

"Sit down, Junior," said Chris, pointing to a chair.

"What's this all about, Grandpa?"

"Mr. Carson will explain."

The man stood up and shook hands with Walter Jr., "Nice to meet you, Walter." He pointed to the chair, too. "Sit down, Walter, sit down."

"Mr. Carson is my lawyer," said Chris. "I've asked him here today. I want to make some changes in my will."

Walter Jr. remained silent, listening.

"Junior," continued Chris. "I'm writing you out of my will."

Walter Jr. looked at his grandfather, a little confused and shocked. "Grandpa, I don't understand."

"It's for your own good," said Chris. "If I remember correctly, the deal you made with Dave, your brother, is when I die he gets whatever I leave to you. Well, now he'll get nothing because when I die, you get nothing. I want you to have your inheritance now."

"Here you go, Walter," said Mr. Carson, handing him a check.

"Twenty-thousand dollars…!" Walter Jr. exclaimed.

"I wish it were more," said Chris.

"Grandpa, I don't know what to say."

"Just promise me you won't spend it foolishly; but I don't want you to let it burn a hole in your pocket, either. You're a smart boy; just think before you leap."

****

After Mr. Carson left, Walter Jr. and Chris sat alone at the kitchen table. Walter Jr. stared at the check.

"Grandpa, you shouldn't have."

"Of course I should. I aint' going to take it with me, or so they say." He reached across the table and placed his hand on his grandson's. "Besides, Junior," he hesitated a moment. "I love you and I'm proud of you." Chris took a paper napkin and blew his nose. "Now don't say anything more or you'll have me getting all misty." He stood up. "Come on, follow me; I've got something else I want to give you."

Walter Jr. followed his grandfather out the backdoor, passed his mother who ignored them both, and then inside the garage. Chris flipped the light switch. There was no mistaking what his grandfather wanted to show him. Against the wall was a large metal machine with switches, dials, and long thick black wires stemming from it.

"It's an arc welder," said Chris. "I was a jim-dandy welder when I was young. I'm going to teach you how to weld." Chris held his palms toward Walter Jr. in a halting motion. "Now don't get me wrong. I'm not saying you have to be a welder. But it's a good trade to fall back on, if your plans are running slow." He pointed to something under the workbench. "Pull out that box, Junior. I got us a heap of scrape metal to practice on." He took up the two welding helmets on the workbench and handed one to his grandson.

****

For the next three weeks they spent most of their time in the garage. Chris showed Walter Jr. every trick he knew about welding. Till one day, Walter Jr. held two pieces of metal he'd just welded for his grandfather to inspect.

Chris smiled. "Well, it had to happen sooner or later. The student has surpassed the teacher. You got a knack for this, son. I'm proud of you. You keep at it; there won't be a welder in Texas who could hold a candle to you."

"It is good, isn't it?" Walter Jr. remarked with pride, looking over his own handiwork. "Say, Grandpa, I really appreciate what you've done for me. I don't know how I can thank you."

"Hearing you say that is thanks enough. Now you keep practicing. There's something I've got to go do. You don't need me anymore."

Walter Jr. took two pieces of metal and clamped them together. Chris stood in the doorway.

"Junior, I want you to know I love you very much."

"I love you, too, Grandpa," said Walter Jr. as he lowered his helmet, and the garage filled with the blue light, as the welding stick touched the metal.

Beth was in the backyard on her knees, tending her garden. She looked up to see her father standing over her.

"Beth, when was the last time I told you I love you?"

She went into a blank stare, calculating the years. "I guess the last time was when Mama died."

"I'm sorry I haven't said it more recently and more often. You turned into a fine woman, a good wife, and a good mother; and I'm proud of you. I love you very much."

"I love you too, Daddy."

"I'm going to my room to lie down. I need to sleep."

"You have a good lie down, Daddy. Walter's working late. Dinner won't be for a few hours. I'll wake you."

Beth's pocketbook was on the kitchen table. A small plastic bottle containing his sleeping pill prescription rested at the top of her belongings. He took the bottle.

"I need to sleep."

****

When Chris woke in his dream on the island, he knew what he had to do. With determination, he started along the shoreline to the far side of the island. The cave where they hide during the storm was easy to find. The matches and the candle were again at the mouth of the cave. He lit the candle, and with his hand shielding the flame he slowly made his way. When he came to the large opening, the main hall, he looked around; it was as he remembered it. He walked to the far wall. The chiseled markings were still there; only now there was one major difference.

The two lines of symbols, one telling of Irene's life story and one of his, both ending at the symbol of the island were exactly as he remembered them. Only now, Irene's lifeline had a symbol after the chiseled drawing of the island. There, now, was a chiseled drawing of a grave, signifying her death.

Tilting the candle slightly, he let fall a few drops of hot wax on top of a waist-high rock, placed the bottom of the candle on the hot wax and waited for it to cool. He let go and the candle was freestanding. He found the chisel and mallet on the ground where he'd dropped them. Right next to the symbol of Irene's grave, he chiseled the symbol of another island; this one was three times larger than the original island symbol. Then he chiseled a line from the symbol of Irene's grave to the drawing of the new larger island.

On his lifeline between the representation of the island and this new island, he chiseled an exact copy of her grave– his grave. As soon as he completed the drawing, he felt his body grow limp and weak. He knew what was happening. In the waking-world, he was dying. He had to act fast.

He chiseled a line from his grave to the drawing of the new island. His life-strength was leaving him faster, now. He stood in front of the carved picture of the old island. He lifted the chisel and mallet and began to erase it from his lifeline and Irene's.

The ground under his feet started to rumble; earthquake sounds filled the air. With each blow of the mallet, chips of stone flew from the wall. The picture of the old island began to disappear, as did the island around him. Rocks and stones fell from the ceiling of the cave, the earth opened up, swallowing itself. The whole world vibrated as if bombs were being dropped. He felt his life force nearly gone. With one final blow of the mallet, the lines of the old island were gone. The candle fell to the ground; everything went black.

****

Walter Jr. lightly tapped on the bedroom door.

"Grandpa, dinner's ready."

Nothing, no sound

He wrapped a little harder.

"Grandpa, are you awake?

Again, there was nothing, no sound.

He slowly opened the door and looked in. His grandfather was lying, face up, eyes closed on his bed.

"Wake up, Grandpa, it's time for dinner."

He walked to the bedside and gently shook his grandfather's shoulder.

"Come on, Grandpa, time to get up."

He started to worry. He placed his hand on his grandfather's; there was no warmth in the touch.

"Mama…!"

****

The ambulance siren got all the dogs in the neighborhood barking. People pulled back their curtains and peered out their windows. Beams of red and white lights from the police car cherry-top swam across the front of the house. Holding toolboxes of medical supplies, the paramedics raced through the house to the bedroom.

Walter Sr. stood in the doorway; Walter Jr. positioned himself behind the paramedics, looking over their shoulders; Beth stood at the foot of the bed, crying into her apron.

"Sorry, ma'am, I'm afraid he's gone," said the paramedic as he removed the stethoscope from Chris' chest.

"Why…why?" cried Beth.

"It's just old age, ma'am. It just happens."

She ran over to the nightstand and picked up the bottle of sleeping pills. "You don't think he…?"

The paramedic examined the prescription bottle. "Was this his?"

"I never allowed him to touch them. I'd give him one and one only before he went to sleep. You don't think he…?" Again she couldn't get the words out.

"I couldn't say, ma'am, not without an autopsy. But I'll tell you this. I've seen my share of overdoses, and it ain't pretty. He looks too much at peace, if you ask me." He took hold of the edge of the sheet. "You want me to cover him up, ma'am?"

Beth nodded. He placed the sheet over Chris' face.

"If we can go into another room, ma'am, there's some paperwork you need to fill out," said the paramedic. They all started out the door. Beth was just leaving when she turned in the doorway to see Walter Jr. still standing next to the bed.

"You coming, Junior?" she asked her son.

He emptied the sleeping pills into the palm of his hand.

"Mama, when did you fill this prescription?"

"Just today, that's a new bottle. Why?"

He looked at her with tears in his eyes. "The bottle says the count is thirty. There are thirty pills here, mama."

Twenty-Seven

I've dreamed of you

I've dreamed of you, always feeling you were there
And all my life, I have searched for you everywhere
I caught your smile in the morning sun
I heard your whisper on the breeze at night
I prayed one day that your arms would hold me tight
And just when I thought love had passed me by
We met

Come dream with me
As I have dreamed of you
All my life

Music & Words by Rolf U. Lovland &
Ann Hampton Callaway

A NEW JOURNEY

Walter Jr. rang the doorbell of 196 at the Emerald Isle Apartments. The door opened, Sandy stood in the doorway. Her beauty took him aback with her hair long, wavy, reddish-brown, her green eyes smiling. She wore a green dress with a paisley print and a thin gold belt that set off her figure.

"You're early, I like that," she said.

"I couldn't wait," Walter Jr. said.

"I like that, too. Just let me get my shawl. Those restaurants always get too cold for me."

He walked a step ahead of her, hurrying to get the passenger-side door for her.

"You don't mind being seen in a pickup truck, do you?" he asked.

"Don't be silly. This is Texas. The only thing better is being on horseback."

She read the sign on the side of the truck door, "Goodman's Welding Company. Walter, I thought you said your name was Bouchard?"

"It is. I named the company in honor of my grandfather. He's the one who taught me how to weld."

"Is he the same grandfather who told you a true woman wants caring and truthfulness in a man more than wealth or looks?"

"You've got a good memory."

"Certain things are hard to forget. That night you bought me a drink at Johnny Friendly's bar, all those months ago, you were so honest. Telling me you didn't have a job or money and that you lived with your folks; that shows character. That's why I gave you my number. You don't think I give it out to just anyone?"

They drove off and onto the highway going north.

"So, where are we going?"

"Dallas, we've got reservations at The Mansion."

"The Mansion, I'm impressed."

"Good, that was my intention."

She rolled the window down. The breeze rippled her hair like red ocean waves. Walter Jr. found it hard to watch the road.

The Dallas skyline appeared off in the distance. The sun was setting behind Fort Worth far off to the west. Large billowy clouds glowed bright pink and orange in the paling sky, as the last of the sun's rays reflected off the metal and glass buildings of downtown Dallas.

The valet held the truck door for Walter Jr. who ran around to the other side of the truck to get the door for Sandy. She slipped her hand into the crook of his arm, as they entered. He felt good; he felt tall.

They were ushered to a romantic table off in a quiet corner. The waiter handed her a bouquet of flowers.

"These are from the gentleman," he said, nodding to Walter Jr., smiling.

"Walter…" she was speechless.

Once seated, the waiter handed Walter Jr. a wine list.

"Any preferences?" he asked Sandy.

"No, whatever you select."

He held the wine list to the waiter and pointed to something in French.

"We'll have a bottle of champagne."

"Oh Walter, make it pink!"

"Pink champagne," Walter Jr. added.

****

Some places seem familiar, more comfortable than other places, as do people. When everything fits into place, they say it fits like a glove. Sandy and Walter Jr. fit like a glove. It's interesting, when a man's attracted to a woman's beauty; through that path he becomes interesting in her. When a woman finds a man interesting, she becomes attracted to him. Either way, the result is the same. The night went too fast and ended too soon for both their liking.

During the drive back to Venus, Sandy sat closer to Walter Jr., not overly familiar or pushy, but comfortable and friendly.

"You're losing the race," said Sandy.

"How's that?" he asked, sounding confused.

"The moon," she said, pointing out his window at the sky. The full moon was low in the night heavens, shining bright and yellow. It was huge, taking up a quarter of the horizon. It hung in the sky a foot in front of them. It seemed to be racing alongside the truck.

He looked straight ahead and gripped the steering wheel tighter. "That's because the moon has an unfair advantage. It doesn't have to follow the speed limit, and it's not afraid of getting a ticket. Just give me five minutes, I'll outrace it."

She pointed directly at it. "Look, you can see his face; you can see the man in the moon."

"That's not a man," said Walter Jr., "Anything that beautiful has got to be a woman."

"Listen to you," she smiled. "Aren't you the romantic?" She began to sing. "*Racing with the moon*...isn't that a song? Who sang that?"

"Darn if I know." He reached over and switched on the radio. "You like music?"

The sweet harmonies of the *Everly Brothers* oozed out of the radio's four inch speaker and filled the truck cab.

"Oh! That's one of my favorites! Sing with me, Walter."

"I can't sing."

"Of course you can."

"*Drea-ea-ea-ea-eam, dream, dream, dream*
Drea-ea-ea-ea-eam, dream, dream, dream
When I want you in my arms
When I want you and all your charms
Whenever I want you, all I have to do is
Drea-ea-ea-ea-eam, dream, dream, dream

When I feel blue in the night
And I need you to hold me tight
Whenever I want you, all I have to do is
Drea-ea-ea-ea-eam"

Just then, the road, which they traveled south on veered to the right, going west to Venus.

"Look, Walter, you were right, you're winning."

With each eighth of a mile, the moon pulled farther back till it was behind them.

Outside Sandy's apartment, they stood face-to-face.

"Do you understand women, Walter?"

"I haven't the slightest clue."

"Well, here's something that should make it even more confusing for you. As a woman, I may or may not kiss you goodnight, but if you don't at least try, I'll be very disappointed."

He grabbed hold of her arms, pulled her a few inches closer, and kissed her quickly and lightly,

She sighed. "That was sweet. . .like you." She opened the apartment door and stood in the doorway. Walter Jr. walked slowly backwards down the walkway to his truck.

"Can I call you again?" he asked.

"I'd be very disappointed if you didn't."

He backed up against the truck.

"Sandy?"

"Yes, Walter?"

"I waited all those months till I got my life together. So many times I wanted to call, but I waited for the right time. I'm glad I finally called you."

"Me, too, Walter; but I knew you would."

"You did? How?"

"The other night, the day before you called, I had a dream and you were in it."

"Really?"

"Really. Goodnight, Walter."

"Goodnight, Sandy."

****

Driving home, the moon was directly in front of him. It took up half the sky and lit the entire night world a soft gold. He began to sing.

"Drea-ea-ea-ea-eam, dream, dream, dream."

THE END

Michael Edwin Q. is available for book interviews and personal appearances. For more information visit michaeledwinq.com

Other Titles in this series by Michael Edwin Q:

Born A Colored Girl: 978-1-59755-478-4
Pappy Moses' Peanut Plantation: 978-1-59755-482-8
But Have Not Love: 978-1-59755-494-7
Tame the Savage Heart: 978-1-59755-5098
A Slaves Song: 978-1-59755-527-5
Fancy: 978-1-59755-540-1
Wistful: 978-1-59755-563-0
Winnie: 978-1-59755-600-2
Sisters: 978-1-59755-641-5
Death in Savannah: 978-1-59755-616-3
Death in Tallassee: 9781597556583

To purchase copies of these books, visit our bookstore website at:
www.advbookstore.com

Longwood, Florida, USA

www.ingramcontent.com/pod-product-compliance
Lightning Source LLC
LaVergne TN
LVHW010615100826
845148LV00014B/2976

* 9 7 8 1 5 9 7 5 5 6 6 2 0 *